D0482657

SORORITY

SORORITY

GENEVIEVE SLY CRANE

SCOUT PRESS
New York London Toronto Sydney New Delhi

Scout Press
An Imprint of Simon & Schuster, Inc.
1230 Avenue of the Americas
New York, NY 10020

This book is a work of fiction. Any references to historical events, real people, or real places are used fictitiously. Other names, characters, places, and events are products of the author's imagination, and any resemblance to actual events or places or persons, living or dead, is entirely coincidental.

First Scout Press hardcover edition May 2018

SCOUT PRESS and colophon are registered trademarks of Simon & Schuster, Inc.

For information about special discounts for bulk purchases, please contact Simon & Schuster Special Sales at 1-866-506-1949 or business@simonandschuster.com.

The Simon & Schuster Speakers Bureau can bring authors to your live event. For more information or to book an event, contact the Simon & Schuster Speakers Bureau at 1-866-248-3049 or visit our website at www.simonspeakers.com.

Interior design by Jaime Putorti

Manufactured in the United States of America

10 9 8 7 6 5 4 3 2 1

Library of Congress Cataloging-in-Publication Data is available.

ISBN 978-1-5011-8747-6
ISBN 978-1-5011-8749-0 (ebook)

For P.D.C.

Contents

Pledge Classes

FALL 2005–MAY 2009

Ruby (Baby Ruth)
Jennifer
Elina (President Swede)
Lisa
Eva

FALL 2006–MAY 2010

Lucy
Shannon
Deirdre
Margot
Marcia (Nala)
Kyra
Janie
Alissa

FALL 2007–MAY 2011

Tracy
Janelle
Stella
Twyla (Twang)
Corinne
Amanda
Kayla

APRIL 2008 DEATH

FALL 2008–MAY 2012 (SMALL CLASS)

Charlotte (Pancake)
Missie (Twinkle)
Noelle (Rich Bitch)
Alexa (Brownie)
Kendra (Prostitot)

1

Sisterhood

-CHORUS-

February 2009

A sleeting night in the heart of February, two weeks before the fall pledge class is initiated, and our housemother, Nicole, is burning white sage in her apartment. We can smell it on the first floor. Ice pings against windows. The trees shimmy and rattle in the woods behind the house. Next door but far away, the brothers of Zeta Sigma whoop and holler, leading a hazing ritual with barefoot pledges in the wet snow.

Room Alpha

Marcia is attuned to all of this. Lying in bed, the window open, cold air skimming every pore of her naked arms and legs, she dangles her head off the edge of the mattress and listens. A tablet of Ecstasy sings through her veins. She is malleable and giddy and completely overwhelmed by the whooshing world.

She is already failing every class. This is her last semester.

But right now that doesn't matter, and she drinks up the euphoria while she can, knowing that when she moves back home she won't feel it again for a long time, not when her grandmother calls her a dumb cunt; not when she goes to the hardware store she worked at in high school to beg for her part-time job back; not when her father won't look at her because she wasted his money on tuition. A brother at Zeta Sigma shouts through the woods, something that sounds like "Chug, Fag!" Silence, then a rush of cheers. Good boy, she thinks.

Room Beta

Before we evicted her, Kyra spent most of her nights gone, never here to wake up to the clanging radiator at 12:22, or again at 1:37, again at 2:52, 4:07, 5:22. Her beta fish swam vicious laps in its scummy bowl, its beady black eyes staring into the dark.

We know that Kyra has slept with twenty-nine boys since she started college. Before the baby she spent her nights sharing a narrow twin mattress with a boy in the dorms, usually a freshman with stale breath and clumsy hands. They were all different and all the same. Earnest. Fumbling. Forgettable.

Room Gamma

Amanda is a virgin. We can see clues of it in her mincing gait, her sloping posture, her arms folded carefully over her chest as she waits for the bus to class. Her sweet, sibilant lisp. It is hard for her to identify the moment when her chastity became a burden. Every night she shares a bed with her stuffed lion, Maurice, whom she pulls from a corner of her closet after she locks the bedroom door. She lies fetal, with her eyes on the crack of light splicing under the bedroom door, until she is sucked into the vacuous space of sleep. Always guarded to the last moment of consciousness. The bottom row of teeth in her small mouth eroded from bruxism while she dreams.

She's the only sister in the house who is genuinely sympathetic toward the pledges.

—You can talk to me anytime, she tells them, often with a squeeze on the arm or a sweet, doleful expression, and the pledges say yes, of course, they'll stop by her room sometime. But they never do. Pledges don't want pity. They just want to endure.

Room Delta

Tracy is writing a French lit essay now, entitled "La Guerre de Troie: Fact or Farce?" In her pauses between the lines, she yanks out her eyelashes with her right hand, one by one, and places them on the edge of her desk. The whitish bulb of each lash must line up, arranged by size. She loves the order of them, these little parenthetical curves. By the final paragraph she will have moved on to eyebrows. Even in her deepest, most introspective moments, she calls this a habit and nothing more. Tomorrow morning she will spend upward of thirty minutes surveying the naked terrain of her face, the exposed orbital bone where brow hair should be, the rabbity pinkness of her lids. Then, with her mouth slightly agape and her right hand clutching a tube of glue, she'll lay a sticky track of fake lashes over the raw. She'll pencil in her brows. She'll hand in her essay, call her mother in Boston, and tell her she's aced another exam.

Room Epsilon

Epsilon was Margot's room.

Nobody lives in Epsilon.

Room Zeta

Lucy is a straightedge. She did the perfunctory drinking during pledging, but after she was initiated she came clean with how boring she is. Even weed scares her.

—I had a bad trip on something once, she says.

She's so vague that we don't believe her. Instead, we've constructed our own theories. Dad's a cop? Brother's a crack addict? Or maybe she's just a wimpy, inexperienced girl, so firmly ensconced in reality that she won't even do a bump with us on the Pledge Room coffee table.

Room Eta

Janelle sleeps with the window open, even if it means sleeping in a sweatshirt and wool hat and turning on the heated mattress pad and burrowing under two quilts. She does this because if she strains hard enough, if she demands her ears to pick up the sound waves through the woods and next door, sometimes she thinks she can hear Wes. He's a brother at Zeta Sigma, a senior on the executive board with curly hair and a profile suited for a Roman coin.

At the last mixer, we all watched as Wes approached her in the Zeta Sigma basement and handed her a solo cup of Chardonnay. Not jungle juice. Not keg dregs. Chardonnay!

—How've you been? she asked. It was an anything-but-clothes themed mixer and she felt her rib cage slick with sweat under the black Hefty bag she'd wrapped around herself, using duct tape as a makeshift belt, cinched so tight it was hard for her to laugh.

—Sometimes I miss you, he said. Parts of you, anyway.

She wondered, why is it so hard to discern if someone is naturally stupid, or just cruel?

—How's Kelly? she asked. And internally she begged, please Jesus give her herpes. Knock her up. Make her fat.

—She's good, I guess, he said, adjusting the newspaper poncho he'd fashioned for himself.

—Tell her hi for me, Janelle said, and hoped that the malice in her didn't speckle her inflection.

—Your ass looks great in that trash bag, he muttered into his Solo cup.

The brothers at Zeta Sigma bellow and drink, bellow and drink, and Janelle listens hard for the pitch of his voice, but more importantly she searches for the absence of Kelly's. He used to hover over her in this bed, his shoulders eclipsing her vision, his eyes glistening in a way that could have been mistaken for kindness. And instead of enjoying him, she'd fixated: was the skin on her heels too rough when she wrapped her legs around him? How flat was her stomach? Could he see up her nose? Strange, how the gratification of faking it for him had almost equated an orgasm.

Room Theta

Two pledges called Twinkle and Rich Bitch moved in here in January. Their real names aren't important until they're initiated; for now, they're just pledges.

Room Iota

Two more pledges. One is squat, loud-mouthed, and dresses with cleavage in mind at all times, so we call her Prostitot. The other is too bland to remember.

Room Kappa

These are Alissa's favorite hours. With the door locked, she opens her bottom dresser drawer and pulls out the knitting needles, the yarn. She will spend the whole night watching her hands as if they were someone else's, capable hands that let the metal needles tick against one another, the skeins of wool at her feet like a sleeping kitten, the drop of one stitch frustrating but reparable. Every project has limitless potential to warm. No reason, then, to unlock the door. There is no need for scrutiny about such an easy little hobby.

Room Lambda

Elina is the oldest, blondest, palest sister in the house. She's also from Norway—*Don't you forget it, pledge rats, don't you forget it.* She finished her term as president last semester, and now she's exempt from all duties. No housecleaning, no sober driver obligations, no volunteer hours. Nothing. She has the biggest room, a room with a king-size bed and the radiator that hisses the least. She had some pledges paint the walls Creamsicle orange and immediately regretted the decision. Orange is not a good color for rest. Maybe for sex, maybe for summer, but in February it's a riotous color that bleats at her when she tries to sleep. Nights, she either goes to the bars in the center of town and drives back drunk on the wrong side of the road, or she sits at her window seat, barefoot and wearing a Beatles T-shirt overstretched at the neck (no bra! we notice) chain-smoking and ashing onto the sill, watching the trees shiver in the woods, wondering why she feels a looming dread about graduation in May.

Room Mu

Nobody talks about Margot anymore. Many of the sisters didn't know her that well anyway. But Deirdre remembers, always remembers.

In bed, the landscape of her memory broadens and Deirdre thinks of the time she and Margot were hazed out in the woods, blindfolded and giggling between shots until the pledge mistress slapped at the backs of their necks with a birch switch and called them lezzies; the time she and Margot were initiated into the sisterhood together, naked under red robes; the time she and Margot did a little blow and went dancing with those two nerdy assistant professors from the anthropology department; the way Margot would sleep with her hands crushed between her thighs; the way Margot drove with one foot curled under her butt; how she would apply perfume by spraying the air and walking through a cloud of it before it settled; the way she smacked her gum in class; the way she looked when Deirdre found her on the floor of room Epsilon on a sunny Friday morning, a streak of vomit smeared across the right side of her face, eyes half-open, whites showing. Glassy.

Everything Deirdre has ever known has had a formulaic ending. Algebra problems have answers. Jokes have punch lines. What does she do, then, with a life cut off in midsentence?

Earlier today, Amanda was in the bathroom when Deirdre was, both brushing their teeth and staring somberly at one another in the reflection of the mirror, and Amanda took the brush out of her mouth and said,

—I still think of her sometimes, too, you know.

And Deirdre spit a bitter gob of foam into the sink and stared hard at Amanda's reflection, hating her sympathy, her goddamn simpering lisp, and said,

—I don't think of her. I live her.

—No need for the melodrama, Amanda said, I was just—

—Well stop, Deirdre said. And then she said to the sink, so quietly Amanda almost didn't hear:

—We are such children. Such pathetic spoiled children.

Room Nu

Shannon is the thinnest girl in our house. We hate her for it, but we know the sacrifice. We know why she only uses the bathroom by the laundry room. The dryers, the washer, the buzz and hum: all of it hides what she's doing. We don't talk to her about it. If we approached her, it would be easy for her to deny. And a lot of us do it, have done it, will do it again. Just with less frequency. Who are we, then, to cast that stone?

Shannon has a coolness to her, a sleekness that coats her body like a varnish. Maybe this is why we put her in charge of writing the house superlatives this semester, which she will read aloud in front of the whole chapter and our dates at Spring Fling. Superlatives are never flattering. Shannon will uphold this tradition easily—her sleekness comes with sharp edges. Tracy peeked in her room one afternoon and saw part of the list on her desk:

Sister Smokes-a-Lot	*Eva Bausch*
Sister Frat Rat	*Stella Tilden*
Sister Walk-of-Shame	*Kyra Clark*
Sister Sloppy	*Elina Jensen*

But we're giving her a superlative, too. Lucy came up with it at dinner one night when Shannon had already left the table.

—What about Sister Binge-and-Purge? Lucy said. And someone

started laughing, and soon we all were, an infection of humor that couldn't be explained and wasn't really funny, and it was decided, yes, Binge-and-Purge, that is just hysterical.

Room Xi

Stella rolls off of Wes and stretches catlike, curling her toes, body extended so taut her breasts nearly disappear. Wes switches on her desk lamp and gets out of bed with sea legs. He saunters over to the window and listens to his brothers whoop outside. Three text messages pulse on his cell. Two from Kelly. One from Janelle. He ignores them and crawls back under the duvet.

Stella curls into him, buries her face in his chest so that he can feel her hot breath on his sternum. She is suffocating him. He counts the tiny filaments of blond hair on the back of her neck; when he gets to forty he will leave.

But for a minute they pretend that this is love, this is nice, this is something that the two of them are willing to hurt other people for and feel justified in doing so.

Room Omicron

Eva is the pledge mistress. She has an impish face, expressive, capable of flexing between a grimace and a grin faster than the pledges can track. It is her job to shuttle them from one mixer to another, shepherd them to safety when frat brothers trick them into their filthy bedrooms, put them in a car and send them home when they're too drunk, clean up their vomit when they're really too drunk. It is also her job to haze them. After all, she reasons, the best things in life are painful to acquire: beauty, her mother's love. And sisterhood.

She locks them in the pledge study and has them memorize long texts about the meaning of sorority support and won't let them out until they all get it right, even if it takes the full night and they're too delirious come morning to know the words bubbling out of their mouths:

In 1864, founders Virginia Wheeler, Lucinda May, and Joanna Howard bonded together to form a private society of womanly compassion and support . . .

She makes them take shots if they recite the Greek alphabet wrong. She tells them they're despicable if they don't mop the foyer correctly and has them get on their hands and knees and lick the floor. But when they pass the tests, memorize the handshakes, the sacred numbers, the Greek phrases and passwords and oaths, she rewards them. She tells them they're ready to be her sisters. Her face will buckle into weepiness but no tears will be visible when she inevitably informs us that the pledges are ready for initiation.

Cult analysts call this love bombing. Eva knows this from a *Dateline* episode she caught at the gym once. She slowed her pace on the treadmill and thought, yes, love bombing, I hate them because I love them. I berate them and make them drink and tell them they're worthless because I love them so fucking much.

Room Pi

Chelsea has a fresh tattoo of Minnie Mouse blowing a kiss. The tattoo is etched over her right hip, and she's examining the work in the mirror and wondering if perhaps it wasn't such a good idea to put Minnie where she did. In this location, Minnie's head peeks over the waistband of her underwear, her little mouse lips pursed, the body hidden. On closer inspection, she looks less like she's blowing a kiss and more like she's trying to whistle. She never should have trusted that apprentice. He'd made such a big deal about using sterile needles. (—*And here*, he said, brandishing the plastic packaging, *is a fresh needle just for you*!) He was so grand about it that she had to consider whether or not a fresh needle was a special occasion for him.

And another thing: when she's sleeping with someone, they'll have an eyeful of Minnie. She hadn't thought of this before. But it's over, and now she has to reconcile herself with the new resident on her skin. Minnie gapes at her vacantly with her six spindly eyelashes and offers no assurance.

Room Rho

This is the pledge study. Nobody uses the study to study. The carpet is mottled with a history of our debauchery: bong stains, burn marks, candle wax, and something resembling the acidic erosion of vomit in one corner, disguised by a judiciously placed armchair. On Thursday nights before mixers, we use this room to do bumps and smoke hookah. It's the farthest room from the housemother, not like she would really care. Tracy in Delta lives directly below this room, and sometimes late at night she hears the rhythmic creak of the guest bed springs in the corner. She usually bangs on the ceiling with a pledge paddle to shut up whoever is above her, but to no avail.

Room Sigma

Twyla had an accent when she first pledged, so we called her Twang. Eventually her accent whittled down to nothing and now it's easy to forget that she's from Oklahoma, with the exception of the state flag she has hanging in her room—blue, with a thing that looks like a dream catcher in the center. She used to play Gretchen Wilson songs on her guitar until her neighbor Ruby complained. Now, the guitar sits in the corner by her desk. She never plays it anymore, but once a week she lovingly buffs the dust off of it with a piece of flannel.

Twyla never goes home between semesters, choosing instead to stay in the empty house, getting paid under the table by our housemother to set glue traps and steam clean the carpets. She works two jobs to pay her out-of-state tuition. One is at the DB Mart down the road. The other is a night shift as a campus security guard. She looks like a punch line in her uniform—drowning in khaki, the weight of her industrial flashlight practically dragging her belt to her knees.

No matter the weather, she always wears long sleeves.

—I'll never get used to Massachusetts winters, she says.

But even in May she's covered from wrist to calf.

Room Tau

At the start of the school year, Ruby painted this room Tiffany blue and plastered posters of Audrey Hepburn on every wall. In case visitors don't get the theme. But why Audrey Hepburn in the first place?

—Because Audrey Hepburn was fucking classy, she says.

So was Margaret Thatcher, we could argue.

Ruby is the fattest girl in the house. She worships at the altar of Weight Watchers and measures her food in points. A piece of whole grain bread is two points. A pint of cappuccino ice cream is forty-nine. Tonight, she faces the wall in bed and stares at the poster of Audrey, eyes roving over the territory of her knobby shoulders, her long fingers, her doe eyes staring back at her in the dark.

Room Upsilon

Jennifer was a psych major. Then she was an econ major. Then she tried linguistics. Now she's in animal science.

—I'm just good at everything, she says.

Except committing.

Father: she never met him.

Mother: only sixteen years older than she. Wears leopard print. Is the secretary to a divorce attorney. Reminds her daughter that she could have been a showgirl, damn it, if she didn't have the C-section scar.

Room Phi

Lisa spent three hours today at the barre, thirty minutes restuffing her toe shoes, forty minutes scrutinizing herself in front of her full-length mirror, and an hour at the gym. But now it's late, she needs a full night of rest for the econ test that she hasn't prepared for, and the only way to halt her compulsive self-analysis is with a bubbler. Five hits exhaled before she settles. The tendons in her legs slacken, time slows, she repacks the bowl, three more hits and she forgets that sleep was her objective. She trundles downstairs and makes a cup of tea that scalds her mouth, tongue to roof. The brothers can be heard through the flimsy glass of the kitchen window, and she wavers there for an eternal minute, listening. Something profound is in their whooping, but she's too foggy to fathom it. She often feels this way high, like she has a scratch ticket but no coin to scrape down to the answer.

Emergency Exit Only. Alarm Will Sound.

This is the Chapter Room; the sign is a ruse for visiting parents and curious frat brothers.

Only initiated sisters are permitted in the Chapter Room, and even they can't enter without the password and the handshake and appropriate attire. This means: panty hose. No open-toed shoes after October 7. Shoulders covered. Mascara mandatory. The dress code in the sisterhood manual is longer than the two-paragraph page on how to report hazing.

Notice the executive board table, the chairs arranged in a horseshoe, the wood-paneled walls, the composites of sisters from years past—1960s bobs, 1970s waves, 1980s perms, then bangs of the 1990s. Candles everywhere. Persian rugs. Fake flowers.

This is where we all met after Margot was found last spring.

The girls who knew her least wept pretty tears, dabbing under their eyes so their makeup wouldn't run. Nobody loves an ugly crier.

And Deirdre sat in the back row, expressionless, her fingers numb, staring hard at a hole in her tights.

Elina lifted the gavel and let it fall on the table and we all quieted, waiting for some heartfelt delivery of insight from our president.

—I spoke with the provost, and for now the university will not shut the house down because of Margot's poor decision, she said.

—Thank God! Janelle said. Heads around the room bobbed in the current of relief. Tracy yanked out four eyebrow hairs in one grab, then discreetly dropped them on the carpet underneath her chair.

—This is an opportunity for unity, Elina intoned. She had written this part of her speech on an index card and glanced at the table before her between pauses.

—Although one of us is now enrolled in the Omega chapter, let us take solace in our sisterhood. Let us seek comfort in our family. Let us mourn with dignity and grace.

—Does this mean Spring Fling is canceled? Alissa asked.

—No, Elina said, momentarily thrown from the formal voice she'd conjured for the occasion. We can't get our deposit back. And anyway—she resumed the voice again—Margot would have wanted us to continue with our sisterhood in her absence.

Sighs of relief gusted through the room. Deirdre's fingers tingled.

—Let us close with a prayer, Elina said. Our eyes shimmered wet in the candlelight, seeking comfort from her in a bona fide tragedy, and Elina's face lit with a flash of pride before she sombered.

When the prayer ended we filed out of the room in pairs, but even in the hush Deirdre caught frayed edges of whispers.

—are they going to do with all of her clothes?

—parents coming for her things?

—she did it on purpose?

The door swung shut, and Deirdre remained. She hooked a thumb through the hole in her tights and pulled. The composite photographs of alumnae peered down at her from the walls, and she stared back at each one, absorbing every single countenance and name, waiting for one to blot out the face she saw whenever she closed her eyes.

Room Chi

Corinne was third runner-up for Miss Northeast last year and this is her year, her year, her year, damn it! She suspects she suffered in the talent portion, when she played "Hey Jude" on the flute and at the end she lost her breath on the E-sharp. Or maybe it was the moment in swimsuit when she popped out of her bikini top onstage. Or maybe it was the interview portion, when she stuttered on the word *amendment* while discussing her feelings on gun control. The memory of flaw—the mere sight of the red bikini in the back corner of her closet, for instance—is enough to make her cringe.

She is the new president of the sisterhood now, her term fresh from January, but she doesn't have time to be apt at it and simultaneously win the title this year. Written on an index card and taped over her desk is the word *Prioritize.* She delegates her presidential obligations to the rest of the executive board, and they tolerate it—because, let's be honest, how great would the sisterhood look if our president won Miss Northeast?

Corinne has a magnified mirror encircled by lightbulbs that sits on her desk, and most evenings she can be found there, bathed in the blinding wattage, pupils contracted to pinpoints, studying the pores on her face. What if the thing that kept her from winning last year had nothing to do with bathing suit wedgies or missed notes? What if, in fact, she had lost because of the tiny hook at the end of her nose? Or the lack of symmetry between her left and right eye? A fissure of a wrinkle is developing on her forehead, and she can see it with perfect clarity even when she isn't in front of the mirror. There is a limited window of opportunity for her to be beautiful.

Room Psi

Janie has a boyfriend with an apartment and an online poker addiction. She spends most of her time at his place, watching him hover the mouse over the pixelated green felt, clicking with fanatical zeal. We used to set up personnel meetings about her many absences. Then, during a chapter meeting, we noticed that she has an annoying habit of tapping pens against her teeth. It's like she's testing to see if they're hollow.

—Can you stop? Ruby asked.

—Sure, she said, but five minutes later she did it again.

Now we just charge her fifteen bucks every time she fails to show up at a meeting and her boyfriend pays the penalties with his winnings.

Room Omega

Our pledge mistress, Eva, is walking down the hall with a pack of Parliaments in hand when a pledge who we call Brownie waves her into this room.

—I'm sorry to bother you, Pledge Mistress, Brownie says. Eva reduces her eyes to slits and waits, body humming for nicotine.

—There's a rumor I think you should know about, Brownie says. She is so nervous she leaves a sweaty palm print on her desk when she stands up and shuts the door.

—Spit it out then, Eva says.

—Is it true that a girl named Margot died here last spring because she couldn't take the pressure of being a pledge?

—Who told you that? Eva asks.

—It's a rumor, just a rumor, Brownie stammers. Some pledges were talking.

—It's a lie, Eva says. Margot was a sister when she died, not a pledge.

—But did she die from the pressure?

—It wasn't a suicide, if that's what you mean, Eva says. She overdosed. It happens.

Both girls are silent. The radiator clangs into action. Footsteps tread up and down the hall.

—I'm not sure I want to go through with initiation, Brownie says.

—Everyone feels that way sometimes. Sleep on it. It's only two weeks away.

—I've been thinking about this for a while, though.

Eva, impatient and jittery now, shakes a cigarette out of the pack.

—Is your smoke detector on? she asks. Brownie shakes her head no. Eva lights up.

—I like you, Brownie. I'd hate to see you go. But if you want to throw away your whole pledge period, if you want to reject an entire house of women who are willing to accept you as their sister, I can't stop you.

—It's not like that, Brownie says. I think you all are great. I just—

—I don't need your excuses. If you think you deserve no love from us, that's not my fucking problem.

Eva finishes the cigarette in silence, taking in the surroundings. She knows so little about this pledge, this Brownie girl, but the room divulges details. Pictures of what must be her parents are on the bedside table, there's a U2 poster over the bed, and her comforter is floral and ragged. She wishes she didn't see these things. It's much easier to haze her pledges when she doesn't know the miscellanea that make them into full-blown people. She gets up to leave.

—Thank you for speaking with me, Brownie says.

Eva lingers at the door.

—What's your real name? she asks.

—It's Alexa.

—Sleep on it, Alexa. Tell me what you choose in the morning.

Outside, Eva immediately regrets that she didn't bring a scarf. She stands under the overhang of the roof and puffs slowly on two more cigarettes, one after the other, and listens to the Sigma Xi brothers finish their ritual and congratulate and shout and spit and slap each other. Somebody retches. Then they are gone, a door slams, only sleet can be heard, and Eva tries to recall in the stillness what it was like to live with the conviction that she was doing the right thing.

2

Thirst

-LUCY, SHANNON-

September 2006

They called at seven o'clock on the last day of rush after I'd already convinced myself that no house wanted me. It took two tries for me to answer the phone, my fingers fat and disobedient.

—Congratulations, someone trilled over the line.

The moment she introduced herself I forgot her name, too jumpy to hold details.

—Are you sure? I said.

—Of course we're sure, the voice said. You fit our house perfectly. Where are you?

—Hawthorne Dorm.

—We'll pick you up in five minutes, the voice said.

I stood rooted in the lobby.

For the first time, a chosen girl.

When the car came, I signed my bid card in urgent cursive on the hood. I swung myself into a sliver of backseat, everyone's perfume mingled sweet and thick, I shook clammy hands, girls cooed welcomes, the car sped through campus, and the girl driving hit the brakes too hard in the parking lot, we jumbled into the yard, the front door of my new house opened, and then I was a pledge.

Balloons hung limp in the foyer and a cake sat on the dining room table, untouched and choked with frosting. Delicious and deadly. My mouth flooded with want for it before I swallowed, ashamed. Sisters flitted from one corner of the room to the other with the objective of studying the new pledges. Were we a pretty batch? Did we look social? Did we look slutty?

It wasn't until then that I saw Shannon. She was talking to another pledge across the room, and whenever she tilted her head the light would refract off her earrings. She felt me watching her. And then, stomach-shriveling eye contact. I saw the outrage in her before she remembered herself and set her mouth in a smile. When she turned away, I could see the knobby ladder of her spine through her shirt.

I had heard from my mother that we had chosen the same college. I had even known that she was rushing. But neither of us had imagined that we would have the misfortune to be chosen by the same house.

Our pledge mistress sat us in a circle of chairs. She was long-haired, with a smoky voice and tiny eyes that were older than the rest of her, and I didn't know it yet but she had hands made for gripping the end of a paddle. Tonight wasn't the night for that. Tonight was the night to dip us in honey until we were too stuck to leave later, when the hazing began.

—Why don't you ladies introduce yourselves? the mistress said. She sat, ankles crossed demurely under her chair, and I imitated her before I realized I had done so.

We were all too nervous to be creative. We stuck to the bullet points:

Name? From? Major?

have remembered being young and female and measured, always measured. She must have remembered the want.

—It's an ethical decision, I said.

—Jesus, she said. If it's ethical does this mean you won't wear those hideous lambskin boots anymore?

My eyes clipped over her. All I saw was her age, her weight. I saw her wrinkles, and the fat on her arms that swung when she hit a golf ball or put away a dinner plate. I didn't see the story her body told.

The first three, five, eight pounds are hard. Then, there is a plummet.

In a season's time, my knees began to bruise against one another when I slept. There was an inlet of nothing between my ribs. My belly button deflated until I could feel my pulse thrum behind it when I lay flat on the bed. The hairs on my arms thickened into a downiness. I could see the tendons crisscross on my forearms.

Nobody said,

—Wow, this is moving a little fast.

Instead I heard,

—You look fabulous!

And,

—What's your secret?

And,

—I see you've lost that baby fat!

And Shannon, skinny Shannon, desired Shannon, said,

—Eat a fucking bagel already.

I knew she was jealous, and it thrilled me. It wasn't long before we were dieting together.

Only when we were high, really high, would we binge on whatever we could find in her parents' refrigerator. Pizza rolls. Leftover vichyssoise. Goat cheese and saltines. Buttered popcorn. Raw hot dogs. Our first binge was an ice cream raid. Mouthful after mouthful of Cherry Garcia until I could feel my frontal lobe crushed into a deep freeze, so high it was hard for me to focus on the nutrition facts, and when I did, something deep within me rioted. I told her that I'd left my purse somewhere, then wandered down the hall to the bathroom farthest from the locus of her kitchen.

When I finished, I rinsed my mouth under the tap and leaned against the sink and shook. Something hideous stared back at me in the mirror. But I felt victory flood my stomach. I had rid myself of the ice cream but it lingered in her, clung to her, ugly, cloying gluttony.

Until, of course, I returned to the kitchen and found that she had locked herself in her parents' bathroom as well.

She emerged smirking.

I wanted to hate her.

Instead, we watched MTV together, sprawled out on her living room floor, and I fell asleep with my head on her heel.

My mother was getting anxious.

She took the laxatives out of the bathroom.

She started making me oatmeal at breakfast and leaving a multivitamin on top of the napkin, next to the fork.

She would say things, infuriating, insincere things, such as, You know you're perfect just the way you are, right?

Or sometimes she would flail about, searching for a mother-daughter bonding experience.

—I know how much seeing Shannon means to you but how about you and I order sushi and see a movie tonight?

Her anxiety skirted the line of bearable until I found the self-help book on raising difficult teenage daughters in her bedroom when I was looking for hidden cigarettes. The subtitle: *How to Reach the Young and Aching Heart.* I was revolted. By the time she got home from work, I was so dizzyingly livid that every eloquent argument about her betrayal had spun away from me.

I had planned to say, I find your neuroticism rather destructive, Mother. But my young and aching heart got the best of me. When she walked through the door with her hair in a windswept swirl, her face lined and appallingly vulnerable, I felt myself surge, and all I could say was, Fuck you. The shock in her face deep enough to split into her womb.

—Fuck you, I said again, and ran, and in the driveway I yelled it one more time—Fuck you!—and the neighbor's dog started braying.

It took me five minutes to get to Shannon's now. Any faster and I'd get dizzy. She wasn't on the back porch, and the light was out in her bedroom. In other circumstances I would have left to avoid interacting with her parents, but the situation was desperate.

Her father answered the door. He had the look of a retired news anchor. Always wore loafers. Always smelled like Altoids.

—I thought Shannie was with you, he said.

—I was supposed to meet her somewhere but I forgot where, I said. Lame.

—Well, she said you were going to the beach, he said. Don't stay out too late.

He shut the door before I turned away.

By the time I got to the beach it was dark and I had to fumble my way up the steps. I found her on the sand with Glen. Under Glen. Everything tinted in lunar blue: her legs stretched out in the sand, her torso pinned and shadowed beneath him, his absurdly exposed ass. I froze, then stumbled away to the dock, sat with my back to them, waiting. The Milky Way cut a stripe above me. The sky had a summer vault to it and the air was warm, but occasionally a billow of cool air would drop on me, like snow. Glen grunted in the distance and then I heard her laugh carry over the dunes. I stood up so they could find me.

She grabbed my hand as if we were still children. Her palm was sandy and warm.

—Hey, Glen said, I got something for us to try.

He took a plastic bag of leaves out of his pocket.

—I'm not in the mood for weed tonight, I said.

—Good. This isn't weed.

Shannon giggled. I wanted to hit her.

—This, he said, is a little something called Datura.

—Never heard of it, I said.

—Glen says it's like salvia, only with more hallucinations.

—I don't feel like tripping tonight, I said.

The whites of her eyes flicked to Glen in the dark. I told you, she said. I told you she wouldn't be into it.

I plunged my hand into the Baggie.

—Do we smoke it or do we eat it? I said.

We ate it. It wasn't like pot at all.

Glen's face was crawling with ants, tiny winged ants, all of them traveling through the tunnels of his nose, his ears, his tear ducts, searching for food. I went to brush them off and they disappeared.

—Stop it, they're just ants, man, he said. And when he laughed more of them poured out of the corners of his mouth.

—You've got them, too, he said.

The waves broke in the hazy dark and I was suddenly aware of their potential. The enormity of them unspooled me until I was too tangled to slow my heart. Surges were breaking over me, again and again, and every time I came out of one I pulled in my breath just in time to go under once more. And then they were gone.

—Where's Shannon? I asked.

He shrugged. Even in the dark, I could see the endless expansion of his pupils. I ran from him. I thought I could feel every individual grain of sand clinging to my feet.

And then it was daylight and I'd found her. She was at the water's edge, building a drizzle castle. I watched her. She was a child again, all rayon and eyes, plunging her fat arm into the bucket and pulling up doughy wet sand, letting it drip out of her fingers into turrets and mortared walls.

When she turned to face me, I was a child, too. The straps of my one-piece cut into my chubby shoulders, and my bangs sprang over my eyes.

—I'm so thirsty, she said. Her voice plaintive. I felt her thirst until it became my own.

—I'll get us water, I said.

I took the bucket from her. The ocean dragged up my shins, then my knees. I walked farther, was struck by a wave, and the bucket filled with water on its own accord, but it wasn't enough, could never be enough, and I couldn't tolerate another minute of this unbearable thirst, and I plunged my face into the water, tasting the salt, the winged ants leaping from my skin, and she was waving at me from a bright spot on the shore to come back but I refused her and I drank and I drank and I drank.

I barely remember the crush back to shore, the waves shunting me, the roll of head over ankle and sand forced into tear ducts and the sizzle of salt in my nose. But I remember after, the sweep of hard wet shoreline, and retching onto the foam, my muscles scraping against the insides of my ribs like they were cleaning the hull of an empty ship, heaving so many times it felt as if I were the one filling the ocean with its water. Some of the leaves I'd eaten came up; I plucked pieces of them off of my tongue and stared at them in the moonlight, in dumb-sick awe at how even the simplest things could be poison.

Shannon's hand weighed heavy on my shoulder. Not a child anymore. I could see the steely edges of her jaw, the sunken depression of eye sockets flanking her nose, her hair frizzled around her temples. She was smiling, ghoulish in the moonlight, on a Datura trip infinitely better than my own.

—You look so beautiful, she told me. Like a skinny, glowing angel.

I gagged again.

It was the last time she ever touched me.

I fell asleep in the sand by the dunes.

It was a beachcombing old couple that found the three of us later that day. They'd been looking for sea glass and instead they found teenagers. The old woman woke me, her breath in my face smelling like a moldy book. Her body kneeling over mine, probing my neck for a pulse. She jumped when I opened my eyes.

—Help me, I whispered.

Once I'd said it, I couldn't take it back. Help me. It travels from one tributary to the next and the words never swim back upstream.

Police were called.

And then, much worse, our parents.

My mother drove me in weepy silence to the hospital for an IV, and when we left she brought a stack of pamphlets with her. She put them in my lap on the drive home. They were all brochures for treatment centers.

—Choose one, she said.

I put my finger on the first one in front of me. A clinic out in Braintree. I spent the rest of my summer there, tracing my body on sheets of butcher paper in a group exercise on self-perception, staring at myself in a full-length mirror for the first time in a year, measuring my food in front of a saccharine counselor, trying to pinpoint the moment where I'd decided to equate success with starvation.

—Your brain doesn't make the right choices, the counselor told me. All you have to do is show up and let other people make your decisions for you.

There was no deadline on the ban on my decision making. They told me to stop calling Shannon. I listened.

I found out from my mother over a carefully monitored dinner of chicken Kiev that Shannon's parents had forced her into treatment, too.

—What made them do that? I asked.

My mother cut hard into her chicken, her knife screeching deep into the plate. I knew then.

I saw her on our first day back at high school. She was standing in the junior parking lot, digging her backpack out of the trunk of a car I didn't recognize. Whose car? A new boyfriend? A new friend? Her new car? I ran to her.

—Shannon.

When she turned to face me I could see the bitterness framing her mouth.

—Shannon, I said again.

I'd missed saying her name.

—You were always such a jealous bitch, she said. But I never thought you'd stoop so low.

—I didn't. My mother called.

It was too late. She'd prepared her own story, swallowed it, and let it sit within her, next to her fury, until it ossified into a truth that would never leave her.

—You just wanted me to get fat with you, she said. You always were a needy, clingy friend. Suffocating.

—I'm sorry, I said. I'm so sorry.

—It's not enough, she said.

Later, after I'd locked myself in the school bathroom, after I'd finished and leaned my forehead on the cool porcelain edge of the toilet like a hand smoothing out my fever, I knew that sorry was the wrong response. I knew that an apology wasn't my responsibility. It was wrong, but I carried the apology anyway. I carried it whenever I saw her in the hallway at school, her arms looped around her binders, her face tilted away from me, always tilted away from me. I carried it on the stage at our high school graduation, when I saw her on the other side of the auditorium, capped and leering when they called my name. I carried it when I sat in the parking lot of CVS in our town and saw her loping toward her car across the street, oblivious of me, her hair cut short now, swathed in a sweatshirt in deep July. I carried my sick apology here to college, waiting to spot her on our campus, waiting for an absolution from her that I would never receive.

A balloon in the foyer popped. All of us jumped and I was sucked back into our pledge mistress's voice, the cadence of congratulations, the stern pronunciations that these women seated in this circle were going to become our sisters, our confidantes, our bridesmaids one day.

We all glanced at one another, sharing portions of hope and skepticism.

The mistress rose and drifted over to the untouched cake on the dining room table. She shook a box of birthday candles into her palm and speared the icing until there were twelve candles scattered over the patina, one for each girl seated. Lights went out. She picked up the cake, her face illuminated from below, her mouth cast in a deep pool of jaundiced light.

The candles guttered as she walked.

—Gather in, she said. And we obeyed, shuffling in the dark.

—To a new pledge class, she said. A new chapter in your lives.

We blew out the candles.

When the lights flicked on, we waited nervously in line for cake that nobody wanted to eat.

Shannon was behind me, I knew, and then her breath was in my ear.

—You going to eat some cake, cow? she whispered.

My desire to apologize to her left me completely, swift and simple.

Why hadn't it come before? But I knew that answer before I finished asking myself: I had learned, in the last two years of our estrangement, that I could manage without her.

—I'm not letting you take this house from me, I whispered.

—I won't have to try, she said. You'll fuck it up on your own.

I could have lunged at her then, taken her skinny body down onto the dining room floor and flailed against her until the two of us were exhausted with our hatred for each other. I could have burst into tears. I could have gone to the bathroom and retched myself deep into the bowl. I explored all of the possibilities at once and settled on none of them.

And then it was my turn in line; a slice of sugar-speckled cake on a plastic plate was in my hand.

The mistress handed me a fork.

—Enjoy, she said.

I stood frozen while Shannon took her slice with the solemnity of communion. The mistress studied us, her eyes in analytical slits.

—You're both the Scituate girls, right? But you don't know each other?

—Never met, Shannon said.

—Well, she said. I'm sure you've got a lot in common.

The mistress held the strings of our arms and legs and we dangled from her, this new puppet master that we'd chosen, ready to obey.

—What did you say your name was? I asked Shannon.

I stuck out my right hand, waiting.

—It's Shannon Larsen. It is such a pleasure to meet you.

We ate.

—How do you like the cake? the mistress asked.

And the two of us said in strange, tinkling unison,

—It's delicious.

We swallowed.

3

Spectral Evidence

-JENNIFER-

April 2005

Mr. Dakota stood in front of me, pacing in bare feet, twisting his copy of *The Crucible* into a tight scroll, watching his actors fumble onstage, especially Tarryn, who leaned against the table on stage left, a dash of tan skin showing between her jeans and her tank top, slipping one foot out of her too-white slip-on and back in again, while Dillon screwed up his lines as John Proctor. Tarryn shifted legs and stretched her hands behind her back. I could hear her joints crack from the front row. Her face was hexagonal and her nose was long, almost too long, and some girls said she'd started getting eyelash extensions when she turned seventeen last year. It wasn't fair. She was already pretty, a senior who was going out of state for college, and on top of that she drove her mom's Miata to school. I wanted to be her when I grew up, but I was only a year behind and worried that I wouldn't be able to accomplish enough in such a short time.

—Give me a word, John, a soft word, she said.

—I c-c-come to see what mischief your uncle's brewing now . . . Line? Dillon stuttered.

If Mr. Dakota didn't already regret casting Dillon, I thought, he had to by now. Dillon couldn't inflect or project and thought that real acting meant flinging his arms outward during his monologues. But that was the way it was at our school. Every girl wanted to be a star and only three or four guys would read for parts. Tarryn sighed and slid her bare foot back into her slip-on.

—Put it out of mind, Abby, Mr. Dakota prompted.

—Put it out of mind, Abby, Dillon said flatly. He adjusted his basketball shorts, which were just seconds away from slipping off his ass.

—John, Tarryn whispered, her voice low, her whole body turned toward him, showing an urgency that I had never felt, let alone been able to imitate—John, I am waitin' for you every night.

—Very good, Mr. Dakota said. Very good. Now hold that for a second.

He climbed onto the stage in his usual way, by swinging one leg and propelling himself up with a flat palm. The soles of his feet had been blackened by the cheap tiles of the auditorium floor. He stood between Tarryn and Dillon like he was the reverend at a teenage wedding.

—Don't forget, Dillon, that you're still in love with this girl, he said. Abigail is supposed to be bewitching to you, even if you don't want her to be. She's supposed to be—

—sexy! shouted one of Tarryn's stupid friends from stage right.

—Ow ow! yelled another.

Mr. Dakota smiled but didn't say anything. He had gotten a haircut over the weekend; he had nice ears.

—Can we take five? Tarryn asked, and the actors hopped offstage before Mr. Dakota agreed with her. He rolled his script tighter and stared at the sound booth at the back of the auditorium until he saw me smiling at him.

—Jennifer, Jennifer. It's like herding cats, isn't it?

He never called me Jen. I was not a cat. We understood each other.

That night I fell asleep in a doze that wrapped up Abigail's lines about knowing John Proctor with the black bottoms of Dakota's soles.

As was tradition, we'd spent the fall semester at Mountdown Academy covering every grievance a white man had committed against another group in the 1500s. Slaves were whipped in North America, Incas were strangled, and China wised up and cut itself off from the rest of the world. We were up to our necks in historical shame. At least with the Puritans in Salem we didn't have to feel so guilty. Now we were just slaughtering our own fellow white people. The academy was known for its collaborative curriculum, so every class for the next two weeks had to be related in some way to the Puritan age in America, no matter how far teachers had to stretch to make it work. In trig, one teacher wrote word problems that required finding the angle of depression in relation from the top of the town stocks. In art, we made our own scarlet letters. I chose *N*, for nail biter. Pablo Esposito created a quilled letter *F* with little tendrils of paper curling inside of the borders.

—What does it stand for? I asked.

—Fornicator, he said.

—Fag, offered another kid.

—I didn't say which kind of fornicator, Pablo said evenly.

We were supposed to wear our letters around the school for the day but instead we stuffed them into the trash, like an alphabet soup of sins.

In English, Ms. Leones, with the bulging eyes and fat neck that she covered with paisley scarves, announced that she had a migraine and told us to split into pairs and discuss what ethical lessons could be derived from a punitive culture of shame. She disappeared into the supply closet with her afghan and a yoga bolster.

—Did you know the technical definition of an orgy is just a group of five or more people not wearing shoes? Sasha said.

—That's BS, I said. That's one of those urban legends, like when people say that you swallow eight spiders in your sleep every year.

—Five, Sasha corrected.

—I'd believe three, I said. I think I'd notice if I ate more than five.

—You just don't want to believe, she said.

—Why would I?

Tarryn was sound asleep at her table, her face cradled in her forearms, her body slumped in complete repose.

Sasha and I stared at her.

—I don't understand how her gut doesn't stick out over her jeans when she's bent over like that, I said.

In college, when my sorority sisters would pass out at the dining room table after a long night of drinking, we'd take pictures of them from the side that showcased their soft, bloated bellies and tape them on the mirror in the upstairs bathroom. By my senior year, it didn't even seem cruel anymore, not even when I photographed a new, dead-eyed sister called Pancake and gave a copy to a guy she had a thing for at our next mixer.

—You know Tarryn's fucking Dakota, Sasha said.

—You are so full of shit today, I said.

—Hand to God. Some of the stagehands saw them hooking up.

—Hooking up, as in fucking backstage?

—Implausible, Roy Coltrane said from the desk behind us.

Sasha swiveled around in her chair and stared.

—You really think so? she asked, overly sweet.

—It doesn't seem likely, Roy said.

—It doesn't seem likely, Sasha repeated. Fuck off, Roy.

—I wouldn't blame him if they were fucking, Dillon said. He grinned at Roy, who had a face so pockmarked I wanted to sand it, and didn't smile back.

—Mr. Dakota's not stupid, Roy said. He wouldn't throw away a job for a slutty teenager.

—What if he doesn't like his job? I asked.

The supply closet door cracked open and Ms. Leones stuck out her bleary face.

—All, I can feel the energy in this room and it is not conducive to wellness and growth, she said. She went back into the closet until the period ended and Lillian Harper gently rapped on the door to make sure she was awake for her next class.

In cultural history, Mr. Blevins told us about witch cakes, and poppets, and shoes.

—The Puritans, he said (long pause), were a very (long pause) superstitious people . . .

Jarred Liotta sketched Blevins with a top hat and monocle, looking like the Monopoly man, in the margins of his notebook.

—Their belief in evil spirits led them to perform . . . unusual rituals . . .

It didn't matter that Blevins was drier than jerky. Talking about spirits had all of us intrigued. Jarred Liotta stopped drawing an erection on Mr. Blevins. He pressed his forearms over the drawing and stared. We waited for Blevins to finish his dramatic pause, but it took too long and finally one of us had to prompt him.

—How did they keep the spirits away? asked Lillian Harper.

—Often, they would combat the evil spirits with the good, Blevins said. In many homes throughout New England (long pause) a single, well-worn shoe can be found buried within the walls (long pause) or under a hearthstone. Any guesses as to why that may be?

—The other shoe decayed? offered Chip Finnick.

—No. He sighed. Any other speculations?

—They got rid of the other one so the good spirit couldn't run away? I said.

—Well done, Jennifer!

No need to tell him that I'd visited Salem on a class field trip before I switched to Mountdown two years ago, where, on the second floor of the Witch House Museum, next to the out-of-place room about medical cannibalism, there had been a rotting shoe in a glass case with a sign saying the same thing, and no need to tell him that, when I saw the shoe, I'd been enchanted by the idea that someone would want to keep a spirit in their house instead of pushing it out, good or not, and the idea that these people with their stodgy little black and white outfits and their fear of dancing were willing to believe in the old-fashioned magick with a *k*. No need. I let him think I was a good guesser.

—Does it work? asked Jarred.

—Does what work, son?

—The shoe? Does the shoe work?

—I mean, it's a hard matter to (long pause) empirically measure, Mr. Blevins said.

—Does the person have to be dead for it to work?

—I haven't tried it, Blevins said drily.

What is the difference between beautiful girls and ordinary ones? My face was symmetrical. I'd taken Accutane. I wore the right things. None of it made a difference next to Tarryn. She had a shimmer about her, a light that I could never fully understand. I couldn't even make eye contact with her. It was like staring at the headlights of a car on a dark road. Later, in my sorority, and even later at my job, I'd meet other women like her and wonder how they were made. They all seemed related. My sorority sisters Corinne and Margot and Shannon had the same shimmer: Corrine, who looked like Grace Kelly, and Shannon, with her sharp chin and small mouth, and Margot, with her impossibly shiny black hair. And even later, I would see it in my boss, with her vicious inflection and the way she could hover for long hours on high heels with calf muscles pumping like hearts as she walked, absent of pain. It was as if they'd inherited an uncanny grace, a physical flawlessness that was not in my DNA. Tarryn was my first exposure to the unattainable, but I didn't call it that then. I only called it jealousy. Onstage, I plodded out my lines as a servant named Mary and found myself hurling my performance into the audience for Mr. Dakota and for Tarryn, for different reasons.

I fake sobbed into Sasha's arms in my first big scene.

—Goody Osborne will hang! I wailed.

—Very good, Mr. Dakota said from the front row. But hold it there for a minute.

Sasha and I clutched at each other and tried not to laugh.

Dakota climbed on the stage before us and sat cross-legged at our feet. His eyes were glistening under the stage lights. If I looked up, I'd see the filters of reds and greens, never understanding how they could cross and transform into something colorless and clean. Tarryn was sitting up in the front row.

—Now, Jennifer, when you cry, I want it to be a real surge of emotion, he said. I want you to channel your terror here. Mary Warren is a girl who has spent her childhood completely powerless and now suddenly she has an influence on other people's lives. She is wracked with guilt and fear. I want you to mine your own life and try to push your guilt and fear into her character.

—I have no guilt, I said.

—Everyone has guilt.

He had wide eyes, and though I'd never thought brown eyes were especially nice, I liked his.

—Not me, I said.

Sasha, still embracing me, squeezed me, the in-cahoots squeeze of what-the-hell-are-you-doing.

—Whatever you have that is conflicting, channel *that*, he said.

He climbed offstage.

—Goody Osborne will hang! I said, and then found myself crumpling into a feeling that I couldn't explain.

—Gorgeous, Dakota said. Really gorgeous work today.

Mountdown Academy had put up magenta flyers in the bathroom about depression awareness. The flyer had a droopy stick figure and some bulleted symptoms to watch out for:

Do you feel . . .

- Helpless?
- Irritable?
- Tired?
- Unable to Focus?

Someone wrote in Sharpie over the poster: if this is depression then im dead.

In pen, someone else wrote: RIP

Jarred Liotta brought a green Croc to cultural history.

—It was my meemaw's, he explained. She died last year but she was the nicest lady.

Someone in the back row snorted.

—What's that? Jarred Liotta said. If any of you have something to say about my meemaw come up here so I can fuck your shit up like a man.

—Now, now, Blevins said lazily. The English language is far too compelling to waste on curse words.

—How do we know your meemaw was a good spirit? asked Sasha. How do we know she wasn't a total creep to everyone but you?

—She wasn't, Jarred said. She was in the Red Hat Society.

—That doesn't make me wanna keep her around, Sasha said.

—Shut it, Sasha, Pablo Esposito said. She meant something to him. It's not a joke.

—We can vote on whether or not to keep Mrs. Liotta's shoe in the classroom, Mr. Blevins said.

—What about absentee votes? Roy asked.

—Quorum is present, Blevins said.

There were twelve ayes and three nays.

We didn't have a hearthstone and we couldn't dig a hole, so we put Mrs. Liotta's Croc on top of the TV with a sign for the janitors: DO NOT REMOVE—EXPERIMENT IN PROGRESS.

We spent the rest of class talking about the nature of spectral evidence in Salem. How you could leave your body and project a curse onto an enemy without making any physical movements.

—Is that a real thing? Sasha asked.

—The Puritans certainly believed it was, Blevins said.

I cast myself out of the desk chair and wandered down the hallways, passing my locker, rounding the corner, seeking out Tarryn and finding her in the bathroom, adjusting a bra strap while she examined her side profile in the mirror, and tried, with all of my bodiless being, to slam her face into the glass.

—Don't fall asleep, Sasha whispered. You'll do that thing where your head bobs back and forth.

• • •

At rehearsal, we reached the scene where Abigail was in court, and I was a follower trying to claw my way back onto her Puritanical good side. I didn't know it, but I was rehearsing for many years of trying to be seen by the women I hated and adored.

—He wake me every night, his eyes were like coals and his fingers claw my neck, and I sign, I sign! I shouted.

In character, I could stare at Tarryn. She was bewitching me. She watched me with a fury that I believed. I blurted and wept my lines and then, as if magnetized, I ran to her and let her hold me in her arms while I sobbed onstage, her fingers stroking and catching a snag in my hair, her neck warm against my cheek. Up close she was poreless. She smelled like my mom's verbena candle at home.

From the audience, Mr. Dakota applauded.

—Tarryn, make sure to keep your expression exactly like that on opening night, he said. You've nailed it.

She smiled at him as he turned away to give the stagehands his notes.

—Nice work, Tarryn, I muttered.

She stepped backward.

—Something wrong? she asked.

—No. I said nice work.

—Is there a problem?

—No, I said.

She crossed her arms over her chest and tucked her hair behind her ear.

—I'm not into games, she said. You got something to say to me, you can say it. You don't need to talk shit about me with your friend in English when you think I'm asleep. Close your mouth. Don't look so stunned.

It was infuriatingly unfair that she could see what a bad person I was.

When the stagehands had switched off the lights and everyone had dragged their backpacks out of their chairs and gone home to their parents and their mundane lives, I stayed. I was compelled. I had to stay. Dakota piled the last scripts into his bag and saw me sitting out in the audience. I sat Indian style and let my head drop down. I was trying to look burdened but not needy.

—You okay?

—I'm just going through some stuff, I said.

—Do you need to talk?

I nodded, faking reluctance.

His office was cramped and didn't have windows, but he'd fixed it by taping posters of shows from years past on the walls. *Our Town*, and *Grease*, and *Much Ado About Nothing*. He flopped into his swivel chair and propped his bare, blackened feet on his desk. He rolled his shirt up at the forearms.

—How does someone know if they're depressed? I asked him.

—Why do you think you're depressed?

—I'm tired and I can't think straight and I feel sort of helpless. And there's a flyer in the girls bathroom that says those are the symptoms.

—Oh, he said, oddly relieved. That's not depression.

—It isn't?

—No, that's just being seventeen.

I was sixteen, young for a junior. I didn't correct him.

—It's not forever, he said. One day you'll go to a good college, and find a nice job, and a great partner, and you'll be happy.

—That's it? I said.

—That's it.

—So all I have of my life is some more school and some paychecks and a marriage and death?

—If you're lucky, he said. And if you're really lucky, you won't be too smart, so you won't notice that it's happening.

—It sounds appalling, I said.

—It is appalling, he agreed. But it's not so bad when you realize that every other person on the planet is doing it with you.

—What if I move to New York and become an actress?

—You aren't going to do that, he said.

—I'm not good enough.

I was staring at him directly now, and he was staring back. I was afraid that if I blinked he'd stop talking.

—It's not about being good, he said. It's about knowing your chances and being smart.

—Did you do that?

—Try to make it as an actor? Sure. It was kind of like *Rent*, but without the music or the love or the fun or even the danger. It was risky but not stage-worthy. It just kind of sucked.

The vacuum of my ordinary life was in front of me. It was terrifying. I couldn't look at it head-on anymore.

—I thought theater was supposed to imitate life, I said. I thought there'd be more.

—No, he said. Life is pretty boring, or it's so painful that nobody wants to watch the real thing. Theater just makes life more interesting.

I knew it was inevitable that I would kiss him. We ran out of words and I was overwhelmed. What were the other options? The script had reached its real purpose, this was the end of the act, and all of my prior moments in front of him had been performance art. Now I was supposed to show him that I wasn't like the other girls. I was braver. So I walked to his side of the desk and kissed him.

The tip of his nose was cold. He didn't put his arms around me. He didn't even put his feet down. I pulled back.

—Jennifer, he began.

—No, I said. It doesn't have to be like this. We could be stupid together. We could go somewhere. We could do something different. You're still young, right?

—I'm thirty-three, he said. And then, as if he needed to explain how ordinary his life really was, he added: I'm taking Rogaine.

My lips and fingers were tingling. I couldn't get enough air. My heart was chugging blood. His nose was cold. He was taking Rogaine. At home, next to the Rogaine, the shelf over his toilet probably had tweezers and suppositories and lotion. There were no stage lights bathing his face in creamy light. His office was cramped. The posters did not make up for windows.

—I can't breathe, I said.

My lungs felt shrunken. I couldn't get in enough air.

He pulled his paper lunch sack from the garbage and shook out the contents and crumpled up the neck.

—Breathe into this, he said.

—I think I'm dying, I said.

—You're not dying. You're just freaking out, he said.

I put the bag over my mouth and inhaled and exhaled.

—I need more air, I said.

—You're getting too much already, he said. Don't talk. Just breathe into the bag.

I stared at the garbage can. There was a Kit Kat wrapper, and some stiff old tissues. I wished it was empty, like a prop.

—Do you love me? I asked desperately between inhales.

—Breathe slower, he said.

—Could you love me? I asked.

I slithered out of my seat. I was lying on the floor now.

—Steady breaths, he said.

—This is such a trope.

I huffed into the bag.

—Yes, he said. But even that should be sort of comforting.

I stayed home from school on Friday. I told my mom that I needed a mental health day, and she agreed.

—Maybe you're having a growth spurt, she offered when I told her I was overtired.

—My shins hurt, I said.

She rubbed lavender oil on my temples and buttoned herself incorrectly into her cardigan while she stared at me.

—Kid, you've got to stop growing up on me, she said.

—I'm trying, I said.

I lay on the living room couch clutching my ratty baby blanket, feeling like I'd been parboiled. I thought of the afflicted girls in Salem, the real girls, long dead, who convinced everyone that they were precious enough for the devil to want them. It was clear now that Dakota had gotten his casting right. For the rest of my life I would play Mary Warren: I would never bewitch and I would barely be seen. Even in college, my sorority sisters would continually forget or overlook me. One year, during superlatives at Spring Fling, they would forget to give me a title at all. I was anonymous in my unremarkable body, and only semivisible if I was pointing a finger or following a girl. Years later, I would pull my sorority composite out of the back of my closet and stare, gazing at Margot's dramatic black plait drifting out of the frame, and Corinne's coy half-smile, and Shannon's sharp little chin, skipping over my own face until I looked for myself row by row.

I was missing rehearsal. It didn't matter.

Sasha texted me.

Where r u?

Home sick

were in the screaming girl part. ur missing out.

best moments?

the part where tarryn is yelling at the audience, y do u cum yellow bird?

I wrote

hahahahahaha

and didn't laugh at all when I typed and pressed send.

And then I wrote a note on printer paper, using my left hand.

The drama teacher is fucking a student.
The student is afraid and won't tell.

I folded it into thirds and ran my thumbnail over the creases.

On Monday morning I taped the note on the door of the faculty bathroom and waited. I was called into Principal McChesney's office before second period.

—There has been an allegation leveled against Mr. Dakota, he said.

—An allegation?

I thought of everything Dakota had taught me. Breathe from the belly. Do not break eye contact. Use your emotional memory to your advantage. I pretended I was a flawless, shimmering girl, a woman really, trapped in absurd circumstances.

—A terrible allegation, McChesney continued. But we think you may be able to help us.

I hadn't expected them to have security cameras in the halls. I knew there was one by the front entrance of the school and a few in the cafeteria, but apparently there was another one, right over an emergency exit sign, that was angled at the faculty bathroom. I had been stupid. I never thought to look.

—Are you the student who left this? he asked me.

He slid my note across the table. It felt like I was on TV. I tried to look at it as if it were a new artifact in my life. I pinched it between my fingers and pictured the version of myself who had written this as a completely different person, a woman possessed.

I considered my options.

Say it was a joke.

Say it wasn't a joke.

—I found the note in the parking lot and thought it should be turned in, I said.

—I see, he said.

He took the note back and smoothed it on the desk.

—It's awfully pristine to have been blowing around in a parking lot, he said.

—It was under my windshield wiper, I said.

—That's helpful, he said. Where did you park? We can check the cameras there, too.

—Good, I said. I wonder who wrote it.

During cultural history, I went to the bathroom and called Greyhound. A ticket to Salem was only thirty-eight dollars, but they needed a license to verify that I wasn't a minor.

I lagged my way back to the classroom. Jarred Liotta was shouting.

—Who moved it? he asked. Who the fuck moved it?

—Language, Blevins said.

Sasha waved me over.

—Someone took his meemaw's shoe, she said.

Jarred was pulling the TV out from the wall now, trying to see if his meemaw's Croc had been knocked backward. Chip Finnick got up and started yanking books off the shelves.

—Open your backpacks, Jarred demanded.

—You can't make us open our backpacks, Sasha said. That's a privacy violation.

—I'll do it, I offered. If I was expelled later, at least I could say that I hadn't taken his meemaw's shoe. I opened my backpack, and Mr. Blevins unzipped his sad little briefcase, and soon our class had opened every bag and watched while Chip and Jarred pawed through the contents. It was like airport security. We all patiently waited for boarding.

—She can't be gone, Jarred said. Where would she go?

—Hey, man, it's just a shoe, Pablo said. He put a hand on Jarred's shoulder.

—It's not! he shouted. It's not!

He was near tears, but none of us laughed. Instead we dug through cupboards and behind bookshelves, combing for a dead lady's rubber Croc.

—Where would she go? Jarred repeated, and I thought of the tiny possibility of a shoe finding its mate and running an invisible body through the walls of the school and across the muddy soccer field outside, the ghost gaining speed, like a thing taking flight, barreling for the tree line at the back of the property, streaking over the clotted grass and ugly fence into a new place, glancing back only briefly to see, just outside the backstage fire exit, beside the generator, Mr. Dakota as he wound his arms around Tarryn's back and she burrowed into his chest, her cheek pressed against him, feminine and kittenish, and the glint of her shining eye, darting, darting, like a wild thing held captive, held safe, wanted, loved, away from cameras, their meeting nothing more than spectral evidence, traceless, unmarked in time.

4

When You're Naked and You Have To

-DEIRDRE-

October 2007

After I saw the body on I-95, just outside of Providence, I called my mom to get some worldly insight, and maybe, if I'm being real honest with myself, some sympathy.

—Oh, Deirdre, she said. (And then:) What was it doing there? (And worst:) besides blocking traffic?

It was worst because I'd thought it, too.

—It was a suicide, I said.

—Oh, baby, she said again.

(My mom's sympathy was strictly syllabic, not content driven. So "Oh, baby" had a sigh and a stretched vowel and a swoop at the end that I taught myself to interpret as *I am sorry that you have seen what you have seen, my precious child, but what you have seen is only a sliver of this world, and—*)

And then she said: Not that I would ever do this, or think of this, but if I *were* to do it, I think it is so selfish to leave a mess that I would probably get a tarp, and leave a check for the EMTs, or something. How was work?

—Boring, I said.

Which was true. I had fallen asleep on the table, for real this time.

—Does the caterer reimburse you for travel?

—Mmm, I said. Traffic was picking up. The lights of the ambulance, fire truck, police all spangled in my rearview mirror, disaster in refracted color. I wasn't supposed to be bothered by the body anymore.

Back at the house, I told my roommate Margot, but I told her in the kitchen, so probably Kyra knew, too, and maybe Corinne, and definitely Ingrid.

And of course Margot wanted to know: What did it look like?

Explaining it was like untangling a dream. When he dropped from the overpass, and I stamped on the brakes and watched him roll off the windshield of the driver in front of me, the car scudding to the right and then shuddering over him again, and then I saw the driver stumble out of the car and root around on her hands and knees, one loafer on, the other MIA, her bare heel white and perfect and naked while she crawled, sobbing, or digging for something on the asphalt, it was hard to tell, and waiting for the police to come, and waiting longer for my lungs to open up and gulp a fresh, choking handful of oil—fat air, all of that wasn't enough to explain it even though it was true. The words were boring and didn't actually describe what had happened as much as hold a place for what it really was.

Margot was impatient with my lack of detail.

—Let's look him up, she said. I followed her back to our room like a duckling.

• • •

Googling "Suicide in Providence October 8" got too many results. "Death on I-95" turned up three for one night.

She said: They aren't calling it a suicide.

—Homicide? I asked. And I thought immediately of a masked man, Zorro's evil doppelgänger, pushing him off the overpass.

She said: Not homicide, just death. I have his name. Wanna know his name?

It was like I was getting an ultrasound, her face glowing over the screen with results, my belly in a knot, and I told her no when I really meant yes.

She said: Tremaine J. Bechetti.

See, I wanted to tell the dead man, I took the time to google you. I care! I am repulsed by your death but I care!

—Darwin said sympathy is our most basic instinct, Margot said.

—Did he really say that?

—It might have been Benjamin Franklin.

The door was closed, so it was okay for her to shut the laptop and crawl under my duvet with me and press her body up against my back. She traced patterns on my neck with her finger. Her breath was stale when I rolled over to face her; it drifted over me like fog. I curled into her chest and thought about crying, but I couldn't really muster it so I made some wiggly motions with my rib cage instead.

—I'm really sorry, she whispered. And then she added, You smell like ginger.

Tremaine J. Bechetti had a Facebook page. His face was broad, as if it had been pressed with a rolling pin. He wore baseball hats, but not backward. He worked in the butcher department at a grocery store in Pawtucket. He liked wrestling and sunglasses and The Eagles and one of those science fiction video games. He had the photos that all of us had; centered in a halo of flash, girls turned sideways at the camera with hands on hips, he with arms in action—either draped forgetfully around someone or holding a drink or both. People had already started posting on his page, a wailing wall:

> trey my man you will be missed but i know your partying with the lord now.
>
> My thoughts and prayers go to the Bechetti family during this trying time.
>
> I didn't know Trey too good but he always had a smile on his face at Fisher, rip.

I didn't want to drive back through Providence, but I didn't have an option. The next morning, still in bed, Mr. Kita called and offered a job for Saturday. They'd pay for my gas and I'd walk out with $500 before tip.

—I'll do it if Manabu's working.

—Maybe he is. I'm driving, I'll look later.

Mr. Kita was always driving when he called me, and he never had answers to my questions.

—Can I shower there? I asked.

—It's a private residence. I'll confirm.

—If Manabu's not working I'm not doing it, I said.

—You want the money or not?

When I hung up, Margot rolled over and took my sheets with her.

—Do you hate your job? she asked me. Because I do.

I watched her get out of our bed and unlock the door. We were roommates again. I wasn't ready.

—I think I dreamed about Tremaine, I lied.

She said: I'd be jealous if he wasn't dead.

And then she leaned into the mirror beside the closet and started squeezing blackheads out of her nose. I could have throttled her with something close to love. But instead I ate a Pop-Tart and spent the morning sequestered on the back patio, skipping a lecture on Israel and Palestine and getting incredibly, stupidly high.

This is not a ghost story. But Trey was the first thing to follow me, the first thing that I had known as vividly, undeniably wrong. I called my mom on the drive again, a repeat of the body without the body. She didn't answer but I made up the conversation on the drive and knew it to be true:

—Hey.

—Hey yourself. What're you doing calling me on a Saturday?

—Driving to work.

—Again? How far this time?

—Not far, the dinner's in Providence.

—Is that so? she'll say, not invested in the *so* of it at all, or the *is*, or the *that*. She could be a voice on an airport intercom: she'll never hear herself, the queen of platitudes.

—I can't stop thinking of the body.

—Oh, baby.

Oh baby. Oh baby. There's a long hiss in my ear.

—I looked him up, I say.

—Oh, baby.

—I thought it would be better for me if I knew him better.

—Stop that. You always hurt when you try to fix.

—Aren't you supposed to have something comforting to say?

—I don't know. I guess so. Other parents would. Think of taxidermy butterflies that flapped their wings in Brazil once. Or something.

Even in fake conversations, my mom doesn't measure up. This is how I know that I am truly hers.

The wife answered the door. She didn't say hello. Instead, she yelled into the cavern of tile and filigree behind her, to no one, or the house, or a hidden fleet of penguined servers: the girl is here! I stepped inside. It was a place designed to hold words like *foyer* and *ottoman* and *dumbwaiter*. I would do well here.

—Can I shower first? I asked her.

She looked as if I'd inquired about her last mammogram.

—I'm sorry?

—Can I use your shower? It helps lower my body temperature.

—The company didn't mention that, she said. Watching her face rearrange was phenomenal. The forehead never moved but her lips could have been the peaks and valleys on an EKG.

—Of course you may shower here, she said, and suddenly her arms were arcs of graciousness, leading, as if I were a shoddy marching band. I followed her past the dining room, where a chef—not Manabu—was prepping the table. I didn't know him. I stayed.

The guest room shower was rococo and tile. I hung my clothes on the towel bar, crowded among layers of guest towels. Naked, in the mirror, my skin rose in goose bumps fat as braille.

This is how you do it:

Pretend that there is a box inside of your skull, a box that you can open and climb into and close, your own control room, a place where you can steer your reluctant, shivering body into the task of acting as a *nyotaimori*. You are a useless geisha. You will walk into the foyer, comfortable in the nothingness that is you, and you will not blink when you meet the head of the household, a man who would be handsome if he didn't hire women to lie naked on a table as the platter of a meal, you will ignore the obvious derision of the wife when you appear in the doorframe of her impeccable dining room, you will ignore the not-Manabu chef who stares at your nipples, first one, then the other, like he can't figure out which pupil to focus on in a close and intimate moment of eye contact with a lover, you will lie on the table, on a slab of wood more expensive than you, and you will try not to think about razor burn, or the leaves being draped over your pubic hair, or the tuna that rests in tiny turrets on your body, of your love at home in your bedroom, of taxidermy insects, or of the body on I-95. It is easy to trust a chef and a chopstick-wielding crowd when you're naked and you have to, so you will die and revive and get paid to do it, and three hours from now you will walk out with an obscene amount of money for nothing, a modern Lazarus, your thighs sore from pressing them together, your eyes adjusting to the light after three hours of fake sleep. In the meantime, sit in the corner of your panic room and wait. Wish that this was a movie with a sound track that could tell you what to feel. Know that the process would be better if you had known him better, if you unraveled him like a cassette tape and were left with sticky black ribbon on the floor, easy to fix, easy to tear. If you could crawl back in time like a half-gilled animal returning to the mud, if you could root beside the woman on I-95, with purpose, finding his feet, then legs, the core, the face half alive half dead, to spread yourself repentant over the shell of his being, then maybe you would have had an answer. Or something.

5

Tend to My Fire and I Will Tend to Your Own

-MARGOT-

October 2007

I like to predict my sorority sisters' futures. Do it all the time. Right now I'm watching them over dinner, shuffling tilapia around on their plates with their forks.

How many will be mothers? All? Mothers are strange women, with their round faces always turned down to their children *à la* sunflowers too fat with the weight of their own heads. Pre-me, my mother was an interesting person. She wore a bikini and drove a boxy green Barbie-ish convertible. Now she's my mother and she says standard-issue banalities about any event (grocery store shopping, nephew's baptism, lunch at Rita's), such as, *Oh, what a riot!* and *We had a lot of laughs!* In a dark moment in high school I asked her why we were all alive. What was the point, etc. She said, Oh, Margot, if you think about it too much it loses all the shine. Then she laughed like she was at a banquet and I'd just told her a joke about a priest in a bar. Mothers come in a few species. That's just hers.

Marcia would make a good mother. She's calm, and she already keeps her hair short in a tiny blond ponytail that sticks straight out the back of her head like a sprig of straw.

And Lisa, too, with those long legs. Easy to picture little children looped around her calves, their arms lassoing her as their own.

Eva would be crap at it. She's leading her third pledge class now. Can't hide her contempt this time around. She could eat her young and then mewl about how they weren't fatty enough.

—They're a shit show, she says to me over dinner. One of them doesn't even have eyelashes. I think she rips them out.

—Who cares, as long as she doesn't rip out anyone else's eyelashes?

—It looks hellish, she says.

—We'll get her some fakes.

—Listen, Margot, she says, I need you to take a little.

—I can't afford it, I say. And I don't know any of them. And I have a research paper on—

—And your dad's best friend's dog has hip surgery, and global warming is an issue. Shut up and take a little, Eva says. You've got to keep your line going, so you may as well do it this semester.

The line. As a pledge, hours were wasted memorizing my big sister's line. It was like learning the most boring parts of the Bible:

Ruby Townsend,
little of
Tiffany Wall,
grand-little of
Sarah Lehigh,
great-grand little of
Deanna Escobar . . .

Upside: If I take a little, when I graduate my name will be another in the forced memorization of others. My life could be completely forgettable, but some haggard future pledges will still have to remember me all the same.

—Ruby'll kill you if you don't take one, Eva says.

True. Ruby loves everything about being Greek. Fat complex, I think. Thought no one would take her, but our house did. They called her Baby Ruth. Her face gets dewy when she reminisces about the days of her pledging, when they drove her to the tennis courts on the edge of campus and made her run laps under the moon until she collapsed. Punishment was to eat the clay off the courts. *I picked grit out of my teeth for weeks!* she told me, grinning. Found myself thinking, do you not floss? But still. Sad, thinking of her running and sweating for devotion under the boulder of the moon.

—I don't know any of the new pledges, I say again.

—Then stalk them, Eva says. I have a lesson with them later. Just sit on the other side of the living room.

Don't want a little.

Do, however, want an excuse to spy.

They arrive at exactly 7:45 and leave their black North Faces teetering on the coatrack in the foyer. They all wear tights and high heels and a mix of skirts and cardigans from Saks Off 5th. Their pledge pins are on the left breast of their cardigans, and they glance down at them often, making sure the faulty made-in-China back clasps didn't break. Not yet allowed to wear the sorority's Greek letters until they're initiated, but the pins have some of our symbols to make them feel peripherally included: two white roses crossed in front of a hearth. They don't know what it means but they know it's something Greek/vaguely Christian/smidgeon occult. They scoop ash out of the hearth and deposit it in a bucket by the poker. They load logs.

They open the flue and light the fatwood. Looking squirrely. Four have already quit pledging. They arrange their chairs in a horseshoe around the fire. I sit on a couch to the side pretending to pick at split ends, though it's too mood-lighty to really do it right.

I was in their place eight months ago, but somehow watching them makes me feel wistful-smug. By now they are thinking of leaving with the four that just quit. By now Eva is a bitch, and no one is feeding them cake, and their initiation date isn't set until February, when Nationals gets a record of their fall semester GPA. They can't predict what sort of hazing rituals we have, so they're imagining what it entails, and the rumors are worse than the reality. On the walks up to the house for their meetings, they say, *What is the point of this?/It's just a stupid fucking house./This is like a cult./ I don't want to buy my friends.* All of them feel ballsy when they say this stuff. They don't know they're already bonded with each other, and what they will never say out loud is that they cling to the possibility of being accepted by the women that scare them, and then, as they age up, of becoming the women that scare.

Most of them stay quiet during the meeting.

Eva goes for the weak ones by pelting them with questions they likely won't know the answer to. It's familiar.

—Tracy, she says. Recite the first stanza of the pledge poem.

Tracy must be the lashless one. I can't imagine her future; she is a girl too nervous to imagine her present. All I can do when I look at her from across the room is picture a rabbit, shivering out in a field. Maybe in a field with a tennis court in the corner and fat Ruby running laps/eating clay. Tracy begins:

A good sister is decent and honor-bound,
Vibrant and composed.

She has the heart of an opal,
The face of a rose.

—Stop, Eva says. Stand up.

Tracy's perfection is in itself an act of insolence. She obeys Eva and watches her carefully, almost ardently. I wonder if she plucks her leg hair, too, one blade at a time.

—Face the fire, Eva says.

Tracy puts her back to the horseshoe and faces the fire.

—Stare into the flames, Eva says.

—I am, Pledge Mistress.

—Tracy, who wrote this poem?

—Lucinda May wrote this poem in 1864.

—Wrong! Eva says, triumphant. It was 1862!

Tracy, who has been nervously swaying from side to side before the fire, goes rigid in the same way a rabbit does when it realizes it's being stalked by a cat. She may as well be roasting on a spit.

—I'm sorry, sister, Tracy says.

Her voice is thinned with tears. Not worth crying over this. Easy to think that, though, outside of the theatrics of pledging, away from the fire, the anxious preening, the rote memorization and quizzes, no longer fighting each minute to prove something. Pledging is like sprinting in the dark without a flashlight.

—It's a shame, Eva says. You have such potential.

—Excuse me, a pledge says from the circle of chairs, but Tracy is right. It was written in 1864. It's in the binders, on page thirty-one.

The pledges begin frenziedly flipping through their Acolyte Sisterhood Membership Binders™, courtesy of Nationals, pages turning so fast they make the candlelight shimmy on the mantel.

—Good catch! Eva exclaims. Well done! Tracy, sit down.

The dispensation of praise is killing her.

—Now, who found the error?

—I did, says a voice at the end. Her hair is dyed Little Mermaid red, and even though the room is sweltering from the heat of the fire, her cardigan's fully buttoned from neck to wrist. She'll have to dye her hair before initiation and cut down on the eye shadow, I think. She's a lip ring away from becoming a scene girl, one of those girls that wears stripes and uses safety pins as a fashion statement.

—Twyla, right? That's your name?

—Do you want it to be? Twyla asks, but there is a wry edge in the question and Eva doesn't miss it. Twyla's voice is flecked with an accent.

—Where are you from, Twyla?

—The Midwest.

—Where in the Midwest?

—Oklahoma. Broken Arrow.

—Broken Arrow! Weird name, Eva says. That's quite the accent.

The corners of Twyla's mouth turn upward, but in firelight it's hard to tell if she's smiling or smirking.

—Is it really called Broken Arrow?

—Last time I checked, Pledge Mistress.

—Do the pledge poem, Twang, Eva demands.

Twyla-now-Twang stands and faces the fire. She says, in a voice slow and careful:

A good sister is decent and honor-bound,
Vibrant and composed.
She has the heart of an opal,
The face of a rose.

While brothers engage in acts bellicose,
She keeps the hearth
And holds children close.

O! my sister of patience,
Too demure for a throne,
Please tend to my fire,
And I will tend to your own.

—Good, Eva says. Now, what does it mean?

—It has to do with the Civil War and holding down the fort at home.

—Go deeper than that, Eva says.

—I'm not an English major, she says. It's like a metaphor for sacrifice and safety? It's not a poem that really grabs me. She pauses. —It sounds a little homoerotic, she adds.

Fifteen heads snap in Twang's direction.

—I think you mean Sapphic, one pledge offers. Homoerotic is for gay guys.

—Sure. Sapphic, Twang says.

—It's not Sapphic, Eva says. Our founders were not gay.

—Lesbian, another pledge offers.

—How do you know? Twang asks.

—Because they don't look gay in the daguerreotypes, Eva says with great authority.

What the hell does Eva think lesbian women looked like in 1864? Did they have artful pixie cuts and wear sensible sandals under their crinolines?

—It doesn't matter to me if they were gay, Twang says.

—Sapphic slash lesbian, says the girl beside her. Several girls nod.

—Sure. Love is love, and stuff, Twang says.

Twyla/Twang's future: customer service manager for a high-speed Internet/cable provider. The lady that they have you talk to after you've gone ballistic on the first two service reps and need someone to tell you in an even, drawly voice that you are going to have to pay the bill, but then she'll placate you with a complimentary twenty-dollar credit on your account that makes it feel like you've at least done something productive with your hold time. You, idiot customer, will feel too soothed by her to assume that she's sketching the word *bitch* in calligraphic script on a Post-it note while she talks.

When the meeting ends, I tell Eva I want Twang to be my little.

—She's not going to last, Eva says.

—I can get her to stay.

Thought I'd start liking Eva after initiation but I just don't. Can't help but remember, as a pledge, the night she and the older girls blindfolded us and stuffed us in trunks and drove. Curled up in the dark with anorexic-steely Shannon, her bony knees hitting me in the back, the two of us conspiring to quit pledging the whole time, then getting hauled out into a clearing in ass-nowhere, hit with birch switches and given shots of plastic-bottle-vodka when we got our facts wrong. At least there was vodka. Belligerent drunk at the end—vodka always puts a mouth on me—and woke up with pine needles in my bed the next morning. *Heart of an opal, face of a rose.* But didn't quit. Deirdre happened. And Ruby. And they were too fun to leave.

Eva's future: will marry a chumpy guy named Warren. Warren will let her get a horde of French bulldogs and they'll live in a duplex in Boston. Warren will make enough money for her to focus on monopolizing the board of a philanthropy program dedicated to raising money to allow underprivileged (whispered—children of color—) access to lacrosse. Those poor ladies. Years spent leaving no impact other than the lipstick on the rims of their wineglasses during luncheons, talking about the best menu options—quiche, or salmon?—all of it ruined by Eva, who interrupts Mrs. Payne's discussion of her son Charlie's most recent adventure with the robotics team at his starchy charter school to push her agenda for the next benefit.

Not the future Eva has in mind for herself, though. My sisters don't get the futures they want. Just the futures I imagine for them. Almost all of their outcomes are mediocre, but none of them suffer. Ask Eva now what her plans are, and she'll say architect, but we can all see that she means architect-that-overshadows-Frank Lloyd Wright, her legacy forever drilled into buildings around the world.

Narcissists, all of us. Lots of click-bait articles about our age group, how we're all the product of participation trophies and helicopter parents and you-can-do-anything preschool teachers and peanut allergies and toys with microchips in them: blame Furby, who told me he loved me, I was important, I needed to give him love like no other person could. Old people say: You think it'll all be handed to you, don't you? Well, yes, old people. We do. We deserve it. We are special. Except now I know I'm not, I don't delude myself with that anymore, and I really wish I didn't know how unextraordinary I am. Still, I feel weirdly superior toward the sisters that have maintained the delusion that they're going to be something significant.

Deirdre is waiting for me in my room. She's wearing her bid-day T-shirt, already ratty, and she's got a bowl packed for me.

—Did you find a little? she asks.

I tell her yes, and by the way, our founding sisters were definitely not lesbian.

—What?

—According to Eva, our founding sisters can't be lesbian because they didn't look the part.

We push open my window and I flick the lighter over the bowl.

It sizzles and immediately turns into a fat cherry of ember. I inhale as deep and hard as I can.

—Slow down, you're toasting the hell out of it, she says. Which little do you want to take?

—Her name's Twyla. We're calling her Twang now.

—What made you pick her?

—She pissed Eva off.

Sitting knee to knee on my bed, turning our heads to the window on our exhales, then facing each other, then window, then back; my heart rate climbs, but time slows and soon it's not so bad that I'm nobody because at least I'm somebody to this person, this specific wonderful person.

I ask Deirdre, Do you ever want kids? and she says What? and I say again, slower, Do. You. Ever. Want. Kids? and she says With you? and I say, Doesn't have to be. Whatever. She rolls on her side to better study me. Slice of her face on the pillow is gorgeous. Tiny threads of white wound in the blue of her irises. Curve of her ear like a bass clef. Some days when she pisses me off all I can see is the misalignment of her bottom teeth. I don't see them now. Lips cover. She's always so serious, like someone took something from her. I want to make her smile. Maybe she's planned a future that'll make her smile.

—I'm not sure, she says.

—Weird. Most girls seem to know for sure either way by now.

—That's comforting.

—I didn't mean it like that, I say.

—I worry I'm a little too flakey to do it. Like, what if I wake up one day and don't want them? Then what?

—That doesn't happen though, I say. All those chemicals in the brain make you stay. It's biological mind control.

—Do you want kids? she asks.

—Yes, I say, but for the wrong reasons.

What I like about Deirdre is that I don't need to explain.

I take her hand in mine and trace the lines on her palm like I can read them. There is a geometric riddle in their creases and I want to pretend that I can find the answers.

—Please don't do it, she says. Don't do the future-game thing. Not tonight.

I fall asleep thinking of her at a hearth, cannons booming outside, children pressing their faces into her damask skirt.

Not much of a secret, but our sisterhood's mythology is tied up in a Greek goddess called Hestia. Other sororities get Athena, or Aphrodite. We get Hestia, frumpy virgin sister of Zeus. She sits at the hearth all day, stoking the coals/scooping out ashes/wondering when she last had her chimney swept, if you know what I mean. Sometimes other gods drop by and show her their newborns, and she checks the fingers and toes and says, Yep, they're babies all right, and the gods trot off with their kids, happy with Hestia's blessing. One time, a pervy god named Priapus tried to rape her, but an ass brayed in the distance and Priapus lost his erection and ran away. That's her big story. Saved by an ass.

The pledges are required to hang out with three sisters before the big-little reveal night. We call it pledge dating. Nationals calls it Friendship Cultivation™. I take Twang out for lunch, and Deirdre, who has also been bullied into taking a little, invites a pledge named Stella. They live in neighboring dorms, and Stella is so excited at the prospect of talking to us that she begins speaking before she even opens the car door.

—can't believe you invited me I am so excited thank you so much for inviting me where are we going for lunch again I haven't been there before but I hear it makes awesome smoothies and do you think they have wheatgrass shots like at—

Deirdre looks at me from the passenger seat like, Oh, God.

Then Twang walks up to our car. Her hair is dyed dark purple, and now I'm the one to think Oh, God, because I'm going to have to tell her to fix it before Eva sees.

But Stella says it for me.

—Twang, what the hell?

—Do you like it? Twang asks.

Stella pauses for the first time.

—It's innovative, she says.

We're in a little café wedged between two of my favorite bars downtown, sitting at a table near the window. The sandwiches are all named after cities in California. Tablecloths are mismatched on purpose. I recognize girls from other sororities here, probably doing the same thing we are. The waiter is skinny and wide-mouthed and has an untied bow tie draped around his neck. Took him a lot of work to look this haphazard. Does this thing where he raps his knuckles on the table after each sentence.

—You ladies ready to order? *rap rap.*

—You ladies need some water? *rap rap rap.*

—Are you superstitious? I finally ask him, and he shakes his head no, clearly I'm the crazy one, and drifts away from the table.

—He's got a cute butt! Stella says.

—I've always wondered what that means, Deirdre says. Do men have cute butts? Men aren't really aesthetically cute, are they?

—I agree, Twyla says. Men are handsome, like, overall, but I don't usually look at their butts.

—You guys! Stella says. I feel like Carrie Bradshaw!

I'm about to tell her she's got the nose for it, too, but Deirdre squints at me, and I have to bite the inside of my cheek to keep from smiling.

—You kind of remind me of her, I say.

Stella is a pretty girl, with high cheekbones and cartoon-Bambi eyelashes. When she smiles at me I feel like I could somehow look past her personality and love her.

—Just out of curiosity, I say, what do you want to do when you graduate?

I think: golden retriever breeder/macramé instructor/Reiki healer.

—I'm studying to be a speech pathologist for children with special needs, Stella says.

My present: cynical asshole.

—I'll be a mortician, Twyla says.

We all stare.

—It's a joke, she says.

—It was very funny, Stella assures her. And then she adds, You've gotta dye your hair before Eva sees it.

—But that was the whole point! Twyla exclaims.

Later, after we drop off Carrie Bradshaw, I tell Twyla I'm going to take her as my little. It's supposed to be a surprise but I don't want her to be disappointed if she doesn't want me.

—That's cool, she says. Thanks.

—Are you going to drop? I ask.

—I'm thinking about it.

—Don't, I say. You're the perfect fit as a sister. You'll just hate being a pledge.

Twyla's eyes drift to the corner of the room, like she's focusing on a ghost, and then drift back over to me.

—I'll stick it out a little longer, she says.

—Can I ask you something? Why doesn't Eva scare you?

Twyla smiles, weary-pleased.

—I've seen scarier things, she says.

—Try not to say stuff like that until you're initiated, I say. You sound a little emo. And seriously, fix your hair.

Some possibilities:

1. Hestia genuinely didn't want to have children and just wanted to be the Greek version of the cool aunt to all. She wanted to kiss babies and feed them Swedish Fish even though their parents had strictly forbidden it, rent them movies with ambiguous sex scenes, and buy them hard lemonade when they were underage. She taught them how to build fires and apply mascara, and not one of the children thought of her as kooky or strange until they hit college and noticed that she was drinking too much at the family reunion; Chianti was splashing out of her plastic wineglass and splattering her tan blouse.

2. Some gods wanted to marry her, but maybe they were the wrong gods. Maybe there was another god, with long thighs and a nice laurel wreath and a jaw that looked chiseled from marble, but he never saw her, mousy Hestia, ashy and forlorn while her sister Aphrodite wiggled her ass and tossed her curly hair over a shoulder. Hestia had read *Jane Eyre* but returned the overdue book at the Olympian library before she could read the final chapters. Inspired, she committed herself to a lifetime of servitude to the women that could have it all. She knew she was not extraordinary. She mourned this quietly, stoking the logs. Poor Hestia, her sisters whispered, she always loved to play the martyr.

3. Maybe Hestia had a thing for women, but that seems unlikely because the Greeks were into some kinky stuff so they'd probably be fine with a lezzie sister at the fire. It wouldn't have been a secret.

Doesn't matter because the outcome is the same. Flat-chested goddess holding a fresh Olympus-born baby, counting fingers, counting toes, cooing over each newborn, glancing at the mothers with strange/protective curiosity. The mothers are bleary and leaking milk through their togas, and they're soothed by Hestia, by her benediction of protection, of keeping the fire, so soothed they could weep. She is the only person who doesn't want to take something from them. She offers protection without a caveat. They clutch her hands in theirs. Their babies lie on the warm hearth floor, briefly fraught.

—Oh, Hestia, what would we do without you?

But maybe Hestia is thinking, Does motherhood make you more significant, or less? Does it make you immortal, or kill you faster? And also: Who thought this job was a good idea?

Maybe Hestia is thinking, Why can't I be a part of this club?

And maybe the mothers are thinking, How can I get out?

Eva has not invited me to this week's pledge meeting. Going anyway. Can't resist the urge to spy. No pledges have dropped this week: everyone wants a big sister. Firelight serves Twang well for the first fifteen minutes. She sits toward the back. Eva doesn't see.

The lesson today is about family lines/why they matter/what they mean.

—Your big sister is like your mom, Eva explains, and I wonder if the pledges can tell exactly how much Eva doesn't buy her own line of bullshit. Then she had them read from the Acolyte Sisterhood Membership Binders™:

Your big sister helps you socially, guides you scholastically, and develops a bond of support and understanding that will last a lifetime. Many big and little sisters become roommates, travel abroad together, and serve as bridesmaids at each other's weddings. A big sister is another opal in the crown of sisterhood.

Even though it's tacky, this is not a complete lie. Still, the expectations are stressful. I think: Twang's all right. I also think: too late to back out of this now.

Eva lobs some perfunctory questions about the founders. Stella and a couple of other pledges deliver rote answers. Lucinda May died shortly after she gave birth to her second child, in 1869. Joanna Howard was the daughter of a preacher who didn't approve of the sisterhood. Virginia Wheeler had three daughters who took the rituals to college and legitimized the sisterhood.

When Eva is pacing the horseshoe, she finally sees Twang's hair. It all goes to hell.

—Twang, Eva says. Are you serious?

—Is something wrong? Twang asks.

Somehow, I feel a new level of affinity for these pledges. All of us must be clenching our jaws in the exact same way.

—Don't play dumb, Eva says. We covered appearance and grooming in the first week.

—My hair is fine, if that's what you mean.

—Read page thirteen in the binder, Eva commands.

Twang flips to page thirteen. She reads, unwavering, small-drawled:

Women of the sisterhood acknowledge that their appearance represents their membership as a whole and will, in turn, be mindful of maintaining a healthy visage. This includes, but is not limited to, using caution with the application of piercings, unusual hair colors, excessive makeup, or tattoos that may be visible in a workspace. While our sisterhood is a place of personal empowerment and individual identity, we acknowledge that societal norms necessitate a standard of professionalism that should be fostered during college years in order to prepare for the working world.

—Is your hair color natural, Twang?

—No, Twang says.

—Did you knowingly do this even though you are aware of the requirements of our house?

—Yes, Twang says.

—Why?

—It's a stupid rule, Twang says. I'm not even wearing Greek letters yet. I can dye it before initiation.

—That's not soon enough, Eva says. This is insubordination. This is the sort of shit that gets you kicked out.

—Is that what you're going to do? Twang asks. She says it so steadily she may as well be asking about the weather.

I know this is a bluff. Eva will not kick Twang out, not after four girls have dropped. If too many drop, people will get suspicious.

—Twang, Eva says, Turn to the fire.

Twang is not afraid. Eva's voice is shaking with rage.

—Kneel, she hisses.

Eva picks up the bucket of ash from beside the fire and dumps it over Twang's head. It's like watching a bomb drop. The ash collapses over her hair, then hits the floor and plumes outward, curling toward the rest of the girls. The carpet is a disaster. Immediately (and in some cases, I think, dramatically/prematurely) the pledges begin to cough.

Eva removes the bucket. Twang is fully covered now. Hair and face and clothes are white.

—That's better, Eva says. Much more natural.

I can't imagine how Twang is not coughing. Did she hold her breath? How did she manage it? She nods benignly at Eva. She does not open her mouth.

—New lesson, Eva says. Clean this up. All of you.

Eva disappears into her room and the pledges open windows. One of them gets the vacuum. Two complain about asthma and leave. Twang walks outside, leaving footprints of ash behind her, and shakes herself off in the front yard. Like a dog.

Hours later. Nearly eleven thirty, and the pledges are still scrubbing at the soot in the carpet, cursing each other, generally miserable, but sometimes I can hear them whisper something and laugh. How did they get here? Why is this important? It's absurd. It's obnoxious. It's impossible to leave.

In two weeks, on big/little reveal night, Twang will appear. Hair dyed dark brown. She will feign surprise when she is led into the living room and I meet her at the hearth with a bouquet of white roses and a silver necklace with our sorority's insignia etched on the pendant. We will embrace in front of the fire. We will take photos of our new family, and weeks later I will give her a puffy-painted frame of the three of us together, all posed with our hands on our hips, arms around each other, all holding our breath while the camera goes off in rapid fire. At least ten shots so Ruby can select the one where all three of us look prettiest/thinnest.

Ruby, Twang's new grand-big, will give her the gifts of our family's line: a seersucker sport coat that she will be forced to wear to a mixer, a small hand mirror that she'll have to do a traditional line off of, and an autographed glossy eight-by-ten of David Hasselhoff that is likely a fake. The gifts are so old that no one knows the symbolism behind them anymore.

I'll take Twyla out in the back driveway and gift her with three more things: an eighth of weed, a handle of rum, and the promise that I will never, under any circumstances, call her Twang ever again.

—What a legacy we have! Ruby will exclaim, and Twyla will light a blunt and pass it, pull up her hair into a pony, and I will see during my turn that the bottom layer of her hair is not quite brown—almost purple/almost red—a hidden mauve.

6

Hush

-TWYLA-

May 2013

My neighbor Jason found me. He'd come through the back door of my half of the duplex to complain about how it was my turn to mow the lawn—Was I ever going to mow the lawn, damn it? Did I even know how? I heard him hollering in my kitchen, and I scrambled in the bathroom to cover the cuts on my arms and legs but it was too much, too fast, and then he was in the doorframe, staring.

He was the one who called the ambulance.

—No need to be so dramatic, I said. But when I went to stand from my perch on the edge of the bathtub, the color blanched out of the room and I staggered into the wall, drunk with blood loss. I left a swatch of red by the light switch.

—Jesus, Jason said. Jesus Jesus Jesus. Twyla, what is wrong with you?

And my father, who's been dead for fourteen years, materialized behind Jason in the doorframe and squinted at me, the whites of his eyes webbed in a net of bloodshot.

—Everything's wrong with her, my father said.

But Jason didn't hear him. Nobody hears him but me.

I didn't have an answer for either of them. Jason stayed until we heard the ambulance crush the gravel drive out front and then he retreated to his place next door. He probably didn't want the paramedics to think he was dating a lunatic like me. My father shuffled off, too. I heard him rattling through my refrigerator, looking for a beer.

I was too weak to fight the EMTs when they found me in the bathroom. I let them handle me like a child.

—Where are we going? I asked.

And the squat EMT, the one with the Burt Reynolds mustache, shucked a sunflower seed from between his teeth and said, Willard Hospital, sweetheart.

So I knew then they all thought I was crazy.

—What about St. Agatha's? Or Greendale? I asked.

But they both shook their heads no.

—We think you'd get better help at Willard, the squat EMT said. He said it gently, like I was going to snap on them. Maybe if I'd had enough blood in me, I would have.

He rode with me in the back of the ambulance, watching me the whole time.

—I just don't get why a pretty girl like you would do this to herself, he said.

I wanted to ask, *What does pretty have to do with it?* But I didn't have the energy to correct him. I closed my eyes and felt my head bob from side to side on the gurney while the ambulance plowed through South Tulsa.

The lacerations on my wrists were clean, well spaced, lined one after the other like the frets on a guitar. A frowning intern stitched me and I stared hard at a perfect dot of blood on the toe of her left sneaker. It took twenty-four stitches to close them all. And then, on my thighs, another seventeen.

—You're required by law to stay on Ward D for twenty-four hours, she said between sutures.

—I'm not suicidal, I said.

—Doesn't matter. If you did this to yourself we have to monitor you before you go.

I melted into a wheelchair and she rolled me into the elevator. Doors shut. Floors rose in monitoring beeps. Too much light, and not enough air.

—I'm not suicidal, I said again. Desperate now.

—I know, she said. But the spun sugar in her voice gave her away.

They took my wallet and my keys and gave me loose pajamas that resembled scrubs. I filled out paperwork, endless paperwork. Acknowledging certain rights. Forfeiting others. Then, they gave me the list of rules. They were the sort of policies applicable to an ashram or a day care:

No electronics of any kind.
No scissors, nail files, unapproved pens, letter openers.
No outside food. No drink. No drugs.
No tolerance for violent behavior.
No sex.
Prescribed medication is mandatory. All other medication is forbidden.

The admissions chick—a young girl, maybe even my age, gave me a Visitor Clearance form.

—Fill out all the people you would permit visitation from at the appropriate hours, she said.

Who was I going to put? Certainly not my mother. And who did I need desperately enough that they would come see me in a nuthouse?

So instead I wrote Cher, Mike Huckabee, Jesus. At the end of it all I put Jason's information. I needed him to bring up some clean underwear.

The admissions chick didn't blink.

—You forgot to write Mike Huckabee's email, she said.

Only later did I realize that she thought I was crazy enough to actually think those people would visit me.

They gave me a sedative I couldn't pronounce. Put me in a single room with overstarched sheets and a nurse who would peer at me through a window in the door every thirty minutes. I slept soundly, so soundly that when I woke up I felt as if I'd missed a part of my life, shot forward through the glass window of my present self and into the future without even noticing.

But then the doctor came in and I remembered. I didn't want to like her, but I did the second she opened the door. She had more gum line in her mouth than teeth and wild eyebrows, mad scientist eyebrows.

—Twyla White? she asked.

—Present, I said.

—Good to hear, she said. I'm Dr. Mercer but you can call me Sadie.

I decided immediately that I would always call her Dr. Mercer. No need to start up a buddy thing with a woman who could have me permanently committed.

—Let's go over the basics, shall we? Is this your first time at a psychiatric facility?

—Yeah, and my last, I said.

—How old are you?

—Twenty-two.

—Hm. And where are your parents, Twyla White?

—Father's dead. Mother's on her way to it.

Dr. Mercer scribbled something on a notepad. She was nice to look at even though she was ugly. Her skin was smooth and pale, like the statue of Hestia that stood in the Chapter Room of my old sorority house. She'd been a lucky statue: girls would kiss her before their exams, or a date, or a pregnancy test.

—What are you writing? I asked.

—Just information. I can show you my notes when I'm done. I don't believe in keeping things from my patients. Now, what brings you here today?

—I cut myself, I said.

—Yes, I understand that part, Dr. Mercer said. What I mean is, what emotionally brings you here today?

—Listen, I've seen shrinks before, I said. How about I condense all of this into one session and save us both the time? My father hanged himself in our garage when I was eight. I was the one who found him. Yes, he was abusive. Yes, he was an alcoholic. No, I don't lie awake nights thinking about it. Yes, I'm an only child. My sex life is fine. I'm afraid of bees and heights. No, I don't need exposure therapy to fix either phobia. And no, I don't hear voices. Is that enough, Doctor? Am I free to go now?

I expected her to say, *Let's explore this anger you're directing at me*, that sort of thing. She studied her hands on the clipboard for a while. Mannish hands. I liked that, too. I didn't really want to blow up at her the way I did.

—I'm going to get a coffee, she said. You want one?

—No, I said. But can you ask the bitchy nurse with the constant wedgie if I can get my phone back?

She didn't respond, but I saw the twitch of a smile around her horse gums when she walked out of the room. I studied the watermarks on the tiled ceiling for a while and picked at the edges of the tape on my arms.

My father watched me from the corner, idly scuffing his shoes against the floor, a Marlboro tarring his fingers.

—You're a stupid bitch, he said. Win her over, or you're stuck here forever.

When Dr. Mercer came back she sat at the foot of my bed.

—Don't sit there, I said. I need some space.

She nodded, got up, and moved to the chair in the corner. My father, bored and sullen and probably uninterested in my ugly doctor, vanished.

—You say you don't want to be here, she said. And legally, we can't make you stay much longer. I don't think you're suicidal; you're not a danger to other people. But I think you should stay.

—Sorry, I said. I have to pick up my dry cleaning.

—Can your dry cleaning wait another night? she asked. Just one more night. Then, if you feel like it, you can go.

I don't know why I said yes. But before I knew it Jason was leaving my stuff with the nurses at the front desk, and every time I speak to Dr. Mercer, she convinces me to stay on a little longer.

After the first day they took me out of surveillance and put me in Ward C. Some religious nut must have donated money to our floor, because the Twenty-third Psalm is painted in giant calligraphic script all over the hallways. Outside my room is the line *Surely goodness and mercy shall follow me all the days of my life.* My eyes buzz with the words.

The anorexics are on the floor below. The suicidals and the self-harming are above, where they kept me the first night. We call them the acutes. If you fuck up on Ward C, if you start banging your head against the sink or telling people that the angels want you to kill the janitor, or you get caught stabbing at your hands with a mechanical pencil tip, then they put you with the acutes. I am a lot of things. But I'm not the top tier of crazy bitches.

The girls on my floor are a catchall. They're just exaggerations of my sorority sisters at school: madness varied, but madness contained. Some of them shuffle the hallways like their veins are filled with cold honey. Some of them fall asleep leaning in doorframes. Some of them are afraid to leave their rooms. One of them tries to eat the toilet paper in her bathroom. One of them tries to fuck all the others. Another girl is an eraser. She rubs at her skin with pencil erasers or old gum or even a rough sock if she can get her hands on it, rubs at her skin until she gets a raw red burn. I can tell when it's time for her meds because she starts quivering with nervous energy like a plucked guitar string that never settles. Ten minutes after she swallows, the muscles in her face slacken. Her chin drops onto her chest, and I can see the greasy part of her hair. I hate that she's like me.

My roommate is a schizo, an overweight chick named Wu Chin with shiny teeth and a tattoo of the Libra scales on her shoulder. She laughs like a dolphin—*eeee! eeee!*—even when I'm not trying to be funny. Especially when I'm not trying to be funny.

—I bet you feel like hot shit knowing that you're staying with a famous person, she told me when they moved me into her room.

—I'm sorry, I haven't read an issue of *People* in a while, I said. What are you famous for?

—Oh, she said. Obama held me prisoner. He released me when the people protested. But he's keeping me here to make everyone think I'm crazy.

—Makes sense, I said. What'd he hold you prisoner for?

Her eyes widened and darted around the room, irises pinballing in every direction.

—Have you got your Social Security card?

—Not on me, I said.

—I can't tell you till I check it, she said.

When she wasn't looking, I took the nail clippers out of her cubby and hid them inside the Kleenex box by my bed.

That night when I met with Dr. Mercer I told her I wanted out. Told her I had no interest in whack job conspiracy theorist roommates.

—Has it ever occurred to you that we all make our own conspiracies? she said.

—That sounds like hippie crap.

—I stand by it, she said. We all trick ourselves. We all scheme. It's just that some of us live in the delusion enough to be hospitalized.

I didn't feel like answering her. I could have. I just didn't feel like it.

—I think you should reframe your idea of whack job. Crazy isn't such a simple term, she said.

My stitches itched, but I didn't dare touch them in front of her. I looked out the window behind her desk. A brick wall in the distance, at the edge of the grounds. I could just picture the evening traffic on Yale Ave. on the other side. People with their windows down, listening to the radio and smoking. The sunset flushed orange sherbet through the trees. When I tuned in again, Dr. Mercer was talking about my mother.

—You said in our first session that she's dying, she said. What is she dying of?

—Breast cancer, stage four, I said.

—Want to talk about it?

I didn't know what she wanted me to say, but I guessed. I thought of all of the Hallmark cards I used to stock when I still had my job at the DB Mart in Massachusetts.

—I've made my peace with it, I said. It's for the best. Her spirit will live on when she's gone.

—Mm-hmm, Dr. Mercer said. So I see we're playing the bullshit game this evening.

—Thanks for playing! I said.

But that night I couldn't sleep. I kept thinking of the last time I saw Mom.

I went to her house to weed the front yard flower bed and make sure she paid the hospice nurse. She had put on her wig for me. Her left arm was swollen, wrapped in a bandage from shoulder to wrist to keep the pressure going.

—I've been sleeping in your room since you left, she said.

—Wanna watch *Wheel of Fortune*?

—I know you won't move back in with me, but what if you just stayed a night or two? It's lonely at night.

—Next week I'll do that.

She nodded, but we both knew I was lying. It had been so much easier when I'd been at college, thousands of miles away from her, away from her need. But since I had moved back to Tulsa I felt her yoked to me again, and my body ached under the weight of the burden.

—You were always so independent, she said.

Could she know what I was thinking? I tilted my face away from her.

—So were you, I lied.

When I glanced back, I found her eyes shut tight, the corners of her mouth drooping downward. She leaned her head back on the couch and her wig shifted out of place. The skin on her face was so translucent it couldn't have been thicker than a moth's wing. I thought she had fallen asleep. I got up to leave, and she spoke.

—Twy. Remember what I asked you after Grandma Gwen died?

—No, I said.

But I did. I just didn't want to say it.

—Yes you do. You remember.

I could hear the mantel clock tick. My dead father cleared his throat and lit a cigarette from the gas burner in the kitchen. He gave me the finger when I looked at him.

—Soon it'll be time, she said. Soon I'll be in too much pain. I'm already in pain now.

—Why does it have to be me? I said. Why can't you just do it yourself?

And she opened her eyes and stared at me, as if she'd never seen me before, the way a child surveys a stranger on a train.

—I've never asked you to do anything, Twy. And I want it to be your face I see when it's time. My baby's face, and no one else's.

—You're sick. How could you ask me that? You're really sick.

—Yes, that's the point, she said.

I couldn't sleep in Ward C. So I got out of bed, took the nail clippers with me, sat on our bathroom floor with my back blocking the door. I decided on the skin above my pubic bone, where they wouldn't look. If they tried I could call them perverts, yell about lawsuits. I dug the clippers in and pinched and yanked. Tracks of skin came up in little strips. It was bloody, it was superficial, but it worked. My hands buzzed with adrenaline. I felt every molecule of myself surge with focus. True Zen meditation, true presence and awareness and clarity.

When I finished, I flushed the skin and the bloody tissues. I stuck a wad of toilet paper against the gouges. The waistband of my underwear held it in place, the blood pasted it closed like glue.

And when I got in bed, whenever I saw my mother's face, I would press hard at the new lines until the sting blotted out the memory. I fell asleep high on the ether of my own pain.

After four days, Dr. Mercer noticed I was still avoiding the other patients.

—I'm not asking you to go to group therapy, or even make friends. I'm just asking you to eat lunch with them. A little socializing would be extremely beneficial for you, she said.

—I'd love to socialize. With normal people, I said.

She was getting annoyed with me, I could tell.

—I'm not sure I understand your disconnect, she said. You can leave here at any time. But something prevents you.

I opened my mouth to protest, but she hushed me. She's good at hushing. Pointer finger extended, thumb pointed out. The sort of gesture Jesus would make in a painting.

—As long as you're here, I suggest you take advantage of your treatment. Meet the others, just have lunch with them. What's the worst that could happen? she said.

—I could like someone, I said.

I'd done the camaraderie thing at school in Massachusetts. I'd had my sorority sisters, and in them, I'd had some friends, before Margot fucked it up.

—What's wrong with liking someone? she asked.

I was remembering viscerally now: Margot on the gurney, zipped into a blue bag, the wheels snagging on the carpet outside of her bedroom door.

—I can't be a part of someone else's sob story anymore, I said.

—This might surprise you, Dr. Mercer said, but these girls don't want to be a part of one, either.

And that's how I found myself at the cafeteria during Ward C's lunch hour, sitting between Wu Chin and an agoraphobic named Lisa who looked ready to throw herself under the table at the slightest provocation.

—Obama called me this morning, Wu Chin said.

—That's a delusion, Lisa whispered. In group we said that's a delusion. You need to accept that if you want to get out of here.

Wu Chin's face plummeted so fast from satisfaction to rage that I felt my stomach lurch with the change.

—You're a delusion! she shouted. And you have sheep's eyes!

—Sheep's eyes? I said.

Lisa put her head in her hands and moaned.

—Look at her, Wu Chin said. She's all glassy and flat. Obeys everyone. LISTEN TO ME, LISA, YOU SHEEPY CUNT!

At the other table, the girl with the eraser burns started laughing at us, the kind of laugh that could shrivel a grape into a raisin.

I left my Jell-O half-eaten, my meat loaf untouched. I stabbed my spork into the top of it, like a flag. I waited by the door for lunch period to end. As soon as it did, I shot up to Dr. Mercer's office and pounded on the door. Rustling papers inside. A woman's voice halted in the middle of the pitch and fall of a sentence. I pounded again.

She only opened the door a crack.

—Yes?

—I'm not eating another meal with those fuckups, I said.

—I'm with another patient right now, Twyla. We'll have to discuss this later.

She closed the door, and I stared at the jamb for a while, trying to figure out why I felt so jealous of the fact that Dr. Mercer had other patients besides me.

—She doesn't like you, my dead father said. She knows you're a liar. You waste her time.

I could hear him following me down the hall. His deep wheeze. The swish of his jeans.

On my way back to my room, the stuck-up nurse with the wedgie found me.

—You have a voice mail from a Jason DeAngelo, she said.

—Did you listen to it?

She nodded.

—It's protocol.

They love that word here. *Protocol.*

I waited for her to tell me what he said. Instead, she handed me the phone from behind her desk and punched in the voice mail code.

Hi, ah, it's ah, me.

Christ. I could have made a drinking game out of his pauses.

I ah, wanted you to know, ah, that your mom's been looking for you. She had a nurse drive her over here and poke around and then she banged on my door and I met her. So I, ah, told her where you were. You should call her. Sorry.

The nurse was watching me. I moved carefully. Swallowed.

—Nobody can visit me here unless I give them permission, right?

—Right. Would you like to add your mother to the Visitor Clearance form?

—No, I said. I want you to make sure she can never get in here.

This morning I could feel the conspiracy, I could feel the nurses collaborating in the hallways and quieting when I opened the door. I'm so sick of fluorescent lights and off-white walls and whispers. I'm not paranoid. But I'm not stupid, either. Then Dr. Mercer calls me into her office earlier than usual, and my suspicions are confirmed.

I don't like the expression on her face. Lips covering gums. Her hands steadier than usual. I sit in my usual spot and feel as if I should check under my seat for a snare.

—I'm starting to suspect something, she says.

Goddamn wedgie nurse. Are there no secrets in this hospital?

—I'm starting to suspect that you're here in order to hide from your mother. But the question is, why?

—She's dying, I say.

Dr. Mercer nods.

—Yes, I remember, she says.

Impatient. She's impatient with me. She doesn't like me.

—Does her death frighten you? she asks.

—No.

I say *no* too fast.

Dr. Mercer sits back in her chair and stretches.

—Let's talk about your father, she says.

—Now we're cooking, my father says from the corner.

—I think we should get to the heart of things.

—I want you to come to grips with the truth.

—Out with it!—Let's have a breakthrough, for Christ's sake—Don't you know what a pain in the ass you are when you hide things—Your denial is toxic, is toxic, is toxic.

Who's talking? Him or her? Mouths are moving and phrases are jumbling in and I can't keep up, I'm behind on the quota, the assembly line is jamming.

—I'm ready to check out of here, I say.

But I trip when I get out of the chair, wobble and knock into the door and I leave so clumsy I'm afraid parts of my body have been abandoned on the way out. But there they are, arms and legs, all moving down the hall for me, blundering, but moving, down to my room and Wu Chin looks up from her bed and asks what the Fuck is wrong with me and I ignore her and go to the bathroom and lean against the door—why don't they put locks on the door? They don't even trust us enough to shit?—and I rip off the tape and start pulling the sutures out of my wrists and my legs, one after another, yanking, skin tearing, and people are pounding on the door, I can hear Dr. Mercer calling my name, but I don't answer and then the door is pushed in, I slide with it, and a pair of hands grips me by the arms, pinning me flat, the bathroom light shines in my eyes until they water and I kick and scream and kick until something cold runs through me, suddenly I'm very tired, so thick and tired, and I drop off the edge into a black corner of sleep in a burly nurse's arms.

I'm in a new room now, back with the acutes, I'm guessing, tongue dry and swollen in my mouth. I go to scratch my nose and can't. My wrists are looped to the bed railings, bandaged and sore. And my father has his back to me—I can see the bald spot of his thinning red hair, and his ugly plaid shirt half-tucked—he's looking out the window, and when he turns around I see the rope loose around his neck as if he's wearing a bad tie.

I press the buzzer on my railing. Over and over I press the buzzer. A nurse peers in the window at me and then she's gone. My father smirks and I can see his incisors, like yellow grains of rice. He gets so close I can see the thread crosshatching the buttons on his shirt.

—Nobody wants to take care of an ungrateful little shit like you, he says. He raises his arm to smack me, just a warning smack the way he used to when I forgot to water the tomato plants or take down the laundry, but then Dr. Mercer comes in and he retreats to his chair to watch the show.

She takes my hand. It feels warm and sweaty and I love it. I'm surprised she wants to touch me at all. She sits on the edge of the bed, still holding the hand. I watch it as if it is an appendage that doesn't belong to me.

—If the door of perception were cleansed, everything would appear to man as it is: infinite, she says.

We're quiet.

—Before you give me credit for such a wonderful line, I should tell you it's by Blake, she says.

I want to ask, How can you cleanse the door to perception? It sounds so easy. Metaphysical Windex. But my tongue is too unruly in my mouth and I can't seem to remember how to speak yet.

—Let's talk about the truth now, she says.

I nod at her. I would do anything for her, to make her stay. To make him leave.

—My father—

My voice comes out with rocks in it. She holds up a finger—so good at hushing—and takes a pitcher of water from the table at the foot of my bed. She cradles my head and helps me drink. I can't help it. I think: *She leadeth me beside the still waters.*

—My father hanged himself when I was eight, I say.

—I know that. I know, she says.

—I was the one who found him.

—I don't forget the things you tell me, Twyla.

I nod again.

—But nobody knows that when I found him, he was still alive.

Her face is expressionless. I want her to tell me I've done a good job. In the corner, my father howls.

—What did you do? she asks.

—I watched him, I say. I didn't run for help until he was still.

My father is writhing now, his legs are curling and kicking at the floor, his face purples, the rope tightens around his neck.

—That's a big confession, Dr. Mercer says. That's very brave. Thank you for sharing that with me.

She squeezes my hand. *She restoreth my soul.*

—How do you feel? she asks.

—Old.

—Good girl. Good girl.

She's watching my eyes. I wonder where she keeps her rod and staff.

—If it's all right with you, before we go any further, I would like you to tell me one other thing.

—Anything, I say. And I mean it.

—Tell me what it is that you're looking at in the corner, she says.

And I tell her, Nothing.

Just a trick of the light.

7

Children of Saturn

-MARCIA-

April 2007

When people lie, they put their hands over their mouths to keep the secret from escaping. If they feel compromised or inferior, they put a palm on the back of their neck and rub. When they feel close to getting caught, they cross the threshold and overcompensate with penetrating eye contact.

The best liars are fluid. They sit still, but not too still. They are worried about being uncovered, but not terrified. Most of all, they are experts at tact, so when my dad asked me about school over the phone and then mentioned, casually, that he was coming up to the sorority house for a visit next Saturday, I told him that I couldn't wait to see him.

—Why isn't Mom coming? I asked, and he told me that her coworker Karen was having a baby shower but he was feeling restless, and wouldn't it be great to have one-on-one time together for a change. I told him that would be great, so great, really great.

I'd taken the call in the living room. Eva, who had been dozing under an econ textbook on the couch, cracked an eyelid.

—Your dad's coming?

I nodded, hand on forehead. (Sometimes liars rub their foreheads when they want to feign exhaustion. Amateur liars.) Eva continued:

—Moments like this, don't you wish we still had flip phones? They were way better to hang up with.

—All I can do is fling the phone.

—It is definitely not as satisfying, Eva said.

—Can I ask you something?

She nodded, and the econ book slipped off her chest and onto the floor. She made no effort to pick it up.

—Do you like your parents?

—I like the idea of them, she said.

—Did you always feel that way?

—No, she said. I used to really, really like them. But things changed when I watched my mom try on a bathing suit in the Macy's fitting room without underwear.

I knew my dad would want to see my bedroom so I went upstairs and filled out the Alert Board. A sorority house is built to look deceptively welcoming. He could see the immaculate foyer, the living room, and the dining room, but he would not be allowed beyond the kitchen doors without notice. Unfortunately, the riskiest sisters are the ones who are garbage at reading the board, so on Saturday morning I knew I would still have to tell Elina to put on a bra.

I don't have a problem with liars, really. Eva is usually a liar. So is Shannon, who purges, and Margot and Deirdre, who make out with each other, and Amanda, who says she's not a virgin. The good thing about liars, though, is that they are so busy playing defense they never notice when you are trying to hide something yourself.

• • •

My brother Nathan lived in the Rosewood complex on the other side of town. He'd dropped out of college four years ago under the pretense of taking time off and now he works as a fry cook at Valentine's and is trying to create a start-up that has something to do with containers designed to store leftover pizza slices. He isn't depressed, but I am depressed for him. The apartment smells like his job.

—Dad's coming on Saturday, I said.

—Shhh, he said from the recliner. Dr. Phil's about to tear this lady a new one.

We watched Dr. Phil's mustache jump as he gesticulated at a woman with a midwestern haircut and runny mascara.

—Janet, let Darryl into your heart! Nathan yelled at the TV. He looked at me, faux doleful.

—Marcia, when will Janet learn to accept true love?

If it were a nice apartment I could have thrown a decorative pillow at him. Instead, I chucked an empty Pez dispenser from the floor.

—You are so empathic, I said.

—I sweat empathy.

—You sweat something. Dad's coming on Saturday, around ten.

—You already said.

—What are your thoughts? I asked him.

—He hasn't called me, Nathan said.

Of course he hadn't gotten the call. Since his dropout, Nathan made guest appearances at holidays and uses work to excuse himself from other visits home. Our parents don't beg for a different outcome. Last Christmas, my mom asked him to take the family photo. I stood in front of the tree, Mom and Dad on either side, my brother hidden behind the shutter. I should have offered to switch places so they could have pictures flanking each child. I did not offer.

—He might call, I said.

—Probably won't.

—You could come meet him with me at the house. My sisters will be around. He'll be nice. It could be nice.

—Hey, it's his thing. I don't want to make him uncomfortable if he doesn't want to see me.

—But I want to see you, I said.

—You're a peach. No wonder you're the favorite.

—Don't say that, I said.

—It's okay, he said. You're my favorite, too. Marcia, Marcia, Marcia!

Nathan did a jokey tantrum stomp into his kitchenette and started thinning the basil seedlings that were sprouting on his windowsill. He nibbled at the tiny double leaves as he pulled. It was weirdly disturbing to watch.

—You look like that Goya painting where Saturn devours his sons.

—There's only one son in that painting, Nathan said, and I wondered for the thousandth time why he hadn't finished college, though of course there are plenty of smart people who don't finish or don't go and lead successful lives and maybe vocational schools are right for them or maybe they find direction in the military and so on and so on, I know.

—I asked one of my sorority sisters how old she was when her parents stopped seeming so perfect to her and she said that she knew it when her mom tried on a bathing suit without wearing underwear.

—Raunchy, he said.

The basil pot had been annihilated. Only two seedlings remained.

—Remember being little and thinking that our parents were awesome?

—Sure.

—I miss that. I used to watch other kids roll their eyes at their parents and I'd feel horrified.

He smiled and nibbled thoughtfully on the root of a tiny seedling.

—I don't know if I ever had the reverence for them that you did, he said. But I get what you mean. I miss thinking they were special.

—How do we get that feeling back?

—You don't. You just get used to knowing that your parents are assholes like the rest of us.

—I really do think he'll call you before Saturday, though.

—Don't count on it, he said.

We watched a full thirty minutes of daytime television before he said, Maybe he'll call. Who knows.

My father was handsome. When I was a little girl, I loved going out with him because I thought everyone was looking at me. He wore Ray-Bans and dress shirts rolled up at the forearm and carried a Zippo in his front pocket, but I never saw him smoke. Up close, I could see the scar on his neck from a tracheotomy that he'd had as a boy. We had a game where I would ask him what caused the scar, and every time he would answer with fresh morals:

Don't juggle marbles in your mouth.
Don't brush your teeth on the stairs.
Don't swallow a whale's eye whole.

Nathan, knowing that it was his job to protect his little sister from becoming a gullible idiot, would shake his head at me from across the table.

Margot's dad stopped being perfect when he took her to play minigolf and told the girl behind the counter that she had a sweet mouth. He didn't compliment her smile, she said. It was the mouth, specifically. It was vile.

Shannon said she stopped admiring her mom when she noticed she couldn't calculate the tip at a restaurant in her head.

Amanda said her granddad was amazing, and kind, and she was so lucky, how did she get so lucky? Her voice was so timorous that I didn't push it any further. She would make a great nun, I thought. She's got that quiet, sanctimonious gusto.

Twyla said that her dad hanged himself when she was a kid. Her honesty was mortifying. I stopped asking other sisters.

For me? I was eleven. He was working in the yard. I came in for a glass of Tropicana and the phone rang, NO NAME on the caller ID. He'd told me time and again not to answer a NO NAME. It breeds more of them, you know. Spam callers just wait for a person to pick up and then they sell the number to other companies. But I was bored, and I answered, and on the other end, I met Sylvie. Sylvie, who was crying. Sylvie, who was asking for him by name. I don't think I spoke after the hello. I hung up. The phone rang again, NO NAME, and she did not leave a voice mail. Outside, my dad was scooping soggy leaves out of the gutters and tossing them onto a tarp below. I crept up to him and jiggled on the bottom rung of the ladder, not enough to harm but enough for him to know that I was there.

On Saturday morning my dad stood outside on the front steps, still handsome. He had a full head of springy brown hair, precisely parted on the side. Wrinkles were converging around the edges of his eyes that made him appear kinder than he really was. He carried a care package filled with my mom's efforts: banana bread, my favorite lilac soap, a jar of night cream, dental floss, and pictures of the family pug, a furry void-filler who had joined the house when I left for school last fall.

—Thank you for this! I said, and gave him an airy hug, trying not to crush the bread. He did not give my mom credit for the package.

—Who painted the lines in your parking lot? They're close, he said. Do you have an assigned spot? Do you park next to someone who is careful with their doors?

I spoke loudly in the foyer: SO GLAD YOU COULD COME, DAD! DAD, HOW WAS YOUR DRIVE?

—Does your mom know that you're doing this with your hair now? he asked.

He ran his hand over my stubby blond ponytail. It was so short I had to use bobby pins to pull pieces of it back.

Doors edged open and shut. Somewhere, Elina was lurking without a bra, and two pledges were hung over and vomiting and sobbing in the upstairs bathroom. I'd found them holding hands under the stalls just minutes before, sisters of suffering. It was kind of sweet. I let them be.

I seated him on the living room couch and noticed, just in time, that someone had left an errant condom wrapper under the coffee table. This was the downside of Saturday visitors. I batted it under the couch with my foot as if it were a hockey puck. God only knew where the actual condom was. I sat gingerly beside him.

—I've missed you, he said.

—I've missed you more, I said.

A polygraph test would be ideal. A cop with Dr. Phil's mustache would sit before us. My dad would have sensors affixed to his chest and arms. There would be a card table. There would be folding chairs. A single lightbulb dangling on a ceiling chain would be too much though, too Hollywood.

The Dr. Phil cop would ask some baseline questions and then the real stuff would begin. I'd wear glasses. I'd be taller. Maybe Nathan could do it and I could disappear from the scene altogether. Nathan would say,

—Tell me about the scar.

—Tell me why Marcia is the favorite.

—Tell me how long you've been cheating on Mom. Does she know? Why doesn't she leave?

—How are classes? he asked.

—I got an eighty-eight on my introductory accounting midterm, I said.

I made eye contact, but not too much. I did not cover my mouth with my fingers. I asked him: How's Mom?

—Terrific, he said. But she sure does miss you.

—Remind me again where she is?

—She's playing a scramble with Sarah, he said.

—That must be why her cell went to voice mail this morning.

—Yes, he said. Her handicap is at twenty-one now. Not bad for a woman her age.

—That's something, I said. How's Nana?

—She's good! They found a new med for her arthritis. She fired another aide.

—What a bitch, I said reflexively.

—Language, he said, and then we smiled conspiratorially at one another.

—It's so quiet, he said. Where are your sisters? If they're your sisters are they my daughters?

—My sisters are hungover and hating their lives, I said, and I uncrossed my legs and turned toward him. He was smiling.

—Let's have a tour.

He nodded approvingly at the kitchen and asked about my diet.

Was I taking a multivitamin these days? Did I get enough calcium? Did I still think I was allergic to cashews?

—You managed to escape the freshman fifteen, he said. Wish I'd been so lucky. I gained twenty pounds my freshman year and your nana put me on Atkins that summer.

He stopped speaking; his lips disappeared between his teeth. (This is a shame gesture, the books say, and it indicates that the speaker feels they have overstepped.)

—Who checks the fire detectors in this house? he asked.

In the bedroom hall, he did not comment on the strange oblong stain on the carpet outside the bathroom door. The Alert Board had been flipped to reveal a framed photograph of our sisterhood's crest, our secret signal for a visiting parent. I showed him to my room. I'd painted it sea green and pushed the twin beds together to make a king. Every night I managed to roll into the gap and edge the beds apart, but at least it looked seamless with a duvet on top. Under the bed, behind a storage bin of salt-stained boots, I'd hidden my pledge paddle, my bowl, my grinder, my wrapping papers, a tiny Baggie of E, and a series of wineglasses covered in puffy paint that had my pledge name emblazoned across them. I had no interest in my father discovering that I'd been dubbed Nala after a long, loopy night on weed rolled in PCP, where I convinced myself that all of my sisters, in their fuzzy-hooded parkas in the snow, were actually lions with terrifying manes.

—Tidy! he said approvingly. He sat at my desk. So, this is where my smarty-pants girl spends her free time.

—You got it, I said. God, I thought, please don't open the drawers.

Elina loped by while his back was to the hallway. She stopped and lazily lifted her shirt to flash me, exposing her droopy tits, before she shuffled out of sight, middle fingers extended. On the other side of the house, out of the clutches of parental purgatory, the doorbell trilled.

He got up and peered out of my window. I had a nice view overlooking the woods. Clumps of forsythia were popping up in the brush below.

—Who trims the trees here? he asked. Do you guys have an arborist? I don't like how this one leans toward your window.

—I think a guy takes care of it during the summer, I offered. I rubbed the back of my neck with my palm.

Down the hall, I heard feet hurrying. Eva appeared. She still had one fake eyelash on from the night before.

—Sorry to interrupt, she said, but there's someone here to see you.

My mother was here. My mother would smooth the strange, halting relationship of a father and his semiadult daughter, but we were doing surprisingly well. He was annoying and proud and sort of nice in small doses. We were reaching across that weird chasm, from making once-a-week three-minute phone calls to something else, something sort of charming and sincere. On the horizon, there were possible father-daughter activities: maybe kayaking? Bowling? Picking out shirts for him at the mall? And during all of this, this strange, fast-flickering fantasy, I saw my father turn from the window and grip at the edge of my desk to stabilize himself.

—Wait, he said to Eva. Wait.

Eva watched us warily from the doorway. She peeled off her fake eyelash.

—Who's at the door? he asked.

—Your wife? she said. I don't know. I didn't ask her name.

Oh god, I thought. Oh god, no.

—Sweetie, my father said to me. Sweetie, sit down for a second.

—You brought her *here*? I said.

—She wanted to meet you, he said. But I asked her to wait in the car.

Eva was transfixed now. She stood in the doorway, her impish face glowing at the obvious drama of our situation.

—I don't know why she's coming in now, he said. I'm sorry. I asked her to wait until I spoke with you. I'm truly sorry.

Sylvie, the poor woman, sitting in his car like an obedient beagle, waiting for her master to let her into the house. It was pathetic. It was gross. I shoved Eva out of the doorframe and staggered downstairs. My vision had tunneled; my ears were dulled with a current of blood. Behind me, my father was begging for a pause that I couldn't dispense.

She wore high heels (on a Saturday morning, of all occasions, I fumed), and her hair fell down her shoulders in absurd, cartoonish ringlets. Her arms and legs were long and slender, but she had a torso like a potato. Her jewelry screamed cubic zirconia. Or worse, it was real. Worse, it was from my father. She clutched at a navy gift bag with a grosgrain ribbon.

—I'm so sorry, Rich, she said. I'm so sorry. I couldn't wait.

—She isn't ready, my father said.

—Marcia, I'm so sorry. It's so nice to meet you. You look just like— I'm sorry, is there a bathroom I could use? she asked, and then she threw the gift bag as if it were a grenade, and vomited on the foyer floor.

I looked at my father's face. Horror left him immobile.

—Help her, I commanded, but he didn't move. So I went. I stood behind her while she retched onto our tile. I rubbed her back.

—Let it out, I told her. Always good to let it out.

Eva, who had followed the commotion, brought a recycling bin in from the mail closet and held it under her face.

—Do you want to sit? I asked Sylvie. She shook her head no between heaves, leaning forward, her hands on her bony knees.

She gagged, and we recoiled and stared, and I kept rubbing her back. I made stupid considerations. Should I walk her to the bathroom? What if she left a trail on the floor? Should I lead her outside? Should I tell my father to take her home? She finished and started to cry.

—Don't do that, I said. You'll mess up your makeup.

I led her into the living room. My father stood dumb.

—Dad, get a grip, I said behind me. He followed.

Eva had already left and returned with tissues and three pledges. I didn't need to look back to know that they were already cleaning up. Leave it to a sorority house to master the efficiency of mopping up after a purge. One pledge brought water. Another picked up the gift bag and put it beside Sylvie. They were benevolent and strangely angelic-looking, with the indicators of their own hangovers on their faces: dark circles under their eyes, scraps of last night's makeup clutching at the skin, ashy hair pulled into identical wild topknots. Of course, out of earshot, I knew they were in the foyer hissing insults over the bucket of suds.

—Do you feel better? I asked Sylvie, and she wept harder.

—Come on, I said. You're not even the first person to throw up in this house this morning.

—I've pictured this for years, she cried, and I never thought it would happen like *this*.

She gestured at herself, and then smiled at me blearily. I wasn't quite ready to smile back.

—Does Mom know about her? I asked my father.

—Which part? he asked.

His hands were crawling over his mouth, rubbing the contours of his face, as if he could erase the years from them.

—All of it. Meeting me?

—I moved out on Thursday, he said.

I was too defeated to feel stunned.

—She hasn't called you because she thought I should be the one to tell you. I'm moving in with Sylvie. Your mom is keeping the dog, he added lamely, as if I cared at all about the status of the overfed little mongrel that I had only met four times.

—Why now? I said. After all of these years?

—We tried to make it work with your mom, Sylvie began, but—

—She wasn't amenable, he said.

I refused to allow myself to interpret what they meant by that.

—We need to go, Sylvie said. I'm so sorry, but we need to go. I wanted us to take you to lunch, and really get to know you, but I think I'm going to be sick again.

She was blanching by the second.

—Should I open this? I said. I picked at the bag.

—Oh god, Sylvie said.

She reached for the bag but I pulled it away from her. It was my gift. If they were going to alter the trajectory of my family's life in one sitting, I at least had the right to open the gift they had picked out for me. The bag was almost weightless.

—We need to slow down, my dad said. This was a mistake.

I picked up the bag and found, inside, a sonogram.

I don't think it's fair to say that my father was the reason why I fell apart. Why, in the next year, I'd start rolling and bombing out of classes and how, eventually, I'd drop out just like Nathan. I don't want to blame him completely. But I do.

When I was little, my dad would come home from work by six and eat dinner with all of us without fail. There were *Sesame Street* place mats, and silly straws for milk. Nathan, depending on the year, depending on the day, resented or adored me. My dad made jokes about Nathan's soccer coach. My mother thawed out fish sticks in the microwave. We used paper napkins. There was no television permitted at dinner, technically, but we'd leave it on mute and gaze at it collectively when we were bored with each other. And then, at nine o'clock every night, my father would leave for two hours. He had a standing meeting with friends at the shooting range, he told us. Some nights, if I felt restless, I'd crawl out of bed and watch television with my mother in their bedroom while she waited for him to come home.

—When you hear the garage door, you've gotta scoot, she'd tell me. And we'd curl up and watch old movies while somewhere, at an unfixed point across town, my father cocked and fired.

So this is how good liars do it: they move slowly, in increments. They laugh loudly at the dinner table. They pick up paper napkins and diet soda for their wives at the store, on their way home from another woman's apartment. They teach their children, through years of subterfuge, that the only way to be authentic is to be colossally destructive.

In the parking lot, my father opened Sylvie's door and let her clutch at his forearm as she lowered herself into the passenger seat. She waved at me from the window, then reclined and disappeared from sight.

—I know you'll have questions, he told me.

—Did you love Mom?

—I still do, he said. His eye contact did not waver.

Why do people lie? I wondered. To protect themselves? Or others? Why go to all of that effort for such a clumsy ending? He was so quietly devastating, his deceptions were so infiltrative in my own life, that sometimes I worried that his decisions would devour my family whole. I just never thought he'd build a new one in the process.

—You're too old to be a father again, I said.

—I don't feel old. Sometimes I forget my age completely.

—I don't.

—May I hug you? he asked. I let him.

I didn't speak.

—Tell me what's in your head, he begged.

—I can't decide if it's worse to cheat with one woman for ten years, or with multiple women.

—Marcia, he said.

—Don't Marcia me, I said. I need time.

—Do you hate me? he asked.

His hands were in his pockets and he was looking down at his shoes. He looked like a boy in trouble. He looked like a liar.

—I have to talk to Mom, I said.

I watched them drive away, and when I was sure they were gone I collapsed on the bench outside of the house. It was too cold to be comfortable but I wasn't ready to face Eva and the others. Everyone would know. I pressed my hands over my eyes. In the parking lot, a car door slammed and boots clopped across the driveway. They stopped at the bench. Nathan stood over me, backlit by a weak sun. He was holding his basil pot with the two remaining seedlings: his best contenders.

—He never showed?

—He already left.

—What happened? What'd I miss?

He sat beside me.

I plucked a scrawny seedling, put it between my teeth and crushed it, stem and all.

8

Wild Things Sorry for Themselves

- AMANDA -

March 2008

I've been keeping the ducklings in a box in my room since yesterday and no one has complained so far. Kyra's room is to my right and she's never home long enough to notice, and Tracy's to my left. She knows about them but doesn't seem to mind. They're blacker than I'd imagined, and they've got nostrils, which is something I'd never really thought about. Sometimes when they drink they dip too deep and splutter, bless their hearts, because they don't understand yet that water and nose holes don't mix and their brains aren't big enough to help them learn, so they do it over and over, thirsty and choking.

When I was a baby and I didn't get what I'd want, my granddad would say, *A small bird will drop frozen dead from a bough without ever feeling sorry for itself.* I found out in my freshman comp class that it was actually a line from a poem and not something he'd made up on his own, but it doesn't take the right out of him. I feel bad for the babies because I can't do it for them.

I found them at the edge of the campus pond yesterday. No preening mom, no father. Was there another choice, except to scoop them into an empty Xerox box from outside the Arts Building? They'd all gone silent in the car ride home, puffing their bellies to catch the warm air from the heating vent. Last night, I fell asleep to feathers and shuffling paper.

I've been feeding them pieces of cabbage and cooked corn but their poop is coming out green, which can't be good, and they all huddle in a clump like they're freezing even though I've got two desk lamps turned over the box. They can't really quack yet, but they chirp in ways that feel huffy. It's like they're waiting for me to be enough for them.

Their first night with me, I read them Ecclesiastes.

—To every thing there is a season, I read, and a time to every purpose under heaven.

When they looked up at me they let their beaks fall open as if they were surprised by what I had to say.

Granddad is losing his ears these days so I had to email him for advice on what to do with the babies. He lived on a farm when he was a kid, just like everyone else's grandparents in the world. He wrote back in under an hour:

> **hello sugar snap my sweet Amanda how's my girl why dont you find yourself a feed store near school and ask for something called starter crumbs you can leave a dish out for them pretty much all day and don't have to worry about them getting too fat ducks are stupid but they are smarter than people and know whenn too much is too much and have you got a bright desk lamp to put over the box that should keep them warm at night you should see the forsythia out here bless the lord this spring is really something and I know it will come up**

to you soon post man didn't show up at all yesterday if you can believe that sleet rain snow but he gets a limp and no one fills in no wonder this country is a mess may god bless you and keep you love from your granddaddy

I could teach him how to press enter but he is just too precious to fix.

The ducklings look at me, heads all on the same swivel. The cabbage is limp and they blink and ruffle at me, like, Is there a main course? Their chirps are always in twos: tee tee, tee tee, tee tee.

I like to talk to people telepathically, but so far no one has said that they hear me. They're afraid, maybe. Or they feel it but their brain doesn't write out the words clear. Still, when Tracy walked into my room I thought at her, you're a beautiful gift from our lord, and in my prayers. Tracy pulls her hair, lashes, and eyebrows out when she thinks no one is looking. It's a shy-girl problem, I think, to go on like no one can see you.

She kneels at the box slowly like it's an altar. Her bandanna is slipping and I can see a bald spot the size of an egg on her hairline.

—Only five, she says.

—Are there supposed to be more?

—I don't know. I guess not. I always thought there would be more in a litter. Is it called a litter?

—Maybe a flock?

—Flocks are for big birds, she says.

I wish there were three of us in my room, one loud person to do the talking for us. But there isn't, and so I say, Their poop is green.

Tracy is a good girl. She nods at me like I've said something smart.

—You know what? We should take them for a swim.

• • •

Nobody uses the bathtub in our house except for pedicures. In a bathroom with three toilet stalls and three showers, it just feels too open to loll around naked in a stew. The radio plays in here at every hour. One night when I was still pledging I found myself on the pink-tiled floor at 3:00 a.m. with sick in my hair, listening to static. I woke up even later curled up in the left shower with my clothes on, the water running. I only use the middle shower now.

Tracy runs the bath and I put the ducks in one at a time. They look healthy but they feel like hollow little accidents. They could disappear with one wrong squeeze.

—They're so cyooooote, Tracy says. And she's right. I worry so much I forget that they are precious. Their feet make tiny currents in the tub and they paddle around, aimless, knocking into one another and leaving trails of poop in the water. The effort they put into paddling is scary.

—Did you ever have any pets? she asks me.

—A cat, I say.

We'd called her Mehetabel. She was an outside cat, half wild. Only my granddad could pet her, and that was only if she was eating. One day she'd shown up with a kitten hanging out of her, long dead, and when my granddad went to pull it out she ran into the woods. We never saw her again.

—My parents never let me have pets, Tracy says. Except fish. But fish don't count.

In this light, I can see tiny speckles of eyebrow hairs, too small for her to pull.

—They don't blink, they don't count, I say. And both of us are quiet and happy with the new rule. I never thought I could have friends in this house. I've tried, but no one wants to hear God's word and so I carry His words alone. Maybe, when Tracy is ready, she will hear His call.

When the water turns cold I start to worry about them catching a chill, so I dry each one, tiny pats on their faces and backs and underbellies. All of them wiggle and writhe at me save one, who is so still that I think he's probably got something wrong with him.

Granddad told me that when he was a boy his toddler sister Ruth fell in love with some baby chicks and wrapped them up in a towel in her arms, and gave them a squeezing hug that smothered them all. She thought they were sleeping because they felt safe in her arms. He told me this when I was just barely not a toddler myself, sitting Indian-style on the floor in a too-big nightgown that stretched over either knee, taut like calfskin. I remember being surprised that I was big enough to kill a chick. I remember thinking, if he ever let me go to the public school, that I would tell all of my new friends this story. Did I ask him this night or another why death happens?

After their bath, I print out driving directions to a place called Old Town Tackle and Supply! Tracy is still in my room, watching the ducklings fluff and hop around the piles of shredded paper I've made for them to sleep in.

—Can you keep an eye on them for me while I'm gone? I ask.

—Huh? Her face is all cheek, like a bunny. She has no eyelashes. So many times I want to ask her why she does it, and then I don't.

—I've got to buy them some supper, I say.

—And you want me to watch them?

—If it's all right with you.

She's got a shy, naked smile. —No one says "supper," you know.

—I know, I say, when I only half do. At home we say it all the time.

—No offense, she says, but sometimes you talk like the 1930s.

I want to ask, why the offense? If I could start myself over, if we could all go back to before we were, wouldn't we?

Before I leave, she tells me thank you, and I say you're welcome, and neither one of us pauses over taking the other's words.

The drive to the feed store is all back roads. This state used to farm tobacco, but now only a few places near my school still do it, and the curing barns I pass look wilted and gray. The feed store, when I find it, is the same color. It's hard to tell if it's a true old feed store from the front or if it's just pretending to be one with the paint job. The parking lot is gravel, the inside floors are speckled with pieces of dirt and melted ice and straw. A bell tattles when I walk in. The racket it makes is unfair. There is a man at the counter and I tell him inside to be nice. He is wearing a shirt with a Browning logo and he's sucking on an e-cigarette.

I don't have any words for these people.

—What do you need?

If I could find a piece of him that I don't want to run from, then I could talk. There are ducks in my room, teeny ducks, so sweet and stupid they don't know how to drink water, with funny black eye markings and little squawk voices and wants. The man has square nails like my granddad's.

—Starter crumbs.

There is blood under one nail, growing out, a slammed nail, I guess.

—Why? he says.

All the true things in the world taught me to turn away from evil. But meanness is an impulse in me that I can't burn out. I look at his slammed nail and think, deserved it, I look at the frayed collar of his T-shirt and think, trash, I look at his hands and imagine all of the dark things I've been warned about that a man like him may have done to girls in hallways, girls at dances, girls at parties. I feel my evil and swallow it, feel it and swallow it when I see these people.

—The crumbs are for baby ducks, I say.

—Ducklings?

—Ducklings.

Does he think he's taught me a new word? And then I cut the meanness in me again, two red slashes over the thought.

I follow him to the back aisle. He walks stiff, like he's been sitting at the counter since the morning talk radio ran into music and then back into talk. He shows me a yellow bag with drawings of chicks on the front. A thank-you comes out of me and floats in the air on a string that follows me on the walk back up to the counter.

—Where are the ducklings at? he asks at the counter.

I don't answer.

I give him my money.

Back in the car I think, there is no corner of me that is good enough for men or God. If I could turn away from evil I'd have to leave myself in the car with my thoughts on him, this poor person trying to sell me a bag of old crumbled bread.

This morning I had taken a duckling out of the box and watched it not be sorry for itself. It took no effort. I watched it flop-walk up and down the bed, then on me. I lay flat and let it wander and peck at my body, fleet feet, walking me, understanding my body in a way I would never know.

The roads are gray with dirty snow this time of year and when I turn corners my tires flip up little gritty waves and I feel like I'm doing a job, moving the water from one spot to another. There are half-melted fields. Every other car is faster than me. Every bumper has a sticker with an opinion.

In the driveway of the house, I step in slush and leave a single wet footprint stamped down the hall. I knock even though it's my room, and the door is opened to me though I can't even remember my hand on the knob. But years later, I will remember the feathers before the blood. Tracy is Indian-style on the carpet and their down is fanned around her, a perfect half-circle halo, with each quill toward her, and she is still plucking when I come in. She is still plucking when I come in. She is still plucking when I. When I.

Here is what I remember with eyes closed.

A stop it, a Stop it and a pull at her hands. The bodies of two, naked and stacked one on top of another, head to toe, still warm under the towel I used to dry them with. The blood is sticky. When I pick one up and rub at it I know it's gone, eyes open and black and dry. Tracy's bandanna is around her neck, the front of her scalp is raw, and if she had eyelashes they would catch her tears and she is saying, why, why am I doing this. I recognize Satan in her eyes and I slap him so hard spit comes out and slides sideways down her chin. In the box, three babies chirp, seeing and forgetting the wrong over and over.

—I didn't know they would bleed, she says. She puts her hands over her mouth and her body stutters on itself, tee tee, tee tee, tee tee.

Ask, and it will be given to you. But even years later I will know that the why is unimportant because it will never satisfy. All I will know is that some things want so badly to be good. Some things want so badly to be good that they can't possibly be at all.

9

The Short Game

-DEIRDRE, MARGOT-

March 2007

Before Margot there had been two boys.

The first was on a living room couch while his parents were at Wednesday night Bible Study, and he was disappointed that I didn't bleed on the Superman towel he'd conscientiously spread underneath me.

—I thought you were a virgin, he said.

—I am.

—Then how'd you lose your cherry?

How did I lose it? Was it supposed to burst for him like a piñata? And he'd hurt me, of course he'd hurt me, but without the blood there was no proof of purchase. Later, I stood in his parents' shower for ten minutes, waiting for the remainder of him to slip out between my thighs. But even the following morning, I could still feel him seeping from me. No one had warned me of this.

I thought I was defective.

The second one I'd fucked on a chair and while I moved he kept angling his mouth for my right nipple like a lamb angling for a bottle. How I didn't give him a concussion I don't know. At one point he'd slid a hand under my skirt, dry fingered and clueless, and although I appreciated the effort I couldn't tell him he was hurting me.

I was gutless with men.

Margot took away the work of explanation.

It is still difficult for me to know if this is because women have better instincts with each other, or if it was just her.

We went slow. Gay men seem to have definitive out moments and women just don't. With Margot it moved in a sequential order, a nice steady drop into minidykedom.

1. Fun night of drinking. In the foyer, we were babbling about first dates. To kiss, not to kiss. Then kisses, and their strangeness. How they should be revolting but are not. That was her segue. She leaned for me, kissed me, full stop, teeth grabbing at my top lip, her thin cold hand slipped around my waist, other hand on my neck, beneath my hair. A sister could have found us at any minute. She tasted like whiskey. A tiny woman, her core so warm I didn't care.

2. Back in our room, undressing for bed, she did not turn her back while she changed. I fought eye contact the whole time.

3. Two nights later, she was cold and asked if she could stay in my bed and I didn't tell her no. She was smaller than I was, her eyes keener, hair darker, shoulders thinner, feet colder. She was shrewder, more decisive, funnier, at some hours cloudier. I couldn't keep up and didn't try.

4. In capable hands, standard-issue seduction works every time. See steps 5–8.

5, 6, 7, 8. The mouth the straddle the foreheads touching the fingers interpreting words like *graze* and *brush* and *trail.*

Wild words, animal words, put in action on a body in the half-dark terrain of a twin bed, and I wasn't sure if I loved her, but my body did. Every tendon in me shortened by an inch and then slackened by two. She put a hand over my mouth and this time I bit back.

9. The streetlight outside our window cast her in pale yellow. She sat on her heels and wiped her mouth.

—I don't know how to do that for you, I said. She was beaming.

—If that's the first thing you worry about I'm sure you'll do fine, she said.

All through grade school I'd felt faulty and done everything I could to blend in so others wouldn't find out that I was a fraud. But belonging to the house had fixed the fear. Every time I wrote a check to the sisterhood, or rubbed the Hestia statue, or told a pledge to shut up, I felt a little safer. Now I had impulses and I followed them, quickly, before I lost the momentum or the bravery to do so. I thought of my older brothers, both in finance, both careful, both wearing creased slacks to Thanksgiving, and of my mom, who panicked if she couldn't mow the lawn on a rainy Sunday because she might get a notice from the homeowners' association. The claustrophobia of their lives: how dare they consider dragging me with them! Margot was my best impulse, my most destructive choice.

10. It came out later she'd always wanted me. I did not ask if there were others.

—Why'd you want to be a sushi model? she asked.

—*Nyotaimori.*

—Saying it in another language doesn't make it less weird, she said.

—It wasn't that I wanted to, I said. It's good money.

She was on top, her hands massaging my breasts. Her thighs dug into my hip bones, and I worried about bruising her, thought about eating more to dull my edges for her. I was too bony.

—You wanted to, she said. Don't lie. You wanted to.

—I wanted to, I agreed.

—Why?

She brought her hands to my neck and squeezed. One second. A reminder of what could be undone.

—I wanted them to see me and not touch. I was tired of being touched and seen at the same time.

—Does it get you off?

—Not anymore.

—It's boring now?

—It's boring now.

—Tell me why.

—You know why.

She didn't squeeze this time. Instead she bit my neck, left side, hard.

—Say it anyway, she said.

—Because (and now I inhaled, hard enough to lift her just a little bit) now I know I'm what they want.

—The game is over, she prompted.

—It's a short game, I said.

—So you'll quit then?

But I would not leave for her. Being bored in my new life was better than being bored in my old one.

In a later day, she truly found me out:

—Is there anything you're not disdainful about?

—You, I said. You make me humble.

—Good answer, she said, and she crawled over me, pinning me, tickling me, until I was consumed by her black hair in my mouth, her laughter in my ear.

10

A Founder's Account

August 1863

In those days it was rare for me to go into town, but when it became unbearable I would steal away to check the P.O. for a letter from Nash, returning either in secret triumph or terror. As time went on Joanna's disapproval grew, and it got harder to leave. I had to hide my trips during her afternoon naps, or when she was busy in the springhouse, and eventually, as his letters dwindled, I terminated my trips altogether. I did not for one moment think that Nash was dead. I did, however, find it possible that he would not want to return to me when it was all over.

But Lucinda craved town. She countered the furtiveness of my trips with a boisterousness that became progressively harder to grasp. She seemed to believe that if she carried on as if the world were unchanged then perhaps it would start to behave accordingly. Now, deep in August, she wore her plum dress, fiddling with the streaming ribbon on her hat. She'd seen a comparable hat in Godey's book and was prideful about her predictive stylistic abilities. Her face was overstretched and spot-scarred, but she knew how to put on style.

—If you don't make the effort then you may as well lie down and die where you stand, she said.

—Joanna won't like it, I said to her. She'll be cross and supper will be a discomfort for all of us.

—Staying here is intolerable, she said breezily. If I don't see a new countenance today I'll lose my wits altogether.

—Your father needs you.

—Father is not going anywhere, she said.

She saw me recoil at her callousness. I never had a good face for hiding my thoughts. She crossed the sitting room and let her skirts gasp around her when she kneeled beside me.

—Virginia, my dear one, I am so sorry, she said. I do not have the compassion that he requires. I am ill equipped.

—I know you are, I said.

It had been intended as an insult, but Lucinda was impervious.

—I'm going to the market, she said with finality. I will buy you a new hairnet.

As we grew, she struck me as increasingly inauthentic, even when she made a thoughtful gesture. She patted my knee and rose and kissed the statue on the mantel ten times.

—I am not in need of a hairnet, I said.

So many other things were needed then, and none of them could be found on shelves, but it was not my nature to say such things in those days. Instead I was sullen.

After she left I washed Uncle's face and resettled him in bed and then I went down to the garden and found Joanna rooting at her potatoes.

—I must look played out, she said.

I said I didn't think it was so, even though Joanna wasn't especially fine-looking, even on cleaner days.

She smoothed her hair and retied her apron.

—Lucinda's gone down again.

Joanna had hair that was nearly red, especially in the sun. She looked to the road.

—She left already?

—She did, I said.

—That's a pity, she said.

—If there were any men left I'd think it was a beau, I said.

—There are none, she said, and she yanked a tuber from the ground with a grim little smile.

When Lucinda returned at dusk she brought me a hairnet, chenille, of all things. Joanna puckered her mouth. Puckering the mouth was an old woman's habit and yet there it was on Joanna's face, not yet twenty. We sat down to supper with admonishment in the atmosphere. There was a great deal of uninspiring talk about the garden. I spoke little and ate quickly. When I finished, I took the blackberry brandy from the sideboard and brought it up to Uncle's room. He did not turn his head when I opened the door.

—I've come with something sweet, I said.

He was staring upward like he was waiting for a god. During the day he would watch the light that pushed through the curtains and swept across the ceiling. At night he would stare at the shadows from the lantern.

I pulled him up and held the back of his damp neck and tilted the brandy into his mouth. Some of it slipped down his chin and I had to wipe at it so it wouldn't stain him. He swallowed but did not speak. He smelled of all the bodily odors that we try so hard to dampen.

—It's a nice pick-me-up for the evenings, I said.

I had taken on a strange tonality with him, as if he were somehow younger in his illness. I spoke brightly and would leave the room extinguished of a resource that I did not know I had possessed. He leaned forward like he was about to spit and a tooth slipped out of his mouth onto the quilt, the root already blackened.

—It's all right, I told him.

I scooped the foul thing into my hand. He looked at me and mouthed but didn't speak, his lips in a crumple, then a hiss, then slack-jawed. He wanted Lucinda.

—I'll send her up, I said.

At the top of the stairs I heard Joanna saying,

—no need for it anymore. It looks poorly on us—

—But who is there to look? Lucinda asked. If they're alive to see me, then they're just as miser—

—It's all distraction, Joanna urged. It's all idleness and it takes us from our purpose.

—Lucinda, I said. Your father's wanting you.

—Yes, Lucinda said. I expect he is.

But she did not rise from the table.

We retired to the sitting room and performed our rites. They'd begun as superstition, when we first heard a rumor that the rebels were just twenty miles away. I could remember the first night with the ashes but could not recall the season or the hour, only their placement on my tongue.

Joanna stood at the fireplace and recited in her best poetic voice:

O! my sister of patience,
Too demure for a throne,
Please tend to my fire,
And I will tend to your own.

We kissed the statue of Hestia on the mantel, five times at the head and five times at the feet. It had been Lucinda's mother's, given to her by a beau when he had seen her reading a book on the Greeks. Of course, this was Lucinda's origin story, and Aunt Bernice had never been one to trifle, so I am uncertain if this was an exact telling. I couldn't imagine men were that thoughtful.

The three of us kneeled at the hearth and dropped our foreheads to the ground like the Moslems in India. The stone was warm on my forehead. Finally, Lucinda rose and took a spoonful of ash from under the andiron. She put it in her mouth without waiting to see if it was hot before she swallowed. Joanna did the same. Long before, when we had first begun the ritual, I had made the mistake of taking a spoonful too near a coal and burned my tongue. I never told my cousins. Instead I learned quickly the tricks of swallowing ash. The mouth must be full of saliva, so one must use the tip of their tongue to tickle the root of the mouth before they take the spoonful. Otherwise the fine powder will trickle into the lungs and cause a horrible choking that will break the custom. Joanna had indicated this bodily rebellion might occur because the lungs are masculine by nature and they want to rebel against the femininity of Hestia's sacrifice.

Nothing was impossible in those days.

That evening Lucinda retired early after her long day at the market while Joanna and I went into her father's room and cleaned parts of him that were shameful to all of us. His thighs were so absent of muscle that I could see his bones. We dressed him in fresh clothing. Tears leaked out of the corners of his eyes and oozed onto the pillowcase.

—There now, Joanna said. She wiped at his withered face and kissed him sweetly on the cheek. He fixed his eyes on her.

—The last good man on this earth, she said.

He smacked his mouth wetly, trying to shake loose the cogs that worked his tongue. He took her hand.

—With much regret, he began, barely audible, but Joanna hushed him and smoothed the quilt, pressing his chest with ferocity. His eyes were shining with a surge of zeal that I had not seen in weeks.

—Your father shouldn't have—he began again.

—There now, Joanna said urgently.

She looked to me and then back to him again.

The clarity left him, his face slackened.

—Lucinda will be with you directly, I said to him.

A residue of ash was thickening in my mouth.

The shadows on the ceiling wavered in unison while Uncle May watched, his feeble hands gripping hard at the quilt, as if something could descend from above and take him.

When I study my memories I find myself wanting to track the date. Perhaps I do this because if I can name the span I can justify the actions. It must have been summer. It was likely August, unless my memory is failing me and Joanna hadn't been rooting at potatoes at all. What if it had been asparagus? But I do not recall a chill in those final days. I have to rummage for other clues. Lucinda's dress. The acrid smell in Uncle May's room. Joanna's hair, lightened by the sun. And how I woke that night thinking I heard cannon fire and thought of Nash. His last letters to me had fresh turns of phrase that I couldn't fully understand. He wrote of soldiers being bucked and gagged. He wrote of his druthers. His sentences swaggered over the page. I thought I heard cannon fire again. So perhaps it truly was August, the loudest month, and I had been sleeping with the sashes thrown to let the air in, when the cicadas and frogs were cricking at one another outside in a way so deafening that I couldn't sleep.

I found Lucinda downstairs at the fire, poring over a book. All of the books in the household had been her mother's. Their pages stuck together and, when gently coaxed apart, revealed troves of accounts by Plato, and musings on Greek gods and goddesses, and numerology. Ten, one book said, was the number of completion. Lucinda had loved the roundness of the statement. In the winter before, when we weren't so somber and we still laughed at the fire, she had admired the ten, tracing her fingers over its shape.

—That's fair, she said. At ten years old I think I felt most whole.

—Surely you'll feel it again at one hundred, Joanna said. A tenfold completion.

—No one should suffer to live to one hundred, Lucinda said. Imagine the jowls.

I had stared at their plain faces, nearly beautiful in the firelight, and wondered how I had been fortunate enough to live with these intelligent cousins.

But on this night we did not discuss numerology, though that was the book in her hands. Instead I coaxed her back to bed. At her door, I asked her, once more, to visit her father.

—Oh, go boil your shirt, she said.

I retired to my room with vexation.

In the morning I found Uncle stiff in his bed. When I went to close his eyelids they skidded over the dry of his eyes and stayed open. That's what I remember. The dry, open eyes.

I went for Joanna's room.

—He's gone, I said.

She sat up in bed like a thing bitten.

—Our lady above, she said.

We stared at each other.

—Did you tell her yet?

—I didn't. I can't.

She looked at her hands.

When we told Lucinda she leaped out of bed and pushed open the door to her father's room for the first time in weeks and stared at him from the threshold. He was a deflated thing sunk into the mattress. I regretted that Joanna and I hadn't been able to fully move him to resettle the tick in the final days. The sun was shining and we could see the dust motes stirring in the air. Not one of us breathed. She closed the door and we tailed her downstairs and waited for her to cry, but she never did. All morning, she sat at the table and drank the blackberry brandy until she fell asleep in her chair and Joanna and I carried her back up to her room.

So one of us was dead and another one was drunk and Joanna and I sat on the steps outside and wept for our sweet uncle, who was, Joanna speculated, in Olympus, since Heaven had likely crashed during the war. Now that he was gone my purpose was rootless. I thought of Nash's druthers and had a few of my own.

—I might have joined the Christian Commission, I said. They needed ladies in—

—You were needed here, Joanna said.

—Perhaps it would have been easier for us if I had—

—You mean you, she said. Perhaps it would have been easier for you.

She faced me.

—Selfishness is unbecoming on you, she said.

It seemed unfair for her to call me selfish when she snatched the ends of sentences from other people on all occasions.

But it could not be said.

That night we took Lucinda's ash on her behalf. We slept by the hearth. When I awoke I found Joanna with fingers threaded around the statue, her mouth drawn even in sleep, and I remembered how, years before, she had only shown displeasure when her father came to visit and he requested privacy for them in the sitting room.

Sun set and rose and we sat in Uncle's room, whispering.

—We cannot allow him to lie there, I said. It's indecent. We have to do it today.

I worried about the odor. It could come on quickly. I'd read about the smell of the dead in the hot India sun after the Sepoy rebellion. But we weren't savages in our country, even during a war.

The gnats were gathering.

—It'll take a day's work, Joanna began, but if we—

—Don't touch him, Lucinda said.

She stood behind us in her stained chemise.

—Lucinda, I said gently, it's time for us—

She stumbled forward, as if still drunk and held my face in her trembling hands.

—Don't touch him, she said again.

Her teeth and lips were stained purple, and when she spoke I saw the flick of a black tongue. Her wide, sallow face was otherworldly, so unlike the woman in plum who left for the market just days before, trussed up and flouncing.

—No one will touch him without your consent, Joanna said.

—I don't believe you, Lucinda said. Her voice was deeper, as if she were speaking from a cellar.

—You are his closest kin, Joanna said. He is not ours to move if you do not feel it is time yet.

Lucinda went downstairs in her chemise and pulled one of her mother's books from the shelf. She wandered outside and gaped at the yard. The grass was scorched and we had not seen anyone pass by the road in a full season. She sat with her back to the house. Inside, Joanna kept a vigil with Uncle May and shooed the gnats. The horseflies were coming. We shut the windows.

—What can I do? I asked her.

I had expected her to tell me to start digging, to get Lucinda drunk, perhaps send for someone in town. Even a gimp-man would suffice in this circumstance.

—Pray, she told me.

Forgive me, my cousins long gone: I failed you. I did not believe in our goddess. Instead I prayed to our old one, the god of my parents, who could flood our earth wholly and collapse towers with a sound. I did not swallow ash if the others were not there. I did not believe in the sacredness of numbers. I did not write poems. I did not believe in coals. I did not appreciate, as I do now, the value of a hearth.

At dusk I brought a lantern to Joanna and the body.

—Perhaps we should inform Mr. Morrow, I said. And the Wilsons should know, too. We can go to town and—

—No one will protect us, Joanna said. You know what happens to young women in a war.

We'd all read about the women down south, and the rebels, and the public women that followed the camps. We knew what men would do.

I remembered the letter we'd received from Nash in the first year, and how he'd talked of the men in his battalion who had done horrible things to the enemy's women, how, when the captain found out, the men had been sentenced to be hung dead by the neck. And the last good man, now dead in our home while Lucinda sat outside in the scorched grass, staring at the moon, her body a wisp of white in the dark yard.

What were my options then? It was too late for the Christian

Commission. All of the men were crippled or old or dangerous and nearly always married. Of course, I fail to elucidate the final reality: I was afraid of leaving, and what came on was so gradual that there were only moments where I felt alarm.

In the coming days we stopped wearing day dresses unless one of us had to go into town for salted pork or sausage. We kept strange hours. One of us always sat with the body. The belly began to bloat. We ate ashes and read poetry. We drank brandy and kissed the porcelain head and feet. At night, Joanna and Lucinda pontificated at the hearth and I listened.

—Cronus devoured Hestia first, Joanna sermonized. She was born and swallowed by him within moments. Imagine the shock, the heartbreak of her mother, Rhea. The female is the cultivator, the man the destroyer. It is a truth that is perceptible, thousands of years ago and today, on our own hillsides.

Lucinda sat at the floor with her fingers laced around her knees and said nothing. She had not slept.

—For eons, Hestia was caught in the acid of her father's belly. And do you know what she did during that time?

We knew but did not speak.

In the morning, I came down and found the number ten written in ash all over the walls. Lucinda sat at her spot at the table with unwashed hands. I went up to Joanna's room.

—This cannot wait anymore, I said. Not one more day. He must be interred.

—It is nearly time, Joanna said.

—It is time, I said, and for once Joanna did not cut off my sentence.

She rose with purpose and I followed her downstairs, but all she did was pour some tea and chew on a soda biscuit. I felt myself unraveling. The house was too quiet.

Lucinda dropped her chin to her chest. Joanna traced the pattern on her teacup with a fingernail.

—Joanna, I said. This cannot continue. This sort of life cannot sustain us for another minute.

She took my hands in hers. Fatigue nearly made her beautiful.

—Let go of Nash, she said. Let go of the whole lot. Give yourself the peace you deserve. We can—

—No, I said.

She dropped my hands.

—No?

—It cannot sustain, I repeated. You're living in a shared madness. You cannot hate every man and call it Truth.

—And you cannot pine for one man and believe in the delusion that he will save you.

—Even if he doesn't save me, another will come, I said. I am not plain.

She recoiled.

—I can take care of you both, I said. I can find a husband, and you can come with us. Both of you can come with us. It will not be such a terrible challenge.

I thought, at the time, that they had chosen to build this new sisterhood to get away from men, and perhaps they had chosen to get away from men because no men wanted them. I understand now that in Joanna's case that wasn't quite true. The wrong man wanted her. Yet even in a war, or if the war ended, I knew that I could find a man. Beauty provided unfair opportunities then as it does now.

Lucinda lurched from the table in her sooty chemise. From the window, I saw her swagger out to the back and begin uprooting grass near the hemlock tree. We had only one shovel. I found a spade and joined her. Soon I noticed that Lucinda wasn't digging deep, but wide and shallow, too wide, and while I kept scratching at the earth, pulling up clods of roots and stones, she was taking the stones and piling them, building a border, and then she started tugging at the grass around the bed, plucking it clean. The sun was high overhead now. If not for the hemlock we would have browned.

At dusk we wrapped him in three bedsheets to keep him whole and carried him downstairs. Maggots had come. We had been so careful and yet they had appeared all the same. I held his blackened feet and swallowed back bile. We lay him in the hole, blanketed by twigs and leaves that Lucinda had gathered.

—It's too shallow, Joanna said.

Lucinda went to the woodpile.

She lay logs over her father.

—Lucinda, I began.

—Do not speak, she said.

Her voice had taken on a hypnotic resonance that couldn't be argued with.

She went back into the house and returned with a taper. We stood over Uncle May and waited. His eyes were sunken now, his head tilted away from us.

—May the fire ever nourish his soul, Lucinda said. She touched the taper to the brush and we stood and watched the flame sprout in the tinder. I circled the fire and saw the silhouette of his good face in the embers, his jaw agape, looking at me as if I were the only thing of substance.

All night, they carried wood and stoked the bones until all that remained was a black gouge in our earth. They came in at dawn and slept in front of the hearth. Lucinda woke before Joanna, in the late afternoon. I could hardly recognize her. Her face was whorled with ash. I stared at her, waiting for her to speak, but she turned away and pressed her forehead to the stones.

If memory serves, the days had shortened and the leaves were browning when we saw Bridget Scriven coming up the road. We scrambled for our day dresses and aprons. I found the chenille net on the sitting room table among piles of papers and dirty cutlery and wound my hair inside. By the time she came up the walk we were breathless and presentable. She had come to tell us that her son was dead, and she was considering a move, she said, to her sister's in Harrisburg. With news like that it was impossible to turn her away from tea. She did not own a black dress or dye. She apologized for wearing deep blue.

—It's understandable, in these circumstances, Joanna said.

Bridget had a severe, wide part that ran down the center of her head, and threads of gray had begun to snake their way through the black. She was not yet forty. I stared. Joanna could not look at our guest at all. But Lucinda had reignited.

—Harrisburg! she said. Don't despair. It's a new life in a handsome town. I think you'll find comfort there.

—I expect so, Bridget said evenly. Is your father well?

She was staring at the ashed numbers on our walls.

—No, Lucinda said.

—Ah.

She saw the spoons glinting at the hearth now. My fingers curled themselves into my palms. A flush began to crawl up Joanna's neckline and spread into her cheeks. I'd forgotten how terrified she was of strangers in our old life.

—You had a decent boy, I said.

—He was too good to live through it, she agreed.

She was staring at the statue. Hestia was looking worn in the daylight, almost haggard. Her porcelain face had a wan, weathered quality to it.

Lucinda's broad features were working themselves into an accommodating smile.

—I'm sure we look in terrible disarray, she said.

—Not at all, Bridget said. She straightened in her chair.

—This is all the aftermath of a silly game, Lucinda said smoothly. It soothes us.

—What sort of game?

I don't recall the exact of what was said after. But I know we began with Hestia's story, and the value of the hearth, and later, once Joanna began speaking, we illustrated for her a gleaming paradise of sisterly love. And, weeks after, when Bridget was visiting regularly and had not moved to Harrisburg, we shared the ashes. And, a year after, Nash found me down at the springhouse, preparing for our Hestia meeting that evening, looking untouched by the war as if bewitched, laughing and gallant and every inch the brave soldier with his whiskers and his scuffed boots. He kissed me behind the springhouse and that is my last true memory of that time: the smell of him, the creases in his coat, the way Joanna looked at us and let her mouth cinch into noiseless wrath. But it did not matter, because Nash had his eyes on me like I was his patron saint, his goddess of the hearth and home.

Now I am old and my own mouth puckers and no man has looked on me in that way in many years. I had been in possession of an enchantment, at the time unwanted, now missed. I had spent the war in a corner of a fantasy of someone else's making, swallowing ash and praying to a resurrected goddess, the goddess of plainness, who, at the time, I had not personally met. But even in these days when I am faced with a challenge, I take a spoonful from the hearth and swallow before the force of my lungs can recognize the noxiousness of what I have consumed.

11

The Ferrywoman

-KYRA-

December 2007

The cute orderly, the one I've seen before with a broken nose and sandy hair, he was the one skulking around the lobby of my grandmother's nursing home. When I last visited he had been in the same corner then, too, reading. I like a guy with a routine.

I can't help it. When I see a guy like him, I feel my hips pivot smoother in their sockets, my torso stretches, and there I am, angling all over him like a tulip stretching in a glass of water.

—I'm looking for Mona Clark's new room, I said.

—Your grandma? She's in one nineteen now, he said.

—Thanks, I said. And then I leaned his way and said, How's my makeup? My grandma hates when it looks too obvious.

I licked my lips, first the top, then the bottom.

—Looks fine, he said. Looks just fine.

It wasn't until I was swiveling my body down the hall that I remembered and pushed a hand into my stomach, hard.

I love the word *zygote*. When it happened it should have rung through my body, as clean as an unmarred gong.

• • •

She was drinking a bootleg glass of wine when she answered the door. Her hair was piled into a perfect swirl of white on her head, like vanilla soft-serve. The weight of her mink coat dragged her down, her gnarled feet were sheathed in beaded slippers, and when she hugged me she reeked of old newspaper and Merlot. I felt nausea ripple in my throat until I gulped it down.

—Your mother didn't tell me you were in town, she said.

—Winter break just started. Is this a bad time? I thought you'd like the surprise.

—Come in, she said. But you're lucky that I do not have a prior engagement.

I had missed her careful diction, the loftiness with which her syllables drifted out of her mouth.

She settled into the deep groove of her armchair, leaving me to close the door.

This new room was bigger than her last, with better lighting and a window seat by the bed. Weeks ago, someone had given her flowers and now they shriveled in stagnant water. I ached to read the card looped around the neck of the vase, to see if it was from my father.

—Nice digs, I told her.

—Nice what?

—Nice place. Nice new room.

—I should hope so. I had to wait for two people to pass on before my name came up on the list.

I wondered if they'd died where we were sitting. On her bed? In her bathroom? At college we practically swim in immortality. In my grandmother's nursing home, the river Styx laps up and down the hallway.

—You didn't kill them to get this place, did you?

She didn't answer. I don't know if she missed the joke or if she felt partly responsible for wishing them into oblivion.

—How's school?

—Good, I said. I switched my major to classics.

—Dear Lord, she said. What on earth are you going to do with that?

—I'm not sure. But I enjoy the coursework.

—Why not a business major? Or accounting? The men in those majors are so handsome.

THE THESAURUS OF MONA GEORGETTE CLARK

Handsome *(adjective): attractive, composed, virile, striking, stately, dignified. Wealthy.*

—How is your house this year? she asked me. What is the reputation on campus?

—It's fine, I said. We have a good pledge class.

—Be sure to network. You never know who will marry a senator. I still keep in touch with my sisters. Those of us that are alive, anyway.

How satisfying it would be, I thought, to drag her over to our house and make her see the dining room at two in the morning on Friday: Marcia, asleep and hunched over the table with her face in her arms, her stubby ponytail askew on the back of her head, reeking of fake cherries and rum. Ruby, gobbling tortilla chips and hummus and slices of cheddar, yapping with her mouth open, laughing too loud and too long. Amanda, pale and sober, frowning like we'd gotten wasted just to personally affront her. Deirdre and Margot singing a bastardization of a rush song off-key, their voices like cracked plates.

Balzac emerged from under the bed and studied me with twitching whiskers. I snapped my fingers at him, beckoning for some contact. I wanted so badly for him to love me. He took refuge behind some dresses in the armoire.

—Balzac doesn't like anyone but me, Mona said. Do not take it personally.

Amazing, the things she had in common with a feline.

—You look pretty, Grandma.

She smoothed the arm of her mink coat carefully, almost petting it.

—I look composed, at least, and that's all one can hope for as they age. And you look—she squinted at me through a cataract fog—you look well, but you better not gain another pound over vacation.

—I know, I said.

I tried to imagine the fetus. I couldn't. I could only picture a seahorse. I felt it back flip, and then I thought: impossible. All of it too early, too insubstantial to feel.

—Dinner is in twenty minutes, she said. You may help me with my preparations. She gestured to her glass-topped dresser and I wordlessly took the brush as I had done since my childhood. I unpinned her hair and brushed slowly, as if she were a horse that could scare easily and kick me.

Family myth dictates that the first full sentence out of my mouth was directed at Mona on one of her visits. Is this my memory, or my mother's? Does it matter? We were standing in the foyer of my parents' house. My father still lived with us. My mother answered the door, and her voice arced above me in an octave of nervousness that I felt but couldn't define, and I studied this woman, this glamorous doorstep relative who carried a hatbox and left her bags on the floor for my mother to retrieve. And I pronounced:

—I like your panty hose.

Mona was thrilled with the content of the sentence.

My mother was thrilled with the syllables.

I offered my arm on our shuffle down the hallway to the dining room, but Mona refused.

—What are you, *a man*?

Instead, she leaned on her walker, not really needing it, but not certain enough with her own footing to slip and risk embarrassment.

—Do not call it a walker, she said. The word lacks dignity.

—What should I call it, then?

—A vehicle. This is my vehicle.

—Are you licensed?

Her face soured.

—Sometimes I admire your wit, she told me. But sometimes you are unbearably proletariat.

When we entered the dining room, her voice shifted and she curled a cold hand over my forearm and announced to no one in particular, Has everyone made the acquaintance of my beautiful granddaughter?

Orphics believed that one drink from the river Lethe in the underworld would eviscerate the memory of mortal life. Unfortunately for them, the Lethe was tempting, and whenever a recently dead human encountered it the urge to drink would be irresistible. To combat this, the Orphics limited their water on this worldly plane. They trained themselves daily to maintain their memories and resist the Lethe, so that when they were reborn they would have the knowledge of their past lives intact.

I want the Lethe.

Just a small dose.

It would take only a thimbleful to forget that I have a father.

I always hated the predictability of Mona's nursing home dinners. I sat at a table with eight slurping geriatrics. Seven were women. Four were conversational. Edward—I knew him from previous visits—Edward sat at the head of the table, silent and morose, while I watched Mona spar with other women for his attention.

—Edward, she twittered, Edward, did you see the new aide yet? She has tattoos on her wrists. Both wrists!

Edward, deaf either by choice or ailment, didn't respond.

Somebody farted but nobody commented.

Mona shifted over to the women.

—My granddaughter just declared her new major.

Squints were cast upon me.

—What's your major? someone rattled.

—Classics.

—Classics, as in Dickens?

—Classics, as in Greeks. Romans. History, I said.

—That is rather impractical, Edward said.

All of us jumped at his voice.

—I have a soft spot for old things, I said.

Mona laughed and simultaneously dug her claws deep into my thigh. I crossed my legs away from her.

—What's your name? Edward asked me. A jewel of soup clung to this chin.

—Kyra Clark.

—Ah, you must be Jim's girl, he said. And then he said to Mona: When will your boy visit again?

Jim's girl. Jim's girl. Jim's girl.

—Soon, I'm sure, Mona said.

Edward studied my face, trying to extract my father's eyes and nose and mouth from the genetic jigsaw puzzle.

—Do you play bridge? he asked me.

—No.

—Your father is a crackerjack bridge player, he said. You should have him teach you.

For years, my mother tried to snag him back into our family. Begging phone calls, and long nights spent in his driveway before the restraining order, and weepy letters. Many weepy letters. And when that didn't work, she asked for child support. And when he slipped behind on that, but she couldn't bring herself to press charges against the man she still loved, my mother turned to positive visualization. And aphorisms. And white sage. And crystals. And witch hazel instead of Band-Aids. And hugs before bed. And, after I went to bed, a little bit of weed. On weekends, LSD.

He never visited after he left. Instead, he sent me books. His handwriting on the mailing labels: slanted, tight, cursive. I traced a finger over every word he ever wrote me. I imitated the loop of his *y* in my name, the deep curve on the leg of the letter *K*.

His packages were always addressed from P.O. Box 446 in Weymouth. Inside each parcel I found a Hawthorne or a Bradbury or a Tolkien or a Hemingway. Always inscribed on the title page,

For my brilliant girl.
With affection, Your father

The books stopped coming my freshman year of high school. I don't know why.

One year later, on the day that I got my license, I drove to the Weymouth post office. It was only a twenty-minute drive. The whole afternoon I sat in the parking lot, watching people come and go, half-afraid of seeing his face, half-afraid that I wouldn't. I never left the car.

Mona wouldn't acknowledge me on the walk back to her room. Her vehicle's tennis ball feet snagged on the rug. I heard a tiny rattle in her exhale, the vapor of a ghost on her furious breath.

—Shut the door, she hissed at me.

She shuffled over to her bedside table, extracted her wine and glass from the drawer, and poured liberally.

—Did you come here simply to exercise your impertinence in front of my companions? she asked.

I didn't answer.

—Thank the Lord Edward liked you. Thank the Lord.

She took an unladylike swig and gulp. The noise—God! The noise of old people! It's as if they carry a bullhorn around for their bodies—the sound was unbearable, the mechanism of throat and mouth revolted me to the marrow. Her coat silhouetted wildly by lamplight. Her shadow could have belonged to a shaman.

—Is it your mission to ruin my reputation?

—No.

—Why, for once, why can't you just keep your tongue in your mouth?

Sometimes, on a train platform, I get the itch to know what it would be like to jump in front of the tracks at the last moment. I'm not suicidal. It's just a doom itch, a what-if itch. I felt the same itch then. It could have been so easy to kamikaze announce: I'm pregnant, you old crone. Then watch her crumple.

—Why did you come here? she asked me.

—To visit you.

—Horse feathers. Why do you visit if you only want to upset me?

—I wasn't trying to embarrass you, I said.

—You want something, she said. You only visit when you want something.

How badly I wanted to tell her she was wrong.

At three months, a fetus has a throat. The head is half the length of its body. A whorl of a hair pattern emerges. It bobs and pulses with the mother, amphibious and parasitic and focused only on its genetic perfection. It has no interest in its father.

—I want Dad's phone number, I told her.

I followed Mona's eyes to the framed picture of him on her dresser. I have the photograph memorized. He's standing on a golf course. Perfect hills ebb behind him. A trophy glints fiercely in his hand. In another hand, a driver. A woman is in the corner of the frame, composed only of hair and an elbow. The woman is not my mother.

—Why do you do this to yourself? she asked me. You're nearly grown. He gives you what he can.

—He gives me nothing, I told her.

—I hardly knew my father, she said. He worked long hours. He had his own life. I let him be. He sent me to a good school. He paid for my wedding.

—Please. I need his number. Then I'll leave you alone.

The coat slithered off her shoulders and pooled on the floor. Spike of memory: when I was a child, Mona would take me to the Anglican church on her visits, and when she did, she was sure to drape the mink coat over the pew, label carefully angled so that those behind her could see, upside down, the quiet declaration, *Le Vison de la France.*

—He's my child, she said. I have to support his choices.

—I'm your grandchild.

—It's not the same. He's a good son to me. A good son.

—I don't want to bother him, I lied. I just want him to know how I'm doing.

She looked so insubstantial without the coat. Practically avian. Had I been a better person, I would have wrapped her in a blanket even if she'd protested. Instead, I stood over her, waiting.

—You are so very like your mother, she spat.

—Because I want him in my life?

—No. Because you are relentless. Get me a pen.

What was she when she was my age? Her mouth is so rumpled, so expressive still, that surely it must have had the fluctuations of a coquette. Puckered one minute, corner-curved the next. She must have worn cardigans, and oxford shirts, skirts breeze-tousled and hinting, and maybe on dates she'd flick open the top button of a blouse, and maybe in her father's absence she had left the house quietly, in slithering high style, running through the town at night on light feet, finding what she needed from other boys, deep in the stacks of a library near her finishing school, maybe, or in the bathroom of an art gallery, or on an empty night-lit tennis court while others danced in a country club ballroom. Maybe she'd filled a different kind of dance card, and maybe she'd done as I had done, throwing the insubstantial core of her teenage body at anyone she wanted, not caring if it was Blake or Alfred or Reuben or Kent, because, she knew, it was the only time that in relinquishing her control that she could gain some in turn, burning through each of them with a reckless quiet rage. So many parts of her were unlovable, but this part, this buried part, was mine. I felt entitled to her past. I was overcome with an urge to reach for her, to pluck that girlish ghost out of her wretched old body and take her home to the sorority house.

Her penmanship was so governed by quivers that it was nearly illegible.

—Is that a three or an eight? I asked.

—Eight, she spat. I want you to leave now.

—I will. I'm sorry I upset you.

—You are a terrible, insolent child. You are no child of Jim's.

—Yes I am.

Balzac mewled from under the bed.

—You don't even know him, she hissed.

—I take only what I need from people, and give nothing in return, I said. If that isn't Jim I don't know what is.

Tears were beading on her eyelids, I could see them.

I took the coat from the floor and draped it over her armchair. When I went to kiss her cheek, she clutched hard at a hank of my hair and pulled until my face was an inch from hers, her breath overwhelming.

—With a disrespect such as yours, you are destined for disaster.

—I know, I said.

Why didn't I say, I already am?

When I opened the door Balzac skittered toward the exit as if it was his last chance for survival, and I crushed his tail with my foot and the trajectory of fur changed course and darted under the bed, followed by a comet of screeching. I shut the door on the pair of them yowling in unison.

Of course the cute orderly was at the end of the hall.

—Everything okay in there? he asked me.

I could see a chain snaked under the neck of his scrubs. St. Michael, dangling on the pendant underneath?

—She always makes a scene, I told him. And she was pissy with me.

—Did you wear too much makeup after all?

I thought of lying, but didn't, because I knew I would never come back to her hovel and I would never see him again either.

—I came to get my dad's number from her.

—You mean Jim?

—Jim, I said.

His name prickled my mouth. I licked my lips to numb the feeling.

—You don't talk to your dad?

—No.

—Why do you want him now?

—He should know how I'm doing. What about you? You talk to your dad?

The orderly itched at the back of his neck. I liked the way the muscles in his arm moved, pulsing with the beat of his scratch.

—My old man's in construction, he said, and I nodded, as if the two statements were in any way related.

—I'll see you around, I said.

On the walk away, I didn't count past two and a half sways before he said, My shift ends in ten minutes.

—I'll wait in the parking lot, I said.

—What's your name?

—Kyra.

—Aren't you going to ask mine?

—I think I'll call you Scott, I said.

Out in the parking lot the wind blew thick and night heavy and I marveled at how, in the soon unspooling of our bodies, in the dark of my car or his apartment, he would never be able to detect the truth in mine.

12

Endings, Bright and Ugly

- CHORUS -

April 2008

There are thousands of ways Margot could have ended.

Start with the easy.

It's a four-hour drive to the Canadian border, dark and snowy and charming, where she landed a job at a titty bar in a scenario without malice: pink pasties, round-faced customers with cold noses, and she renamed herself something demure and kicky all at once. Candice, or Lorenna. And one night (of course it's a late hour, and of course the roads are snow clotted and empty) she leaves work a little toasted and drives dreamily into a white ravine, tapped unconscious. Sleeping Beauty in a bikini and parka and yoga pants, hemorrhaging gently into an exhale. Her pristine blue face and ashy dye job are beautiful in the sunlight when the Mounties find her in the morning.

Or maybe, she dissolves far into another future that never happened, where she is reduced to an unflattering oil painting on the wall of her third great-grandniece, who removes it because it is an ugly portrait, anyway, and there's something morose and clumsy in it. The mouth is too flat, and the nose is too squashy, and that just doesn't jive with the upholstery.

And then there's the easy option, the headstone cleaved in two after years of rain and sun, hauled off unceremoniously by a maintenance worker in a dirty polo shirt and a wheelbarrow, for even in the future, surely, there are wheelbarrows.

A novice hacker in search of something profitable accidentally wipes the courthouse holding the last existing scan of her birth certificate.

A daughter and son-in-law, standing on the dock of a beautiful fake lake in Arkansas that she'd always found detestable in life, dissolve her ashes in water.

—She would have liked that, her daughter will say. And her son-in-law, a nice man who never felt he could stare her old wilted face down at the breakfast table, will squeeze his wife's hand three times, their secret grip.

All of the hairs on her head that have drifted out the window on long car trips or been left behind in airplane seats, on hotel pillows, in the water filter of a pool in Thailand, swept in the corner of a restaurant in Barcelona, wrapped around the squeegee handle in the bucket beside pump nine at the Sunoco in Tennessee: all of them will burst into dust—some of them well before their creator does—and some, frail and gray, not long after.

Or maybe she won't disappear until a perfectly executed midlife crisis, complete with breast implants and the revelation that everything in her life that she resents falls on her spouse. A tidy solution that unravels two years later, living in a sublet in Des Moines, with the ugliness of her dissatisfaction waiting at her doorstep, disheveled and collared, loyal as a Saint Bernard that followed her stench through every forsaken hillside, trailing a noose behind him, whiskey sloshing in the tiny barrel on his collar.

It could be a tumor: pick a spot.

A seizure behind the steering wheel.

A bat caught in her chimney that bursts into the living room and scratches her tidily, so lightly that she doesn't go for the shots. Now that's a way to go, a real way.

Why, then, do we find her on the floor at the age of twenty-one? She's been on her side a while, and her skin is punched in white and purple. Her eyes are matte, her mouth is open. Urine has released around her hips and is nearly dry, sticky and acrid. There is no blood.

Deirdre found her after a late night at her sushi model job. Let's rubberneck and follow her down the hall, shall we, a camera on her goose-bumped neck, a slow zoom when she turns the corner and makes a long sleepy trudge to her lover's door (of course we know they're gay, we're not stupid), texting and walking, and then the agonizing search for her keys in her jacket.

Everyone enjoys a sturdy Before and After. The change is so fast that time has to be double-slowed to see it absorb after she opens the door. It will take time for Deirdre's eyes to adjust to dawn bleeding through the window before rods and cones register the body. Then, Deirdre's brain, then sympathetic nervous synapses, then tingling in the marrow: the utter fact of her living knitted into her revulsion, her horror. Nobody remembers her screaming but all of us remember waking and finding the body, finding her with the body.

And decades later, bumping down the hallways of untrustworthy memories, each of us feels as if we discovered Margot first, because in a way we did. It was as if we'd come across a shattered mirror, and each piece of her had winked at us, a variation on hair and smirk and rigor. We gripped at her doorframe as if she could reach out and clutch us to her chest. *Come here*, she'd whispered, and our own bodies turned toward her in recognition of our deadlines, long scattered and imminent all the same.

13

The Deposition

-ELINA-

April 2008

I didn't see Margot's body. Amanda and Twyla woke me with the news. They both were crying, looking at me like, What do we do? I'd been president of the chapter for almost a full term, but my experience didn't make a difference. It's not like there was a section on this in our handbook.

My room was far from Margot's on the other side of the house. My first instinct was, *Maybe we can move her somewhere else.* But that wouldn't do. Girls were already crying in the hallways.

—Elina, what's going to happen to us? Amanda wailed.

—I don't know, I said. Are we sure she's dead?

—She's dead, Twyla said, and she sounded so flat that it had to be true.

—Let's get Nicole, I said. Twyla looked at me with relief, as if involving our idiot housemother might cause a complete revival. The three of us ran barefoot down the hall and tapped at her door. What if she wasn't home? What if she failed to answer? Her apartment was near enough to Margot's room that I recall waiting for her to open up and being disturbed by the fact that I was in the vicinity of a dead person. But maybe she wasn't really dead, I thought. She could just be blacked out. She wasn't in my pledge class, so it was hard to remember what kind of a drinker she was. Then Twyla got impatient and banged on the door with the heel of her fist like in the movies. Nicole opened up and stared.

—We think Margot's dead, I said.

—You think she's dead?

—She's dead! Amanda cried.

Nicole grabbed something that looked like a rosary with a tassel from the door handle and hung it over her neck. She started rubbing at the beads. She was like the patron saint of old hippies, standing there in an ugly kimono.

—How do you know she's dead? she asked. Are you sure she isn't just sleeping?

—She's dead, Twyla said.

Now all of them were crying. I was still composed.

—Let's go, Nicole said, and ran toward Room Epsilon. Amanda and Twyla followed, but I couldn't do it. I stayed at the doorway to Nicole's apartment and called 9-1-1.

—*How do you know she's dead?* the dispatcher asked, like she was bored.

Down the hall, the girls got silent and Nicole walked into Margot's room. Deirdre was already inside. She was yelling. Nicole shut the door, then opened it again and stuck her head into the hall.

—Who here knows CPR? she asked, and fat Ruby plunged into the bedroom like she'd been training for this moment her whole life.

It went like this: fire department, ambulance, cops. The walkie-talkie people. Yellow tape went up around our parking lot. I found a piece of it twisted around a birch tree many weeks later. I was told to order my sisters to their bedrooms until further notice. That was fine. I did not want anyone to leave before we were united on the story.

A gurney rolled in. The brothers from Zeta Sigma gathered around the yellow tape and watched. They wore puffy jackets and hats and their faces were red, like pigs shoved into people clothes.

—Is Margot dead? one of them shouted.

—Yeah! Eva yelled from her upstairs window.

—Fuck! a brother shouted.

—I know! Eva yelled.

—How?

—Shut up, you fucking assholes! Ruby shouted.

—Did she kill herself?

Ruby pulled her head out of the window, broke the rules to stay in her room, ran down the hall, and grabbed me.

—Tell them to fuck off in Norwegian, she said.

—Why?

—Because they're scared of you and if you swear in a different language they won't know how to respond.

I hung my head out of her window.

—Hey, President Swede! they yelled.

—I'm Norwegian! I yelled back.

—You're missing the point, Ruby said.

—*Dra til helvete*! I yelled.

—What? one of them said.

We shut the windows.

We could still hear them through the glass, same question, Did she kill herself? But it was not really a bad question. Margot's cause of death was tied up with our house's endurance. If this were a fluke young-age thing like an aneurism then we wouldn't be punished. An overdose would be another kettle of eggs. Papers would read, EVIL

SORORITY DRIVES SISTER TO USE INSERT DRUG THAT EVERY COLLEGE KID USES HERE.

Eventually, the walkie-talkie people started leaving and took the gurney with them. Men in suits started coming in. College administrators. Social workers. All of them scrunched around the coffee table in Nicole's apartment. I joined her. There was crying. I got teary eyes, and Nicole leaked the whole time. Her skin was starting to look like a plucked chicken. There was instant coffee. The men had fat fingers and typed notes into their tiny phone keyboards. They kept asking me,

—Was she a drug user?

—Was anyone with her?

And I said I didn't know her super well.

—Weren't you friends? one asked.

—We were sisters, not friends, I said.

They didn't understand.

Then the suited men stood in the front yard and spoke for a long time with two cops. Nicole and I watched from her window. By now the rims of her nostrils were raw. She kept dabbing with a hankie and I thought how strange it was that Margot was dead, a full body, and here was Nicole's hankie, a tiny world of bacteria, alive.

—You poor girls, she said.

There was no nice way to ask if they were going to shut down our house, so instead I asked, What's going to happen to us?

She rubbed my back, palm up and down like she was trying to burp a baby.

—You'll suffer and heal, she said.

Then Margot's parents came and I cried in the shower, finally.

That afternoon the provost said we were not to be shut down during the investigation. I called a meeting in the Chapter Room. I wrote down what I wanted to say in nice language. I used the thesaurus in Microsoft Word. I said things like, *This is an opportunity for unity,* and *Let us take solace in our sisterhood.* By the time the meeting ended, I got a call that Nationals were coming on Monday. I spent the night telling each idiot sister to do a room check and hide their stuff. Someone took the bong out of the Pledge Study and stacked the paddles behind the washing machines. We vacuumed. Girls were still crying.

Three women with the same haircut had been flown in: the vice president, the head chapter consultant, and the president of Nationals, who had, by far, the worst face job I'd ever seen. They were dressed like former beauty pageant ladies turned judges, you know, with the pencil-skirt-suit-jacket combination and blouses in different shades of pinks. Each one of them wore the opal pin with the Greek letters. They were calling it an informal deposition. My understanding of *deposition* would mean that it could not be informal, but no one seemed to care about the contrariness. It was annoying.

Our meeting was in the Chapter Room. Someone had put out a tablecloth and a bouquet of our house roses. This made things look pretty and it hid the graffiti carved into the wood, stuff like KYRA SUCKS A CHODE or FALL '04 BEST OF THE BEST.

—Elina, we're here to give you the benefit of the doubt, the president said. We are your sisters, and your word has value to us.

—Thank you, I said.

Legs uncrossed and recrossed and the tannest woman, the vice president, clicked at her pen over and over until I wished I could reach over and take it out of her hands.

—Tell us about Sister Margot Glenn, the president said.

—She was a good sister, I said.

—A good sister, the president repeated. Can you expand on that?

I wanted to say, not really, because I'd only hung out with her a few times. She was not in my pledge class, and she was one of those sisters that was a little skanky. She liked arguing. She was a snoop.

—She was really nice, I said. One time, I ran out of quarters for the dryer and she helped me. And she was good at making rushes feel welcome during recruitment.

—"Rushes" is inappropriate language, the president said. Her eyelids were so big I could see eye shadow even when she tried to open wide.

—Please bear in mind that rushes are to be referred to as Potential New Members.

—I apologize, I said. English is my second language.

It was an easy excuse. I don't even dream in my first language anymore, and when I last spoke to my grandparents I felt like we were talking on laggy Skype even though we were in the same room.

The women were unimpressed.

—Can you tell us about what happened on Friday morning? the chapter consultant asked.

—We found her in her room, I said.

—We? said the chapter consultant. Who's we?

—A lot of us saw her before the ambulance came.

—Who called the ambulance?

—I did.

—Ah, the vice president said. That's very good. Good initiative. Was anyone in with Margot when she passed?

—I don't know, I said. Maybe Deirdre. I don't know.

—Deirdre who?

—Ah, said the vice president. She nodded and jotted something in her notebook. I wondered what she knew.

—Deirdre is her best friend, I said.

—Who had been with her that night? asked the president.

—I don't know, I said.

—You don't know.

—No.

Glances were traded so swiftly that it was as if they had practiced. The chapter consultant was getting impatient. I thought about what her life must be like. She probably drives a black Escalade and has au pairs for her Ritalin babies. Stupid woman. The consultant turned toward the vice.

—Go get Deirdre, she said.

The vice nearly ran from the room.

—Do you think I'm here just to be fucked with? the consultant asked.

I had never seen such a pretty woman over forty say *fuck*. The president looked offended.

—Joyce, the president began, I would like you to keep yourself composed while we discuss with Elina—

—Your chapter is in serious jeopardy, do you understand that? the consultant said.

—Yes, sister, I said.

I thought dumbly about how these women reflected exec boards in every chapter. The president had to be sneaky plus steely plus attractive. The vice had to be demure. The pledge mistress (or in this case, the consultant) had to be a bitch. Four hundred chapters across the country, all the way to the top, this was how it went.

—This death has struck a chord with all of us, the president said.

—I agree, I said.

—It wouldn't do to withhold information, she said.

—I agree, I said.

—It wouldn't do, say, to deceive us about goings-on in the

house. We know you want to reflect well for Nationals. That is truly admirable. But in this room, we need to be transparent about the activity of your sisterhood.

I didn't say anything.

—When I was in college, the president began, our chapter threw a party one night where someone managed to bring a horse up to the second floor. It climbed the steps beautifully and spent the night pacing up and down our hallway during our party. Unfortunately, horses are terrific at climbing steps and not so satisfactory at getting down. We had to call the fire department to get it out. What a mess! But those were different times!

She laughed at her own story, but her face muscles didn't move and her mouth hung open in a strange circle.

—How did they get it out? I asked.

—I don't remember, she said wistfully. Plywood, I think.

—Is there, to the best of your knowledge, any illicit drug use in this house? the consultant asked, and the president looked at her sadly, trying to say with her eyes that the story she just shared was meant to change the mood so that I, the silly chapter president, would be superenchanted, you know, and more willing to talk about my house's violations.

—I do not allow drug use in my house, I lied.

The president leaned in and placed a hand on my forearm.

—Are you from America? she asked.

—I was born in Norway, I said. But I've been an American for most of my life.

—Your English is impeccable, she said.

I nodded.

—Isn't Norway the one with the wooden shoes?

—That's Holland, I said.

Both of them needed a good smack.

—My apologies, the president said.

—I am not here for her biography, the consultant said through her teeth.

We were quiet.

—Elina, my dear, the president said, your sister is dead. Her parents have ordered an autopsy. There will be an investigation. Any drug use that is traced to this house could lead to its immediate disbandment. However—

Deirdre stumbled into the room, the vice trailing behind her. She wore a pajama top and a pair of boxers. She was shaking.

—Oh. The president breathed, and somehow dead Margot did not seem so mythical anymore, not when we were staring at Deirdre's blotchy face.

—Oh, you dear girl, the president said. She stood, and Deirdre crumpled into her pink blouse and wept.

—There, there, the president said. What a shame. What a shame.

Why do Americans repeat themselves when they're sad?

Deirdre let the president hold her. The vice bunched up her hands. The consultant watched them carefully, like she was looking for mistakes. The president sat Deirdre in her chair and stood behind her with a hand on her shoulder.

—Now this is true sisterhood, she said to us. Look at this girl. This is true friendship. Her devotion shines even in her loss. My dear girl, know that your sister is in heaven with the angels.

I know it was sad and everything, but god, if Margot had been alive in that moment, I would have killed her myself. What a bitch. What a stupid, selfish bitch. In Oslo, people who kill themselves do not get rewarded with angels. My cheeks were blushing.

—I can see how distressed you both are, the president said. It's a terrible business, and I'm so sorry to have to have these discussions with either of you, but we have to know, Deirdre, what did Margot do before she died?

—I don't know, Deirdre said. I was working.

—You work nights? the consultant asked. I could almost see her thinking: stripper.

—I work for a caterer, Deirdre said. The party went all night and we weren't dismissed until four. Then it was a long drive home.

—You poor girl, the vice cooed.

—So you don't know where she was, the consultant said.

—I don't. But I just got off the phone with her dad.

Deirdre wiped her eyes with her palm. Her inhales were making her chest tick and shutter. I could not tell if she was suspending us on purpose or not.

—Yes? the consultant said.

—The coroner found a heart defect, she said. Isn't that ridiculous? Her whole life, and she never knew it, and it kills her in her sleep? It's so—

—Abnormal, the president said. That poor girl.

They were gone within ten minutes.

I went to Room Epsilon. They had stripped the bedsheets. Deirdre lay on the mattress without tears.

—What was it really? I said.

—It was a defect, she said. A defect, and a shit ton of Molly, and some other shit, too.

I did not want to stay. I did not want to sit on the edge of the mattress and pet her and make her cry again. I was so tired of all the crying. So many girls were sniffing through the house with tissues balled in their hands. If they were truly sad then there was nothing I could do to fix it. If they were just following a trend then I didn't want to encourage it and let it continue. It could be a sad thing in church, or alone. The rest of it was just a display.

—Do you believe in any of it? she asked.

—Any of what?

—Is it worth lying for?

—Yes, I said. I have no doubts.

—It's doubt. Singular. You have no doubt.

—Are you actually sad? I asked her.

She looked at the ceiling above her, unblinking.

—Sometimes, she said. When I believe that it's real. Are you?

—No, I said. But I didn't like her.

I could see that she was struggling with liking my honesty or hating it. She crossed her arms over her body, like she was in her own coffin.

—We were in love, she said.

—I know, I said.

—Everyone likes to act like they knew. But if they knew the whole time, why did we have to be so secretive? Why couldn't you all be accepting? Why did we have to hide?

—There are regulations, I said.

—Society, and shit. And image. It's all such a sham. Is that what you're going to say? Did you think we were going to infect you?

—No, I said. And then I had one of those moments, like I do in my meetings where I felt like I had something real to say. This is a moment for unity, I thought. Those had been good words. Sisters had liked them, and I liked saying them.

—People just want to belong, I said. And sometimes we have to set up expectations so sisters can meet them. It makes people feel safe.

—It's all such a sham, she said again.

There was no way to reach her, and I did not really want to anyway.

I left her in Room Epsilon with the door open. I walked past Nicole's apartment, through the halls to my room, where I lay in bed and thought of the consultant—*Do you think I'm just here to be fucked with?* Yes, I thought, that's the point. That is how we pass time.

14

Autopsy Report

COUNTY OF SPRINGFIELD
DEPARTMENT OF CORONER

AUTOPSY REPORT

I performed an autopsy on the body of
➔

No.
2008-013-46
GLENN, MARGOT GRACE

at THE DEPARTMENT OF THE CORONER
in the city of Springfield, Massachusetts
on 28 April 2008 @ 0900 HOURS

From the anatomic finding and pertinent history I ascribe the death to:

A) Due to or as a consequence of SUDDEN CARDIAC DEATH

B) Due to or as a consequence of VENTRICULAR FIBRILLATION

Other conditions contributing but not related to the immediate cause of death:

A) METHYLENEDIOXY-METHAMPHETAMINE EFFECT

B) BENZODIAZEPINE EFFECT

Anatomical Summary:

1. Toxicology findings (see separate report)
    a) Methylenedioxy-methamphetamine, alprazolam, and clonazepam identified in blood samples
    b) Methylenedioxy-methamphetamine and alprazolam identified in stomach contents
2. Evidence of therapy
    a) Resuscitative abrasion-contusion of central chest
    b) Resuscitative fractures of sternum, right 3rd, 4th and 5th ribs, and left 4th and 5th ribs
    c) Resuscitative alveolar hemorrhage of lungs
    d) Resuscitative transmural hemorrhage of stomach

CIRCUMSTANCES:

The decedent is a 21-year-old woman who was found unresponsive on the bedroom floor in room Epsilon of her sorority house on April 25th, 2008. She was taken to Mercy-Pratt Medical Center, where she was pronounced dead.

CONTENTS FOUND ON THE DECEDENT AT TIME OF DEATH/DISCOVERY:

The decedent had one black denim miniskirt and one light blue pair of underwear that are urine-stained. The decedent had one gray bra and a dark red polyester blouse cut vertically in the process of attempted resuscitation. There is a vomit stain on the right shoulder of the blouse. There are no shoes or socks. There is no jacket. The decedent's Massachusetts driver's license and Bank of America debit card are located in the posterior right pocket of the denim miniskirt. The left front pocket contains a packet of cigarette rolling papers. All items are in a two-gallon plastic biohazard bag and will be returned to the parents at the conclusion of this autopsy by a social worker, most likely Joy, who will give them too many pamphlets.

<u>EXTERNAL EXAMINATION:</u>
The body is identified by toe tags and is that of an unembalmed refrigerated adult Caucasian female who appears to be approximately 20 years old. The body weighs 114 pounds and measures 64 inches in length. Lividity indicates a right lateral recumbent position upon death.

The body is young. The body is blue-eyed and has a long, sixteen-inch plait of straight black hair braided to the right side of the skull and secured with a purple elastic. The body has six bobby pins in the hair. The body has an excessive amount of black kohl around the eyes. The body has three ear piercings in each ear and is wearing one set of faux pearl studs in the lobes.

The body has a four-inch bruise over its sternum that indicates an attempted resuscitation, most likely by Dwayne Ellison, the young medic who has hands like oven mitts. Dwayne has a dogmatic belief that he can bring bodies back if he compresses them hard enough. (NOTE: Someone needs to tell Dwayne that bodies are not walnuts; they cannot be cracked to unveil the meat of a soul buried within.)

The body has a tattoo on its right hip, three inches by two and a half inches, of a dove holding an olive branch in a facsimile of Picasso's work. The legs are shaved. The fingernails are short and painted in light pink polish. There is an oblong scar less than one inch long on the left knee. The soles of the feet are dirty. Three superficial puncture wounds approximately ¼ inch each are located on the ball of the right foot. (NOTE: This is conducive to reporting that the decedent took off her shoes on the walk back to her residence during the early morning of her demise.) The toenails are painted light green. It is an unflattering color.

The body has no right to be here. The body does not belong under my instruments. I submit to you, friends, a stupid body. Do not allow the undiagnosed arrhythmia to be an excuse. This body was a fool. This body had two parents: a father who will read this report in horror at the words *lividity*, *rigor*, *abrasion-contusion* and wonder if he could have done something—if he had taken her to a cardiologist and a youth group would this be different?—and a mother who will be inconsolable enough by the fact that this report exists. She will be unable to read the contents. This body is the reason why my insolent intern James will have to run the autoclave later. This body is the reason why I had to reschedule my annual physical for the second time. Nobody picks a convenient time to die in this godforsaken county.

This body came from a fancy, mostly white overprivileged college up the road and is likely already the subject of urban legends about the dangers of recreational drug use, but more bodies will come over the years with the same affliction anyway, each of them with the faulty opinion that they are immune to the rules of mortality. This body will likely make the news because she is young and pretty and white.

This body is another reason why I hope my daughter Maya gets into Notre Dame.

This body deserved to be more than the parts on my table. The body had not fallen in slow-plodding adult love, or carried a baby, or seen a wrinkle, or paid a phone bill. The body is lost to all futures and now it lies here, cut down the linea alba, its pale organs shining, its hands slightly curled, its mouth agape at the horror of what it has done to itself.

I affirm that all of the information above is true to the best of my knowledge:

LaTisha Majors

LATISHA MAJORS

SPRINGFIELD COUNTY CORONER

15

Fisher Cat

-STELLA-

May 2008

From a distance, the cabin was pretty, with little dabs of vines on the exterior and a green tin roof. This was according to Grant, handsome Grant, who was so good and so charming that I believed him. I believed him on the drive up when he told me about the time his father was struck by lightning and survived, and I believed him when he said that he once caught a fluke that came back to life on his cutting board hours later. I believed him when he said that he was going to be something more than his family's HVAC business. Of course he was, how could he not be, with those cheekbones, with his thick hair that fell over an eyebrow without effort, dark as otters' fur. There was something strange about his handsomeness, which I think, maybe, is true of all handsome people. In game shows when the host calls on an audience member they're usually stunned—who, me?!—and their friend has to say—yes it's you! get up there!—before the contestant runs up to stand under the lights and beam. That's how Grant made me feel. I reached a hand across the gearshift and rested it on his leg, then regretted it. It seemed like a manly gesture. But he kept talking about the cabin, the fisher cats, the species of trees, and I drowsed a few times, stirring whenever the Jeep hit a rut or a branch reached out and dragged a limb against the side panels.

It had been a lot, you know, on our house. It was nobody's fault and I never would have wished to be somewhere else but a break from them was in order, we were tired, over a month of sadness was heavy on my sweet girls. Twang and Deirdre and Ruby took it hardest, I think. She was their family. In the real world families fall apart in this sort of situation but our girls stayed. They'd darkened but they stayed. Twang stared at corners when she thought no one was watching her, like a ghost had pulled up a chair. And poor Deirdre, she stopped drinking and quit her job and spent the last month of the semester sleeping in her room. I'd leave plates of food on her desk and she'd say thank you from the bed and nothing else. Ruby was furious all the time.

—All of you are too young to suffer through this, the minister had said to us after the service, which was kind but not consoling, not really.

But Grant was consoling. The sisters hadn't gone next door to Zeta Sigma for three weeks after Margot died, but he hadn't seen anyone else. He'd waited for me. He was the one who suggested the cabin when classes ended, this place his big brother owned north of I-95, with a skylight cut in the tin roof, and a woodstove and a big bed, he said.

I've always been a romantic thinker so I had this image of me in an oversized red flannel shirt, legs for him. Grant stoking the wood, and rain on tin, and sleeping on his chest while he stroked my hair. All of these images were possible, inevitable, even. It was the best time with him, the time before either person says love but each is earning the letters for it, one at a time. So my sisters mourned and

I mourned and drifted a little, thinking about what to pack, what to wear, how to cover my black eye, and then felt guilty that I didn't feel guilty enough about these plans, while in the moment around me my girls suffered.

The road was too narrow for the Jeep; we walked the last half-mile. I wore jean shorts even though it was chilly, a navy sweatshirt that was too long at the arms, aviator sunglasses, and my hair carefully braided in two, so that later, when I undid it by the fire, it would shake loose in fairy-tale waves. The two of us walked through a spiderweb. Grant swatted it off in one smooth motion but I could feel it pinned in my hair, even after three swipes, like an invisible veil.

—Poor thing, I said. We're home wreckers!

He grabbed my hand with a surge of affection.

—You know what I like about you, Stella? If you saw a mouse, you wouldn't climb on a chair. You'd find a way to feed it.

—I always liked Stuart Little, I said.

—Who?

But we were at the clearing. The cabin sat in the middle, next to a covered woodpile. The outhouse was farther. I followed him up the steps to a narrow screened-in porch. The holes in the screens had been lovingly patched, and there was a fresh coat of yellow paint around the sills and doorframe. A burner and propane tank sat in the corner. He gestured to it.

—Your kitchen, my darling.

—Divine, I said.

There wasn't a lock on the door, just an eye hook catch. It worried me, but not enough to say something aloud. I quieted myself by poking around the cabin. Everything I touched, Grant commented on, mansplaining it to me as if I were a child. He showed me where the flint was, and how to turn the vents open on the woodstove, and where he kept the washbasin, the extra bedding, the newspaper and kindling. He hung the shotgun on its rack over the table and put a box of bullets by the drainage sink. Months ago, we'd fired some practice rounds into the deep tract of woods behind Zeta Sigma, spattering tree trunks with our shaky shots. I'd asked him then if what we were doing was legal, and he'd told me yes, as long as the cops didn't get called.

He took me outside to show off the water pump. He explained about the red tint in the water, how it was good water, don't worry, full of iron and manganese.

—Water, Helen, water! I said.

—You're just so damn funny, he said. Really. You're a barrel of laughs. His face shifted. Take off your sunglasses, he said.

—No.

—I want to see it in the light, he said.

—Why?

—Just take them off.

I obeyed.

—I bruise easy, I said.

—Poor kid, he said, and held me close, pressing my face into his collarbone. I won't let it happen again. I swear on Helen's water pump.

And of course I believed him.

Later, when he went out to pee, I put some water on the stove and snooped around our bags. In my backpack: some apples, some Ramen, some jerky, some Xanax, some clothes, some bug spray, *Walden*, and makeup, hidden in a corner pocket. In his: shotgun shells, and carabiners, and protein bars, and condoms, and a pile of clothes.

I heard him on his cell phone through the flimsy walls, a swelling rise and fall of sound. He came in frantic.

—My mom's locked out of her house, he said. I have to go.

—I'll come with, I said.

—You've already got the water boiling, he said.

—I can turn it off.

—She's an hour away, he said. It's a boring drive. I'll be back by dark.

I didn't push it because we were new still, and maybe it was too early for me to meet his mother, which was disappointing but understandable. So I stayed. I watched the back of his dark head bob out of the clearing, his hands in his pockets. Later, thinking back on how abrupt it was, I would replay this scene and feel completely foolish. But at the time I believed him.

As soon as he left, silence flooded. It drowned my ears with an endless ring. I had expected to hear sparrows, cicadas, squirrels. Things living and dying. It was warm still, but I lit a fire in the woodstove, hoping that the crackle would override the ring. It didn't. I sat at the round wooden table with a kerosene lantern by the bed. It was difficult for me to imagine Grant sitting there. He was smart, but not bookish. He carried his intelligence around like an awkward rucksack, stashing it on the backs of chairs and forgetting it under barstools. I sat at the table with my copy of *Walden*, my eyes scudding over the words about minks and muskrats, reading the same lines until they didn't make sense anymore. I started thinking about all of the things, the less romantic things I would say to Grant when he got back, the things I should have said about last week on the drive up. I would say those things and then we could move on to bare legs and flannel.

All I could think of was the night I met him, back in January, when my pledge class had gone out with our older sisters and I'd tumbled through the door drunk and blissful and crazy for my girls: Margot's long gorgeous braid, and Twyla's funny punch lines, and Shannon's ability to boot and rally, twice, and keep on partying. We careened into the sticky basement of Zeta Sigma, Michael Jackson remixes playing, brothers in hoodies and snappy T-shirts, lobbing awful shots at beer pong, and Grant found me in the corner and pressed a dime into my palm.

—That's what you are, kid. A perfect ten.

—Did you know dimes are ninety percent copper? I said, and his brothers laughed so hard that I felt in on the joke while Grant grinned at the complete failure of such a phony pickup.

—What an ass, Margot said at my shoulder, but it didn't matter. He was gorgeous, he was mine.

Later, I followed him up to his bedroom and he kissed the insides of my wrists, the divot at my collarbone, kisses that were even and tender and hard to find in someone his age.

At dusk it was dinnertime for bats; they dipped low and lifted again, searching for meals I couldn't see. I watched them and knew, with sudden and awful accuracy, that Grant wasn't coming back. I did not call him. I would not be that girl. I should say now that this is not a story where I will have an answer for where he really went or why he left. Maybe he was ashamed when he saw my eye in the sun, or maybe I said something awful that I can't remember blurting, or maybe his mother truly was in trouble and what he found at home was so distressing that he couldn't bring himself to talk about it. All I know is that afternoon was the last time we spoke, and by September, when I saw him with his brothers on campus, we would pretend we didn't know each other at all.

I cried ugly tears that no one saw and then I got to work. I pulled stacks of wood for the night. When I bent down, I could feel the blood surge in my eye. My nose ran. A chipmunk regarded me suspiciously from the other end of the woodpile.

I pumped a pitcher of reddish water, poured it over the roots of my hair, pumped another pitcher, soaked my face. Later, as my hair dried, I would absorb the smell of smoke and grit from the cabin and feel purified.

Night came. That cabin wasn't large, but it took nine tapers and the kerosene lantern to keep from feeling the dark. Cold air slinked in from the crack under the door. I added a log to the fire and curled myself into bed.

In Margot's obit they called her *wry*, which I loved, because it made her sound smarter than a sorority girl. She was wry. During rush she'd sat with me in the living room and listened to me nervously chat about my hometown, how we have this amazing firemen's fair every year, and how my parents ran a local protest about how non-judiciously people sprayed DDT all over the place and how that stuff was poison, and my family cooked with a lot of garlic because it was really good at repelling mosquitoes naturally.

—Wow, she said drily, I don't think I've ever learned so much about someone in five minutes.

She could tease without injuring; I don't know how she managed it.

Later, when I was pledging, I joined her for lunch along with Twyla and Deirdre and she called me Carrie Bradshaw.

And then later, after pledging, I saw her with Deirdre in the back stairwell and the two of them had stared at me, and I said nothing and left. She was grateful, I think. I could see it in her face at dinner later, when she came into the dining room and no one looked up and stared. She was so compelling—another unearthly beautiful person—that she could have robbed a bank and I would have been honored to sit in the backseat during the getaway, Deirdre at the wheel.

She was clogging my dream.

The fisher cat woke me.

There was no cadence or art in the noise. It struck in bursts, circling the cabin like sonar. Grant had warned me about how fishers yowl—*They sound like banshees*, he said. Outside, it screamed and paused, screamed and paused, puncturing the ringing in my ears.

The woodstove was out. I'd left the vents too far open and now the cabin was dark and freezing. She screamed again. Was she hungry, or sick, or aimless?

There were thousands like me, I knew, who scampered into the woods: Thoreau, and that kid who ate the bad berries, and the Unabomber. But those people were dangerously strange. They had chosen solitude, but it had been thrown at me. And maybe it's the fisher cats that make loners crazy, or the way the branches cross one another into oblivion in the night, like a pen scratched in one spot over and over, or maybe madness compelled them into the woods first and then aloneness nursed it for them.

Every nerve in me flared each time the fisher keened. Even with ears covered, I could hear it through the pillow. It wailed until dawn; I didn't get out of bed to relight the stove until it stopped. I was childishly afraid for my body, half-naked in the dark, while something circled the cabin and screamed. With a sound like that, I thought, it must be afraid of itself.

It's natural, the minister said at Margot's funeral, to think that each of us missed signs of recklessness because we were too busy with our own lives. A strange noise came from Margot's father in the front pew, a choking sound, and the man beside him put an arm around him.

Grant sat toward the back with his brothers. Anticipating this, I had twisted my hair into a chignon before the service, exposing the back of my neck.

—All of us have vanities that obscure the signs of that which is around us, the minister said. But in some ways, these obfuscations are holy tools. They are put there with purpose. We are not meant to see the suffering of all. It would make life unbearable.

I wondered if my skirt was too short, and would Grant leave his pew before I passed by him at the end of the sermon?

—But, the minister added, if we can just see a sliver of the suffering of others, then we will be rewarded with a bounty of goodness. Compassion for suffering is a precious gift.

Coals were tucked deep in a nest of ash. I restoked and sat cross-legged on the floor, letting the heat tighten the skin on my face. I ate nuts for breakfast, drank the reddish water, and ached for caffeine. How could I have forgotten coffee? Apples were wrapped in layers of clothing in my duffel to prevent bruising. They tasted mealy but I swallowed anyway. Outside, in a pool of sun, I broke down and called Grant, again and again, until his phone stopped ringing and went straight to voice mail. There was no medium. I would look aloof or crazy to him. The reality of this was hideously unfair. I tried once more. Then I called Shannon.

—He just *left*? she said. I breathed slowly so she wouldn't hear my tears.

—He may have had a good reason, I said. But I'm up here and don't have a ride home.

—Why didn't you call last night?

—I think a part of me wanted to make sure he really wasn't going to come back.

—I'm leaving now, she said.

—Don't. Not yet, I said. Let me take one more night here.

—Why?

—Just to say that I did this by myself. And if he ever asks, I can tell him that I so enjoyed my time alone that I stayed on and didn't even miss him.

—If you already called him fifty times then I don't think you'll get away with looking casual, she said.

—He could think I adapted, I said. Do you want to come up and stay, too?

—God, no, she said. It sounds awful.

I tried *Walden* again, and the writer begged for truth instead of love. It was absurd.

I tried meditating, but the ringing in my ears drowned out the calm and I abandoned the search for nirvana. The only time I'd ever been close is when I slammed a finger in the car door and the reverberation of my pain rattled through me, like a gong. Every atom in my body drew its attention to my ring finger, and I felt marrow, nails, veins, with a clarity I would never know again.

I went for a walk and hung a camera from a strap around my neck, which I knew I would not use. The land near the cabin was flat, but a twenty-minute amble northeast revealed a drop of rock face. Exposed quartz descended into the woods far below, with the occasional sturdy pine pushing out of a crevice. Moss hung off the rock like a bad toupee. I could see for eons.

Not a single living creature was visible. Only the trees moved in the breeze.

• • •

Last week, he'd taken me to dinner at an Italian place in the center of town. I needed to get out of the house, he said. It was too much darkness. And he didn't know Margot well, he said, but if she was like any other girl in my house she would have wanted me to live. So okay. There I was. He ordered us a bottle of Chablis and pasta with shrimp staring dolefully at us from their little mire of noodles and sauce. He drank more than I did, and then he wanted to drive home and I told him no, I should drive, and he insisted, and I said I didn't feel comfortable, and usually I wouldn't have pushed this issue but I was frail and tired and sad and so I started crying, blubbering really, and then I was ashamed of my tears, which made me cry more, and he said come on Stella, take a breath, and I couldn't, I didn't have it in me to get it together anymore, and somehow I was pressed against the car and he had me by the wrists but I was wriggling and an elbow hit me in the eye, an awful mistake that stopped both of us immediately. He dropped my wrists and backed away like I'd shot him.

—I hit a woman, he said, agonized.

—No, no, you didn't mean to.

—But I grabbed your wrists. I grabbed your wrists! he said.

—It was an accident, I said.

—I hit a woman, he said again, in awe.

When I got back to the cabin, it was well past noon. My legs were sore when I hit the clearing and I was so thirsty I drank directly from the pump, water splashing over my face, spluttering like an animal.

The door was open slightly. The eye hook was unlatched. Holy God. The eye hook. Had I forgotten to lock it? No, I was sure, I could picture my fingers slipping the hook in its metal noose. I was sure.

I yelled Grant's name. Nothing moved.

—Don't mess with me! I shouted at the cabin. I know you're here!

I kicked at the door so hard it bounced off its hinges and drifted back to me.

Nobody was inside. Not under the bed, or on the porch, or under Grant's table, or in the outhouse. My paranoia embarrassed me, but I couldn't shake it. It followed me inside like a stray. Did somebody move the duffel one centimeter to the left? And where was my comb? My other apple? Did I pack my Xanax? Where the hell was my Xanax?

I ate beef jerky, gnawing on it until it thickened into wet gristle in my mouth. I lit every taper in the cabin, then the woodstove, and shut every window and door. It wasn't even sunset. Sweat curled the hair on the back of my neck. The soreness in my legs amplified. I thought of calling Shannon again but couldn't, not yet. She would ask for the whole story on the drive home. All week, I'd been wearing sunglasses in the house and hiding out in my room, because it was finals and my sisters were still emotional and no one said or noticed anything. But if she asked, I'd have to tell her: he did it by mistake. It was an accident. It wouldn't sound believable. I wasn't ready. My ears rang, and rang, and when I pulled the quilt over my head I could smell my own exhausted fear.

The fisher woke me. Three hours asleep, or ten, I didn't know. All the tapers had extinguished in mottled stubs. Only embers were in the woodstove.

Its wail was closer that night. Everything about its pitch was loathsome. Three seconds and then the shriek. Two seconds and then the shriek. Advancing like lightning on an approach. It was mocking me, its keen imitating a woman in pain, and the way it circled had to be planned. It had to know I was there.

Moonlight sluiced over the floorboards in luminous patches. I was careful not to step on them, as if they could be disturbed. It was not hard for me to see the outline of the shotgun on the wall. A twelve gauge wasn't as heavy as I remembered. I nudged open the door, tiptoed through the screened porch, and stepped quietly onto the front steps of the cabin.

How strange it must have looked: a thin young woman, dirty, barefoot, holding a shotgun in her underwear. Wild-eyed. But does it matter, does it really matter, if no living man can see? The air plucks every goose bump on skin. A raise of the gun, resting the cheek against the smooth wooden stock, and a stare down the barrel into darkness. It's like riding a bike. Grant would be so proud.

I waited for the glow of the fisher's eyes.

16

Lovable Persons

-CHORUS-

Fall 2009

Ruby: Pledging is basically an excuse to go to parties and get drunk with your best friends for months with a legit reason. The girls that complain just like having something to bitch about.

Jennifer: Pledging is like buying a day pass to a really small water park. It's great for the first three hours, but eventually you'll have been on all of the rides so you'll just have to keep riding them, over and over, even though you don't really wanna anymore, just so you can say you got the most out of your money. By the end of the day, you'll have a UTI from your wet bikini and the antibiotics will cost more than the admissions ticket, but on the bright side, you'll be really good at chugging pretty much anything, including twenty-four ounces of unsweetened cranberry juice.

Kayla: People think it's like the movies. It's better than the movies. My sisters have taught me how to be a better person. They've taught me unconditional love. And there's always food.

Elina: If you have to ask about what it is like then you should not be allowed to get the answer.

Lisa: I mean, it sort of sucks. But it could be worse, you know? I've heard Iota has it worse.

Marcia: Pledging gives you structure when you didn't even know it was what you needed.

Shannon: Pledging is basically boot camp. You know that you'll be stronger when you finish, and everyone on campus will have a new-found respect for you.

Amanda: Pledging is an incredible opportunity to connect with a generation of precious women who will be your best friends for life. No matter what happens, your sisters will accept you and cherish you for who you truly are.

Janelle: Pledging is the best thing you will ever do with your life no seriously it's incredible. It's so much fun that you'll barely notice that there is work involved and at the end of the process you're going to be part of a secret group that connects you to thousands of women across America and you can even get discounts or job interviews from it so it's not just about mixers and Greek week, though those are definitely a plus lol.

Janie: My mom is still pissed that I didn't go legacy and rush her house. She wouldn't even write the check for house dues my first semester. I had to ask my dad to do it.

Twyla: Pledging is like going to a debutante ball where you announce to the world that you are a lovable person. At the ball, you wear a white dress and gloves that go past the elbow and everyone tells you that you have incredible poise on the dance floor (the waltz is truly a dying art), and then later you go home and your sisters threaten to post pictures of you in your Spanx on the Internet if you don't give them your dress immediately.

Lucy: When we were pledges we had to take turns as the sober driver from Thursday to Sunday. We'd post our cell phone numbers up in the lobby and we'd spend the weekend on call, waiting to pick up our wasted future sisters. It sounds obnoxious but it was actually kind of fun. On weekends we'd line our cars with trash bags and when cops pulled us over for speeding we said we were picking up drunk sisters and they would tell us how awesome and responsible we were and let us go.

Corinne: Pledging is like trying to eat a powdered doughnut without wiping your face or using a napkin. You'll do this weird thing with your lips where you'll have to pull them away from your teeth in order to make a clean job of it. If you do it right no one will know that you ate the doughnut, but in the meantime you'll look like a dope.

Tracy: Pledging is awesome like eighty percent of the time. The rest of the time, you'll wish you were home.

Alissa: We share secrets, drinks, mascara, shoes, mono, pinkeye, class notes, gossip, textbooks, gas money, leftovers, herpes, grudges, lies, songs, Halloween costumes, puffy paint, thread, blunts, tweezers, compliments, curling irons, and the flu. We are experts in taking group photos, making jungle juice, braiding hair, cleaning floors, sewing pledge pillows, and making paddles. And sometimes we say "Love you like a sister" and really mean it.

Stella: Pledging is like having a boyfriend that calls you every day and tells you he loves you and picks you up from class, but one time he accidentally hits you when you are being obnoxious, and after that it's sort of hard to forget that he did it but at the same time he's still a great guy so you forgive him for the most part and aren't willing to leave him over something so small.

Deirdre: Margot used to say that pledging is like sprinting in the dark without a flashlight.

Eva: Get a grip, Deirdre. Jesus.

Kyra: There are so many other things to care about. After they asked me to leave I'd look back at it and laugh at how stupid all of it was, if I thought of it at all.

17

Scylla

-KYRA-

February 2008

Week Twenty

I made it to the end of February when you began to have consequences, my girl. It couldn't be helped: my sisters noticed when I quit drinking, and then I got too fat to button up my peacoat. I loved that coat. Before you bumped I would tie that belt tight at the waist, so tight I would feel like a magician sawing myself in half. I had to stop cinching and leave myself unbuttoned with a long, gauzy scarf draped around my neck, its fringe grazing my belly. My sister Margot, who could never seem to stand still long enough to hear another person, pulled me aside.

—What's happening to you? she asked. She shifted from one foot to the other, and I couldn't help it: I followed her feet with my eyes.

—I don't know, I said. I think it's a thyroid thing.

—You're not fooling anyone, Kyra.

—I'm probably fooling some people, I said. Isn't that enough?

—What're you going to do?

I called the first clinic on Google. I could have gone to University Health but I had a not-so-irrational fear that you—my condition—would be reported to the school and I would be forced to make an academic decision before I was ready.

The clinic was called Family Care. No one was in the waiting room, and I didn't bring any of my sisters along. I had different friends at the time, boyfriends, mostly, and I didn't like staying in the house around women when I had so many opportunities for romance.

A girl my age came out with a name tag—Agatha! What a name!—and gave me a cup to pee in. You were already announcing yourself in my blood, in my urine. We sat at a card table in an overheated room with staccato fluorescent lights. I started to sweat but couldn't take off my hoodie; I was wearing my letters underneath.

—Would it feel pain? I asked.

—You're a good person to ask that, she said. Most women don't ask.

—Is that a yes?

—Yes, she said.

—For how long?

—You'll get a shot, and it will take twenty-four hours to work. So it could take twenty-four hours for the baby to die. We just don't know.

Her connotation should have been a hint about exactly what sort of family planning center this was, but I was sufficiently terrified. I didn't think of her phrasing until later.

—I have to do this, I said. But I already knew I wouldn't do it; I just hadn't admitted it in a full sentence.

—I understand, Agatha said, and she held my hand in hers. Her palms were warm and clammy. But first, we should do an ultrasound.

—I'd rather not.

—It's recommended. If it's an ectopic pregnancy then we'd have to react differently.

The proclamation of *we* was comforting.

On-screen, I saw your blue profile bobbing in the blackness. I could see the outline of your nose and the fingers of your left hand curled in a fist. It was all over for me. We were moored together now.

In my meeting with the executive board, I was asked to submit my resignation to avoid the shame of disaffiliation from the house. I had to leave immediately. They told me to forfeit my letters, my pin, and my room key.

—We will give the remainder of your boarding fee back, Elina said.

—How generous of you.

Elina was indifferent to suffering. Her term as president was nearing its close, and her responses were clipped short, as if she'd run out of the required ingredients for softness.

—We are being generous, she said. If Nationals looked hard at this they would say we had no obligation to return your money.

She handed me a check for $622.45.

A box of tissues sat in the center of the table, prepared for my tears. So much of my body was water by then, I was nothing if not a reservoir of bloat, and I refused to let my last commodity fall for them, not a single drop.

When the meeting ended I thought I would be left to pack on my own, but some sisters joined me in their final gesture of goodwill. Elina scooped my clothes into a trash bag, and Margot and Marcia hauled my stuff to the car, armfuls of jackets and books and blankets. My beta fish sloshed gently in his little bowl, wedged carefully between shoe boxes on the passenger seat. He scudded against his glass and gravel. Elina went back into the house and returned with a razor blade. She scraped the Greek letters off of my rear window and stuffed the sticky, crumpled vinyl into her coat pocket.

—Best of luck to you, she said. She shook my hand.

—Call me if you need me, Margot said, her back already to me, trotting up the steps and into the house.

Only Marcia lingered.

—I don't know where to go, I said.

—You could go to your mom's.

—I'm done with the house; I'm not done with school, I said.

My mom was a three-hour drive away from campus. She was likely at home at that hour, smoking pot and wandering up and down the backyard in her parka and pajama bottoms, bare feet jammed into rain boots, waxing poetic to a telephone psychic about the life ready to burst forth, life that was miraculously buried under the layer of frost.

—I haven't told her yet, I said.

—But she's cool, right?

She would hug me for long hours and call me an earth mother and discuss my yoni. She'd research doulas. It was too much.

—I can't go home, I said. I rested a hand on my belly. I was just learning the power and vulnerability in the gesture.

Marcia sighed.

—I know where to take you, she said.

I found myself caravanning behind her little Toyota to her brother's apartment in the Rosewood complex across town. I'd been there once before, when he was throwing a Super Bowl party where no one watched the game and my primary concern had been how to make a jersey look sexy. I'd woken up on his couch the next morning without underwear, but he'd been nice about it and offered me a half a bag of stale Raisin Bran before I left. Now I followed her car and worried that she'd change her mind if I lost her at a yellow light. I felt like a Russian nesting doll, fogging the glass of my windshield with our breath, two exhales in one, braking slowly so I wouldn't throw any water out of the beta fish's bowl. I never dreamed that I'd suddenly be adrift in the world as a civilian and not a sister. All of those long hours of carefully curated approval, the insane litany of songs during rush, the perfection of the head tilted just so at cameras, the sluggish dinner talks about what was on TV then and what would be on TV later and who had notes to Intro to Linguistics, all of that fraudulent cultivation of superficial friendship, gone. There had been so much potential to have people to love. I'd wasted all of my time on boys.

Her brother Nathan opened the door, his face absent of surprise. Marcia must have called him during the drive. He was fatter than when I last saw him. The ratty beard was gone, and now his cheeks stood out like dough. Hair curled from under his beanie. He still had an easy grin.

—Have we got a stray? he asked.

Marcia looked at me.

—Go ahead and bark, she said, and I was a little dazed because it hadn't occurred to me that Marcia could be funny.

Later, after Marcia left, he asked me if you were his.

—Do the math, I said.

—I did, he said. I'm half-joking. But whose is it?

—I don't know who the father is, I said.

—You feminists get weirder every year. What wave is it now? Sixth wave? Is it a tsunami?

—It's still the third wave, I said. How long can I stay here?

He rubbed his hand over his bare cheeks, looking for his beard.

—How long do you need?

It wasn't a bad apartment. It was messy, but not squalid. A fire detector chirped its low-battery death knell. Little clusters of herbs were sprouting on the kitchen windowsill.

—I don't know, I said.

—You can stay until you cramp my style, he said.

We spent the evening watching sitcoms that were filmed live in front of a studio audience. When he fell asleep, I wrote him a check for $100 and left it on the refrigerator. Weeks later, it was still there, and I didn't remind him to cash it.

Week Twenty-One

I drove home to tell my mother.

—Kyra, my girl, oh Kyra! she cried. The tendrils of her hair were catching in my mouth. She gripped me so tightly I felt you nudge in between us, she a rock, and me your hard place.

—I'm so glad you're coming home, she said.

When I told her I wasn't, she dissolved.

—But motherhood will transform you! she cried. You can't stay with that boy without a job, without a future. You'll have the baby and you'll become an animal. You'll do anything to survive.

—I don't know if that's true, I said. But I hope that's true. Right now I can't think past the next week.

—Pregnancy makes you complacent, she said. It's a drug. Get a job.

—I'm not much of a candidate right now, I said.

—I'll take care of it. Give me a few weeks and you'll have something.

Week Twenty-Two

There were perks to my living situation. Nathan insisted on the couch. He said he couldn't handle the idea of keeping a pregnant woman out of a real bed.

He never flirted with me. At first I thought that he was kind, or maybe even reverent about the fact that I was busy forming life out of nothing. Then I realized that he was likely repulsed by my bloating body. But he was fat, and he had no excuse! How dare he not want me! I was fat for a real reason! At first it was outlandish, then easy to be friends with a man without the anticipation of more. Still, nights, I missed it all the same.

My belly felt firmer than I'd anticipated, less gelatinous. I couldn't understand the riddle of how many flimsy parts made something so solid. I stared at my popped navel in his bathroom mirror and willed it to retract. I was asexual, practically genderless.

Week Twenty-Three

The apartment was at the end of the complex by the Dumpster, a war zone of chittering raccoons and cats after dark. Our next-door neighbor was a Hispanic woman with two little boys. One warm morning in late March, she saw me waddling with a bag of trash to the Dumpster, the belly swelling before me.

—Ah, she said. *¡Estas embarazada!*

It sounded like she was asking if I was embarrassed.

—Yes, I said, I truly am.

I wondered if she had a spare crib, or if her babies weren't in big-kid beds yet. I was going to be a terrible parent. I didn't even know when children could graduate from sleeping behind bars.

Week Twenty-Four

I withdrew from two classes but kept going to my classics courses. My professors showed slides of Olympian gods with tiny penises, of the rivers of Hades, of naiads, of Scylla, her six necks coiling themselves around the torsos of men, her mouths agape, teeth glittering.

Week Twenty-Five

I found myself spending long hours in Nathan's tub, the belly rising out of the water as an island, your small kicks trembling it on its own tectonic plate. In the bath I was a goddess. I had hewn you from nothing. In the mirror I was a monster. I had destroyed this body for nothing. I dreamed of putting a soup can on the belly and yelling through a taut string, then holding my ear to my own can and waiting, and you would speak to me in another language, a voice of tin. I wondered if you could see red if I shined a flashlight on myself, or if you were always blind in the primordial darkness. I wanted to know: How much of you was made of me? Of my mother? My father? Of my grandma Mona?

Nathan bought those little rubber flowers that grip the tub floor to prevent slipping. He stopped cooking with onions when I couldn't handle the smell anymore. I complained of strange aches in the very middle of my back, and he didn't touch me, but he researched the dangers of Advil during pregnancy. He worked late hours and came home ruddy-faced from time in the kitchen. We'd watch cooking shows together and he'd fall asleep on the couch with a hand tucked into his waistband. We had skipped dating, love, and marriage, and now we were a dog-eared couple with a baby on the way.

Week Twenty-Six

Nights, I'd wake up on my back and panic—it's bad for the baby—and then pause: What if I stayed where I was? Would it make things easier? I would hold my breath and wait and then lose the nerve.

Why do I tell you this, my girl?

You earned my love. You worked for it, and that made its dispensation better. To say that a mother loves unconditionally is a lie. To say that a mother needs her child: that is true, and fair.

Week Twenty-Seven

This is when I found out that my ex-sister Margot died. I didn't even know until after the funeral. She'd spent the night with a graduate student from the university, rolling, and my sisters—ex-sisters—found her dead on the floor the next morning, maybe from dehydration. Molly makes you forget to drink, and you sweat yourself out on the dance floor until your blood is gummy. The heart can't take it. It's a fool's drug, my girl, and Margot was a fool.

Marcia sulked at our apartment. She was glum but not sad, disturbed but not destroyed.

—The house is a hot mess, she said.

—The house was always a hot mess, Nathan fired back. Let's be fair about this. Margot didn't turn it into one.

—Yes, but it's worse now, she said. The reputation is shot. First the pregnancy, and now this.

—I'm right here, I said.

—I'm sorry, she said. But let's be realistic. I can't believe our house is standing right now. You're lucky that you jumped ship when you did.

—I didn't jump ship, I said. They pushed me into the water.

—What did you expect? she snapped. Pregnancy ruins everything.

—None of it means anything, Nathan said. It's just a system. It's not the important stuff. Here, he said, and he dragged Marcia's hand to my belly. The two of them pressed their palms and held their breath, their eyes closed, waiting. When I'd still lived in the house, if I made too much noise with a guest in my room, Amanda would gently tap the wall and I would tap back or ignore her and keep up the ruckus. It was the same game. We waited for you to kick, but you lay still until they removed their palms.

Nathan left for work and Marcia stayed, lolling on the couch.

—My dad's girlfriend just had a baby, she said.

People were starting to do this. They'd stop me in the gas station and tell me about how their friend's sister was pregnant, too, or how they had a little newborn at home, as if I were in a new sisterhood and I just hadn't met the members yet.

—Congratulations.

—I guess, she said. What's the deal with you and Nathan?

—There is no deal, I said. We're roommates.

—He might love you, she said.

—Look at me. I'm a manatee.

—It doesn't matter if you're a manatee. Nathan could love anything.

Week Twenty-Eight

For six nights in a row I woke up at exactly 4:07 and tried to uncover the significance.

I ate white foods: cauliflower, popcorn, mushrooms, goat cheese, chicken husked of its skin.

At dusk I didn't turn on lights to save electricity, though I never saw a bill and Nathan never asked me to pay.

I took hotter baths now, scalding baths, and when it was too much, I'd displace the water in a tidal wave and lie overheated on the bathroom floor like a fat old golden retriever in the sun. I drank water, peed, drank again, and thought of the myth of Tantalus.

I couldn't decide which was more frightening: that Margot's life could be taken so easily by error, or that she could have gotten to a place where she wanted it to dissolve.

Week Twenty-Nine

My beta fish died. He must have swum himself into a frenzy and self-ejected from his bowl because I found him on the kitchen floor, looking stunned and dry. My failure to keep even the smallest thing alive was impressive.

I threw him out in the Dumpster so he wouldn't haunt the pipes in the apartment. I wondered about reincarnation. Would you be my beta, unblinking? Would you be Margot? When did you become official in the depths of my own body, when did you gain access to a soul? Some days you were profoundly real to me, and others you were just an extension.

Week Thirty

There was no more snow, and the mountains of winter ice plowed in parking lots had melted into nothing. The white was gone. The world was gray, and goldenrod with edges of green was creeping in. Spring was late that year, my girl.

I bought a box of Crayolas and ate the white crayon, paper and all, then left the box by the Dumpster. I watched from the window. I daydreamed that the raccoons and the cats would descend upon it and learn to draw, like those elephants that can paint with their trunks. At dusk a raccoon trundled up to the box, sniffed, and left it where it was.

I called my father. I have news, I said in the voice mail. Call me when you can. I said my phone number twice. He didn't call back.

Week Thirty-One

I wrote a final paper about Scylla's origins as a nymph gone bad. The professor called my insights "muddled, with hints of originality." I got a B. I took multiple choice exams that asked how many children Medea killed, and who was the goddess of shame.

Nathan's hours at the restaurant dropped off and he picked up a side job cleaning pools.

—It's like mice have a death wish, he said. You won't believe how many little bodies I pull out of filters.

The town emptied. My ex-sisters went home, and the line at the grocery store shortened, and I started walking on the empty campus, watching the ducks churn through the pond. Faculty nodded at me during their liberated strolls, saw the bump, and kept walking.

Week Thirty-Two

My mother did take care of my job. I started telling fortunes over the phone. I named myself Cassandra and listened to lonely women across the country ask why their men had cheated, or were they cheating, or would they cheat and when. I said maybe, yes, maybe, and I told them which constellations were guiding them. I told them about women's intuition. How the most destructive creatures in Greek myth are female, and that should say something about our power, shouldn't it? Medusa didn't even have to blink, and sirens just needed to trill a few bars. Circe turned men into livestock, and the six-headed Scylla would consume them like carrot sticks.

Leeann from Boise was convinced that Terry was cheating on her and told me that the new moon was very significant to her, and she was going to try to dream of the moon that night so that Terry would stay with her through the luminous power of the goddess Diana, and maybe Terry just needed some time, you know, to decompress, some space to really see Leeann's true beauty, and she needed to derive her inner power from the white glow of the moon.

—Sure, I said, and she didn't want to pay another five dollars so our consultation cut off abruptly, and I listened to the dead air, thinking of lonely lunar Leeann in Boise.

Nathan shuffled into the kitchen.

—Men will kill you with their idiocy but women will kill you with their brilliance, he said.

I smiled at him and rested my head on the table. He touched my hair.

Week Thirty-Three

I ordered a breast pump off of Amazon, then ate the white packing peanuts within.

I blew bubbles in my milk like a child and consumed the foam.

You wiggled less, slept more, and occasionally aimed a square kick at my bladder.

Week Thirty-Four

My father called.

—I've heard about you, he said.

—Have you.

—You're in trouble?

—I wouldn't call it trouble, I said.

—Your Grandma Mona is so ashamed.

—She was ashamed of me before this happened anyway, I said.

—Why didn't you fix this before it was a problem? he said.

I thought of Agatha, weeks ago, and the way she held my hands. I thought of Margot's stopped heart on her bedroom floor, of my dead fish, of the mice in Nathan's filters, and how all of the boys I'd thought I loved were gone now, away for the summer, lifeguarding and interning and dating lean, leggy girls named Ashlee.

—Are you still there? my father said.

—I failed at being a good granddaughter, I said. And a good daughter, and a good sister. Maybe I could be a good mother. Maybe it's my calling.

—You're too smart to waste yourself on parenthood, he said.

—You hardly know me, I said. I could be a mouth-breather.

—I'd considered that, he said, but I think it's far more likely that you're just ill-advised.

I wanted to say, whose job is that, *Dad*? After I hung up I thought: it isn't impossible. I can be a good mother, even if I failed all of the other tests.

Week Thirty-Five

I trawled for cribs on Craigslist, white cribs, pink cribs, cribs with children that didn't exist anymore, that had grown past the length of a child's mattress and now slept in beds with cartoon-patterned sheets.

My ankles swelled, and Nathan and I started playing a game where we would poke at my flesh and count how many seconds it took for the skin to return to normal.

—You're like one of those memory foam pillows, he said.

—So are you, I said. At least I have a reason.

—Shouldn't you be getting checkups and ultrasounds and stuff? he said.

—I do, I said. I go when you're at work.

—That must be expensive.

—It's not bad with the co-pay.

—How much is your co-pay?

I made up a number, and he was satisfied.

We watched an infomercial for a stain remover. Someone poured red wine over a piece of lace, then dropped it in a clear basin of liquid, and we watched, transfixed, as the stain disappeared and the camera panned over a crowd of women applauding in ecstasy.

—About the baby, he said.

You and I were all ears.

—Have you considered a better place to live?

—Oh yeah, I said. I'll be out before the birth. Don't worry.

—I'm not saying you have to—

—I've already made plans, I said. It's all in the works.

—I'm really not saying—

—It's fine, I said. It's really not a big deal.

When he fell asleep I drove to the store and ate an entire container of whipped vanilla frosting.

Week Thirty-Six

I ordered a crib from Amazon, finally. One reviewer wrote, *This crib changed my life*. I wanted to ask her, how? And if the crib changed her life, what sort of impact did the baby have?

Week Thirty-Seven

During one fortune-telling phone call, a woman with stomach cancer asked me how long she had left to live. She wanted to know if she needed to renew her husband's AAA membership now, or if she could wait. She was worried he'd forget and then he'd wind up, eight months later, with a flat tire and no one to call for help.

—He won't get a flat tire, I assured her. He'll be very careful on the highway, especially after you're gone.

—He might get preoccupied, she said. He might miss me so much he'll drive off into a ditch.

—He won't drive into a ditch, I said.

—But when will I die?

—I don't know.

—It's your job to know! she said.

—September fourteenth, I said.

She was satisfied.

Week Thirty-Eight

The belly had been the first transformation. The breasts were heavy with milk now. The ankles, hands, and face were waterlogged. Who knew where my organs had been pushed. My stomach felt like it was where my heart had once been, and I couldn't inhale all the way, not even when I yawned. The transfiguration had already felt completely monstrous, so it didn't feel particularly unusual when, on an afternoon in mid-June, my water broke and I began to grow new necks, first one, then two, five fresh necks, all hewn from the original neck in long stalks, and then some heads sprouted from them, my faces in different expressions of disgust and regret and shame.

Contractions began.

I locked myself in the bathroom and ran the tub. I put my faces under the spout and drank in shifts, one mouth to the next. We all had something to say, we all agreed with what was said, and finally I had built-in sisters, finally I had some women to love who were my own.

Some hours passed. We had plenty of time. We crooned at one another. A surge came and went and we would congratulate each other on our incredible fortitude. We needed no one.

Nathan came home from work and pounded on the door.

—Are you in labor? he called, and I said with six forked tongues: open the door and I will show you.

He didn't open the door.

—Which hospital are you supposed to be at? Do you have a bag packed? Isn't this too early?

—Come to me, my six heads hissed. I have a problem and you are my answer.

The belly was covered in dark scales now. They shimmered in the shower and dulled out of water. We picked strands of kelp out of our wet hair and tossed them into the toilet bowl.

I heard the apartment door open, then close.

The heads commiserated.

—You're doing your best, said one.

—Nobody understands the pressure you're under.

—This little one is so lucky to have you.

—Everyone loves you. You are so loved.

—Adored, really.

—There is no need to be ashamed.

Our faces were salty. We kissed cheeks and leaned our heads against one another, like flowers in a vase.

Another surge began, deeper this time.

We heard the front door open. On the other side, Nathan and the Hispanic woman were speaking over one another.

—Should I call 9-1-1? he asked her.

—No! My heads shouted in unison.

—*¿Cuánto tiempo ha estado así?* the woman said.

We heard the drill going at the hinges on the bathroom door.

—No need for this! The heads shouted. It's fine!

The door was gone, and the woman entered. Her two children sat on our living room couch. One watched in awe; the other was engrossed in a Game Boy. The woman knelt before the belly. We felt like a queen. Nathan was pale.

—Nathan, we said, do you remember when we first met? Our first night?

He couldn't speak.

—Do you remember?

—I remember, he whispered. You were so beautiful.

—It was raining, we said.

—Yes, he said. Lightning illuminated your face. You looked otherworldly.

—Tell us we're pretty.

—You're stunning, he said.

The necks were bigger now, so strong they could have reached around his body and crushed him, squeezed his floppy abdomen until he divided in two. He was pale and salty and waiting to be consumed by us, standing still, even, as if he knew that he had to be sacrificed.

—*Es la hora*, the woman said.

We bore down.

You pulled away, covered in brine, skin glinting, gasping at the forced plunge into this world that you were not ready to love. You were wound in a mainsheet and you started to cry. The children in the living room were unimpressed. Maybe they were lashed to the mast. Maybe their ears were plugged with wax.

—I can't believe she's here, Nathan said.

I waited for the slither of placenta. You were laid on my chest. Six heads crooned. Our baby, we whispered, our baby. You did such a good job, what a girl. When you wailed there were no tears and we thought, that's our girl, don't waste your tears on this.

The woman was in awe.

—*Ella tiene ojos como una serpiente*, she said.

—I know, we said. Isn't she beautiful?

You were quiet, your pupils enormous, and when you yawned we could see the glittering of thousands of tiny teeth.

What's her name? Nathan asked.

—Mona, we said.

He stepped forward and held out a hand. Your little face went still when you saw him. You curled a fist tightly around his thumb, then squeezed.

18

Louder, Dirtier, More Fun

-CHORUS-

May 2009

In the distance only steeples are able to burst out of the trees, and farther on, the hills are always gray, as if they'd run out of ink. Janelle and Lisa lie on the roof of their house with their arms flat at their sides, legs straight, both in shorts, with little paper cups over their nipples because even the tiny strands of a bikini top could leave tan lines. Janelle has tanning oil, and soon they will shine and smell like daiquiris.

If one were watching them with an aerial view, angel or apparition, they would witness the strange scowl in Janelle's mouth and maybe, if the watcher was truly absorbed, they would see the edgy little twitches of her right hand. Meanwhile Lisa is lax and nearly asleep.

Perhaps the watcher would be aware of how astoundingly, achingly alive these two are, even in repose. Inside of both girls skeins of rosy, functional cells are aligned, pushing themselves through the colossal effort of living. There are no malingering issues in their limbs or organs. Deep inside of both of them, the eggs of future people are lined up like strings of microscopic pearls. All of it is both paltry and transfixing.

The cells in Lisa's body are shrinking away a blister on her heel, and her toenails have to be cut weekly so she won't suffer on pointe. Hip bones push under her shorts like two parallel shark fins underwater. All of Lisa's body parts are sharp: chin, and elbows, and earlobes forming sylphlike slants. Except for her cheeks, which are puffy.

Janelle's pale hair is gleaming in the sun. Her lips are so red they look as if they'd been sucked. Even the thin discs of her kneecaps are flawless to the watcher, if the watcher was, say, disembodied and no longer in possession of their own kneecaps.

The watcher could spend eons analyzing the details of things taken for granted and now lost. The watcher could easily envy the perfection of the living and forget the more exasperating fragments: the feeling of wet jeans, or what it's like to have a head cold, or the way an arm can wake up a sleeper in a horrible prickle if slept on at the wrong angle. That is why, even if it's an intrusive violation, it is necessary for the watcher to look into the skull of its subjects and listen. It's not unlike viewing a soap opera in another language: at first there is a lot of staring at the curves of bodies and the hyperbolic expressions, but eventually the plot takes over, and the watcher sets the remote down and forgets about their own place in time.

So:

Lisa had come up here to get high on the roof and watch the treetops execute their tiny shivers until she fell asleep. Janelle had come up thinking she could hear Wes better next door. The trees are fully leafed now; they cut out the sound and she can't hear him from her bedroom anymore.

—I hate this time of year, Janelle says. It gives me allergies.

—You're crazy, Lisa says, barely moving her lips.

—It's just so unnecessary, Janelle says. Why go home and forget everything for three months only to come back and do it all over again?

—At least you get to come back, Lisa says.

Lisa is graduating this month. She has already accepted a job as a customer care professional at a car insurance company. She is not fully sure what the title means but it pays $33,000 and her major in modern dance hasn't panned out the way she'd hoped. Maybe she can dance at night. Join an amateur group and keep auditioning. Being discovered would have been nicer in college, sure, but this is what she has now.

—What's your earliest memory of this house? Janelle asks her.

It's sort of like asking a grandparent what their childhood was like, but in condensed time. Lisa can impart some sort of interesting tidbit about hazing four years ago and Janelle can share it with future pledge classes, embellished, so she can demonstrate how easy they have it now.

—There were more of us, Lisa says.

—Was initiation the same?

—No, Lisa says. It was louder. It was dirtier. It was more fun.

—Margot really screwed us, Janelle says.

She hopes she's said it to the right sister. Half of the house would be offended.

—She did, Lisa agrees. The new pledge class . . .

She never finishes the sentence. She dozes off. Janelle moves her hand off of her belly so she won't get a weird tan line and listens again for Wes. If she sits up and squints, she thinks she can see him down in the parking lot talking to the little whore.

• • •

—It's because of Grant, isn't it? Wes says.

—This isn't about Grant, Stella says.

It is absolutely about Grant. Stella can't get over him. She can't be in the same house as him. She wants to cut herself off from every stubbly, creepy guy at his brotherhood. Start fresh, and maybe meet a nice man at her internship this summer.

—I thought we had fun, Wes says.

—We did have fun, Stella insists. And I really want us to be friends. I know that's a thing that people say, but I really do.

There is no way that she can offer this to him without sounding banal and insincere, but she is no longer willing to try trusting this guy. She thinks he's just hard up all of the time and he calls her when he needs to get laid. It's been a year of this. She's tired of it, and tired of sleeping with him and waiting to love him and never really managing it.

Wes has never been rejected in his life and can't fathom that it's happening to him now, on a beautiful day, with a girl who can't get over Grant, who is two inches shorter than he is, and who doesn't like the taste of Hennessy.

—He's a weird guy, Wes says. He and his mom are a little too close, if you know what I'm saying.

Stella looks at him with abject pity.

—Don't throw your brother under the bus, she says.

—Don't give advice when I'm not asking for it.

She wants this to end nicely but doesn't know how it will.

—I'm sorry, she says.

—You know, Wes says, you're only going to be hot for a few more years, max. You haven't got a lot of time.

—Thanks for the tip, Stella says. She's near tears now. He wishes she'd get angry. It's not fair. He watches her cross the parking lot and disappear into the house. Now that he knows he can't fuck her again he wants her, savagely, in a way that he's never wanted someone, almost like he loves her. He wants to yank her by the hair and call her exquisite. Bash her head against the rocks. Curl all of her toes.

—Wake up, Janelle says. She taps Lisa's foot with her own.

—Mm, Lisa says.

—I think Wes just dumped Stella, she says.

—Mm, Lisa says again.

—Fucking finally, Janelle says. What a mattress surfer.

Lisa is not interested. She rolls onto her belly. She looks striking, clean-lined, with a curve at her waist and strong shoulders, her elbows bent like the arms of a cartoon cactus. Others may look down at her from above and remember what it meant to feel healthy and unburdened.

—Word of advice, Lisa says. You need to let go of Wes. It looks desperate. You're like one boiled pet rabbit away from being a bad movie.

—Why do I do this? Janelle asks. Why do I let him hurt me?

—A part of you has to like it.

—It can't be love, then.

—I dunno, Lisa says. Love has to have a little bit of pain involved.

—Or shame.

—Sure, Lisa says.

Over by the Dumpster, Ruby hurls tattered posters of Audrey Hepburn into the trash. Audrey's limpid, childish eyes are peering at her from their new post. She's holding one of those cigarette extension thingies from Back in the Day. Ruby wonders if Audrey Hepburn is still alive. She wonders if Audrey Hepburn ever got fat. She wonders if Audrey Hepburn ever suffered a strange, quiet humiliation inflicted by the cruelty of others, perhaps equivalent to a group of collegiate men calling her Butterball.

Eva and Shannon are splitting a cigarette down on the back patio. A catbird chitters in the brush, looking for grubs and coming up with nothing. Shannon is taking over Eva's position as pledge mistress. Both of them think she'll be terrible at it.

—Are you going to miss initiating sisters? Shannon asks.

—God, no, Eva says. Somehow we managed to pick even bigger pussies every year.

—The new ones aren't so bad, Shannon offers. I like that Pancake girl.

It's obnoxious, Eva thinks, that Shannon caught her in the hall and is now bumming this cigarette off of her and forcing her to talk. The tobacco tax is going up and it's not cheap to share anymore.

Elina and Jennifer are packing their cars.

—You need to put your backseat down, Elina advises. You can fit more that way.

—It's broken, Jennifer says.

—Have you ever really tried?

—Yeah, Jennifer says. I fishbowled with Boz and we hooked up in the backseat this winter.

—Sounds nice, Elina says.

It did sound nice. It sounded especially nice because Jennifer left out the part where he pulled out and came on her face, which she hated, and how cold the leather was on her naked back, and how she'd just finished her period a few hours earlier so she kept worrying that she wasn't really and truly done.

• • •

Marcia trips onto the back patio while Eva and Shannon are still smoking.

—Have you guys seen my shoes? I can't find my shoes, she says.

She wobbles around the patio, and it is easy to remember what it felt like to be drunk. The memory of the feeling is enviable.

—You didn't bring them out here, her sisters say.

—I did! she insists. I did!

Marcia walks into the ivy and pulls down her pants.

—Bathroom's inside, Eva says.

But they can hear her piss falling on the leaves.

—Hey! Janelle calls from the roof. Get your shit together!

—I'm trying, Marcia says. She's laughing at herself in the ivy.

—God, Eva says. She hands her cigarette to Shannon and follows Marcia into the brush. She yanks her upward and pulls up her pants.

—Go inside, Eva says.

Marcia obeys Eva at all times, even when she's sloppy.

The gesture reminds Shannon of Eva during initiation: her cold hands, the way she'd push sisters through the door.

—Before you initiated me I thought you were going to lock me in a coffin or make me walk on hot coals or something.

Eva exhales through her nose.

—Do you wish we'd done that instead?

—Sometimes, she says. The real thing is so goofy.

—I'm not going to miss eating ashes, Eva says.

The watcher overhead can remember, with an intense clarity, the swish of red robes in the Chapter Room, the candle wax, the taste of ash in the mouth, the rules about no makeup, no nail polish, no colors to be worn during the process except red, vivid red, and how, after long, tedious hours of chanting and leaning against plywood altars, the newly initiated sisters have their blindfolds removed and can see, for the first time, the artificial solemnity. The bust of Hestia is chipped and grimy. The sisters' faces, removed of makeup, are plain and long-shadowed under the candlelight. Their bored expressions make them look distantly related. But still, it is a relief to burst out of the room when it's over and pop cheap champagne together. The red robes are left in a pile on the laundry room floor. The new sisters put on their lettered shirts and do each other's makeup. Dance music pours out of bedrooms and into the hallways. The housemother suddenly realizes she must visit a relative in the next town. The boys come over. The house is transfigured into a refuge for clumsy euphoria. There are fights and tears in the hallways and long, sloppy hugs and proclamations of eternal friendship, and everyone wakes up in the morning feeling as if something momentous had been accomplished. Parents call and ask about initiation and their daughters are coy and thrilled with their new secrets, the things that belong to them and no one else, no matter how idiotic the secrets actually are.

They've made, as the oath says, a gleaming paradise of sisterhood: clumsy in its execution but smoothed by memory until it is something sacred, something pristine.

19

The Putting Green

-CORINNE-

June 2009

Twelve years ago, imagine there was a girl called Corinne who was home from college for the summer. Whether or not the girl is me is irrelevant. There are only two things to know about the girl: she was good-looking, in the way that only twenty-year-olds can be, and she was very protected. She was aware of both fortunes in a vague way, in the way that healthy people are grateful for their vigor, which is to say: the stakes for her gratitude were low.

Corinne's mother, who was also pretty, but wilting, was studying her daughter's figure as she stood before the mirror on her armoire. The house was old but updated: Corinne's parents had gutted it upon its purchase years before and gone to great lengths to install central air. Outside, fireflies and crickets put on a show that none of the family noticed through closed windows.

—Oh, it just looks ridiculous on you, Corinne's mother said. It's so boxy.

Corinne's dress hit halfway down the thigh and was high-necked and sleeveless. It had a pretty pattern that reminded her of lilacs.

She admired her legs in the mirror. She had nice legs, nicer than her mother's.

—I think I look pretty damn good in it, Corinne said.

—It doesn't do your waist any favors, her mother said.

She stood behind her daughter and yanked at the fabric to demonstrate the young body hidden inside.

—That figure, she said. If only I had that figure.

—You still have it, Corinne offered, albeit absentmindedly. But this is the look now. All the girls will have this, and I'll stick out in a different cut. You'll see.

Her mother's cocktail dress pleated close around her waist, and the hairs on her arms were almost white against her tan.

—Whatever became of the little black dress?

—Black is over, period, Corinne said.

She reached behind her neck and yanked off the tag to demonstrate her commitment.

—It's your loss, her mother said.

Technically, it was Corinne's father's loss. He hid in a nook in the house, likely the sunroom, and drank Dewar's with his bare feet resting on the coffee table, listening to people with exotic names and perfect mid-Atlantic accents hum out the news on NPR. Meanwhile, a floor above him, mother and daughter picked up their drinks from the bureau and sipped. It was Corinne's first summer where she could say damn and drink wine away from the dinner table without admonishment. These leniencies, and the quietness with which they happened, made her feel unusually generous toward her mother.

—You look really young, Mom.

—It's all smoke and mirrors, she said. I went to the stylist this morning with a photo of myself at Duke and asked her to make me look like the girl in the picture. This was the best they could do.

It was not true. She'd said this line before, fishing for a compliment that others had already let her catch.

—Where's Yvette? Corinne asked.

—Probably in the kitchen.

Now she was pacing her daughter's room with her hands on her hips, examining the crowns and sashes that had been carefully arranged on white shelves along the western wall. She frowned, but didn't say anything.

Hard to believe now that the summerhouse had been so beautiful, and maybe twelve-year-old memories make it more stately than what it was: a tall yawning thing with gray shingles and tall boxwoods on the corner of Astor's Neck and Hodgeman Lane. The family could see the inlet from the second floor. When they arrived in late May they had ordered tulips in vases throughout the house. June brought the peonies. July was hydrangeas. August was something imported because Corinne's mother thought sunflowers were vulgar.

Yvette spent most of her time in the kitchen, working or watching her stories on the tiny plasma television that had been installed for her beside the microwave. She would spend hours leaning her elbows on the counter, butt jutting out, gaping. She'd been with the family for so long that even her sloth seemed charming, and in memories she was easily reduced to a stereotype: the chubby black housekeeper with a mushroom haircut and a face like a walnut. This time Corinne found her making a Caprese salad. Tomatoes slipped off the cutting board and bled onto the marble.

—Look at you! she said. Just like Ingrid Bergman.

Corinne always wanted to ask her why she didn't say Grace Kelly, who was clearly more beautiful and memorable, but at the time she didn't think Yvette was smart enough to administer such a backhanded compliment on purpose.

—Can you pick me up from the country club tonight?

Yvette's lips thinned but she didn't disapprove.

—How late'll you be?

—Not very. Maybe ten?

They both knew it would be twelve, and she would wait. She hemmed and hawed and oversalted the tomatoes.

—As long as it's ten, Yvette said. My sister's visiting tomorrow. I took the day off to see her and I can't have you keeping me up.

Corinne remembered she had a sister who sent the family Christmas cards every year but she could not recall her name. She lingered at the counter.

—Are you nervous, sweet pea?

—What if they know about the pageant?

—They don't know, Yvette said. She smoothed Corinne's long, pale hair, tucking a piece behind her left ear.

—How do you know they don't know?

Yvette ran a tongue over her teeth and turned back to her tomatoes.

—They might know, she allowed. But if they do they won't care enough about you to talk.

—You're out of line, Corinne said.

Yvette turned and stared at the girl, now taller than her, with her mother's almost-crooked nose and her almost-arrow eyes that looked, nonetheless, wholly ethereal, the girl whom she'd cared for since she was a toddler, who used to sleep in her bed during thunderstorms and who had asked her Montessori schoolteacher why other families didn't have an Yvette, too.

—I didn't mean anything by it, Yvette said.

The families with children were already at the country club: young mothers in floral sundresses with scoops of cleavage, fathers in salmon-colored shorts, with offspring all varying shades of blond. Corinne watched the younger children scatter onto the putting green, their saddle shoes pressing indents into the wet grass, their soft hands grabbing up the red metal flagsticks and brandishing them like swords. The adults were lazy with their admonishments because they had done the same when they were small, on the same green. Music, jazzy and forgettable, poured over the ballroom and out of the open doors. She admired the square lines of her father's retreating dinner jacket as he strode into the ballroom with her mother and noticed with satisfaction how the other fathers in his age group were using blazers to hide old-man potbellies. She ordered a drink and walked purposefully upstairs, acutely aware of the flex of her calf muscles and how the older ladies glanced and looked away as she ascended.

Her summer friends were at the upstairs deck overlooking the putting green, a group of young people with identical tans and white teeth that she had known since infancy. This was the debut year where they had stopped hugging or waving hello and had started kissing each other on the cheeks instead. It was the first real weekend of the summer, and more of them were home from college now. Dina was there (with ten extra pounds), and so was Sophie, who wore the same espadrilles from last summer, and so was Adam, who'd had his ears pinned back. They looked much better.

—So good to see you! Adam said. His upper lip left a damp impression on her cheek and when he turned to pick up his glass from the railing she dabbed carefully at the mark, not wanting to upset her foundation.

—Did Dartmouth keep you late this summer? she asked.

—No, but a girl did, he said.

—Congratulations! she said, and felt a little, inexplicable stab even though she'd never wanted Adam, ears pinned or no.

—Where are you again?

—Up in Massachusetts, she said.

—Harvard?

—No, she said. The minutes seemed to slow in the gravitational pull of her awkwardness. She did what her coach had taught her in pageants and clenched her buttocks—(put all the stress in your ass! she'd said)—and asked, How are your parents?

They all seemed so civilized. Adam switched to talking about his parents, his weak-chinned sisters, and their boat.

It was a relief for her to be with this crowd again instead of back at the college, running the sorority house, monitoring each of her sisters for signs of slovenly attire or unmade faces before they left for class. They were just so casual at school, so oblivious to their reputation. *You don't just represent you, you represent your sisterhood*, she'd tell them, but still some of them would slouch off to class without straightened hair if she didn't stop them on their way out the door. At home, these people understood. There was pride in the order of things. Even if her friends here were ugly, they at least tried to be stately.

Now Roman appeared, with his square head and wolfish incisors and wide, asymmetrical grin. She hadn't seen him since New Year's. She became very aware of what she was doing with her arms and let one rest on a wicker chair. She pulled her cheeks ever so slightly between her teeth. She angled her face toward the porch lights. They exchanged platitudes. Cheek kissing ceremony commenced. She had a flash memory of him striding toward her in the pool room last winter, the shadows predicting where the wrinkles on his face would eventually lie, his teeth clumsily clicking against her own in the dark.

—That's a nice color on you, he said, and his eyes flicked down her dress and up again.

—I wore the same color in my last pageant, she blurted.

—My mom heard that you did well, he said. And she said you're president at your sorority? Not a bad year for you!

Corinne had learned to swat compliments away as if they were mosquitoes. It was the right thing to do. It was especially easy in this case, because what he claimed his mother said was likely a lie.

Roman leaned over the edge of the deck and yelled to his little brother on the putting green—Sebastian, don't mess with the hydrangeas or I *will* take you home!

She excused herself and ordered a second vodka tonic with lime. Couples were dancing in the ballroom now, repeating the same cha-cha step over and over. Hands on waists, hands on shoulders. The women's hairs were already curling on the backs of their necks and the men were wiping their foreheads but refused to relinquish their blazers to chairs yet. The ceiling fans ran at full speed, high above, useless. Corinne's parents minced little steps near the band. Two more songs, just to make an appearance, and then they would leave. In ten years, she knew, she would be in their place, with her husband, hopefully the right type of man. All day she'd wanted to come here and now she wanted to disappear. Instead she returned to the deck and laughed at someone's punch line, something about the way old Jeanine Wilder looked on the tennis court, something about her varicose veins. Down on the putting green, Sebastian had found a stray golf ball hidden under the hydrangea bushes and lobbed it at a little girl in a seersucker dress.

Mr. Cline materialized in her line of vision, frighteningly close, so close that she could see the gray in his eyebrows, and he said in a voice so unctuous it could have oiled a squeaky wheelbarrow,

—Corinne, you look beautiful, just beautiful! I'm so sorry to hear about your last pageant.

—Thank you, she said.

—It could have happened to anyone, he said.

She was doing a frantic equation as he spoke, trying to derive who had found out, and who had gossiped, and how many people in that moment could overhear. These people had taught her everything: how to disguise all expressions into pleasant amusement. How to cheat and ignore others cheating. How to drink scotch and soda and do the twist without a bellyache. She smiled at him.

—You are so considerate, she said. Thank you for your kind words.

Roman intervened as soon as he disappeared.

—What a dick, he said.

—It's too early for you to talk like that.

—I've had two drinks, I can call him a dick. What a dick. But what happened at your pageant?

—See, asking that makes you a dick, too, she said.

—I'm sick of this fraudulent mire of societal nicety, he said. Is that better?

—Oh, I love the fakery, Corinne said. It's just the people I can't stand.

The Von Wooten couple, who had been standing within earshot, shot nasty looks in their direction.

The night was almost full-mooned and shimmering; the putting green was still overrun with children. Some lay flat on their backs, looking up at the stars. Others still were pinwheeling around the green, chasing one another, shrieking and tripping over their own shoes. Corinne's group was on their third round of drinks now, and the band downstairs had transitioned to playing pop hits in a jazz style. It was the club's way of appearing contemporary without sacrificing much. Downstairs, she knew, older couples were leaving.

Newly marrieds stayed on and danced a little spasmodically, without rhythm but with plenty of fervor.

—Let's take a walk, Roman said. Corinne felt a little dab of adrenaline and looped her arm through his. They walked outside the pool of light framing the clubhouse and up the fairway of the first hole.

—You smoke? he asked, and shook two cigarettes from a pack and lit hers first, like they did in the black-and-white movies Yvette watched when she ironed. She stood on one foot, then lost her balance, tried standing on the other, lost her balance. Finished her drink. Took off her shoes. She hadn't had much dinner and the drinks were melting her blood. They stood in the full dark of the fairway. Trees stood in indistinct blots of darkness on either side, and moonlit grass gleamed before them, and thin skeins of clouds stretched over the sky. She lay down.

—What are you doing?

—It feels nice, she said.

—If you knew how many pesticides they put on that grass, you wouldn't be lying on it. The golf pros can't have kids because of it.

She flung an arm over her eyes, as if she'd just fainted in a Victorian novel and the fairway was now her chaise lounge. It occurred to her, as it occasionally did with some people, that she could easily dislike Roman if he wasn't so handsome. He was too dramatic. Who was he fooling with the whole I'm-tired-of-the-fakes act? He'd probably taken her out here to pull her pageant fuckup out of her, then sleep with her and leave. They all still acted like they'd never left high school; they were just getting a little more artful. She could predict the next hour with perfect accuracy, but she wanted it all the same. He kept standing, scanning the fairway.

—What would people think if they saw this? he asked.

—They wouldn't call it fraudulent, she said.

He sat beside her.

She traced a finger over his mouth, running into the divot of his upper lip, and he lay still, watching her, waiting to see what she would do next.

—People might know what we're up to, he said.

—They might know, she said. But even if they know they won't care.

He followed her into the trees dividing the first and ninth hole. She needed his help with her zipper, but she didn't let the dress fall off her shoulders. She studied him as he shook out of his blazer and shirt and tie and belt and shoes and socks and finally pants, underwear.

—Women are so lucky in the summer, he whispered.

She let her dress fall in the grass and they stared at one another, tense, until he moved toward her, his teeth shining in the moonlight, his face joyful in the way she had seen in him when he was a small boy, tussling with her in a sand trap at a party not unlike this one, his asymmetrical smile still the same, whispering childhood myths into her ear.

She let him put an arm around her waist on the walk back to the clubhouse. Her new dress had grass stains. She had sobered somewhat; she walked in a straighter line.

—I lost my shoes, she said, placidly.

—Should we go back and look for them?

The lights loomed before them.

—No, she said. I want another drink.

—Will you tell me about the pageant now? he said.

—It was awful, she said flatly. It's on YouTube. It was awful.

—Will you show me?

—No, she said. Google it if you care. You'll hear soon enough.

—What did you do?

—I tripped during swimwear, she said.

They were near the party now. She noticed, dimly, that the music had stopped.

—That doesn't sound so terrible, he said. He almost sounded disappointed.

—No, she said. It was. It was terrible. I tripped, and fell, and I popped out of my bikini.

—Oh my god, Roman said.

He broke into a run, his tie flapping over his shoulder. Frantically, she followed, her dress catching between her legs, her hair flagging behind her shoulders, losing its curl.

—It wasn't that bad! she yelled. Roman!

She chased him through the club crowd until she saw Sebastian, sitting up on the putting green, picking at a scab on his ankle, his face expressionless, with a metal flagstick impaled in his right eye. He wasn't crying. Was he too shocked to cry? Dr. Houghton sat next to the boy, gingerly holding the other end of the flagstick.

—Hi, Roman, Sebastian said cheerfully.

Roman lurched sideways, as if he were going to faint. Mr. Cline grabbed him by the shoulder.

—Keep your nerve, he said.

Corinne breathlessly gripped at his arm. He was panting, staring at his little brother.

—Why won't somebody pull it out? Roman shouted.

—We can't do that, son, Mr. Cline said. He settled Roman in a wicker chair away from the scene.

—Why won't someone call an ambulance! Corinne shrieked.

The crowd stared at her.

—The ambulance is coming, Adam said. You would have known that if you'd been here ten minutes ago.

Corinne looked for her parents and couldn't find them. They'd already gone home. She found a frantic waiter and told him to call her house and tell Yvette to come. She was in possession of a strangely sobering alacrity that stunned her. She was too drunk to feel so aware. Nobody seemed capable of looking at Sebastian with the exception of Dr. Houghton, yet they all gathered around him like some sort of bizarre wagon train barrier between the boy and the elements.

—Remarkable, the doctor muttered. Truly remarkable. Tell me again how it happened?

And Sebastian recounted how he had been running with the flag as if it were a spear, had caught his foot in a hole, and had fallen on it, with part of the flag jamming itself into his eye before his free elbow hit the green and stopped the rest from entering.

—Am I going to have to get a shot at the hospital? Sebastian asked.

His blond hair was shining. There were grass stains on his knees and a tiny spatter of blood was on his white polo. Corinne wondered wildly at how there wasn't enough blood. Maybe it was a joke.

Dr. Houghton was not one to sugarcoat, and certainly not one to lie to a child.

—I'm sure you'll get several shots, he told the boy.

Only then did Sebastian start to cry out of his good eye.

—Keep both eyes closed, sonny, the doctor said. When you move one, the other goes with it.

And so Sebastian wept with his good eye closed, still picking at the scab on his ankle.

The red and white lights of the ambulance strobed over the

hedges, and the paramedics sprang out before the brakes were completely thrown. Corinne thought, stupidly, of how the tires would destroy the appearance of the green, and then was immediately ashamed that this had occurred to her at all. Another thought intruded: Margot had died a year ago, freakishly young. Surely, people had to have a quota for tragedy. Wasn't it possible, then, that Sebastian would be fine because Margot was already the one shitty death in the periphery of Corinne's life?

Roman was stewarded closer to Sebastian. He couldn't look at his brother's face. He glanced down, turned ashen, and then looked away.

—He's going to be a freak! Roman shouted.

It seemed a bad idea at this point to put him in the ambulance alone with his brother, and so Dr. Houghton volunteered to join them. The paramedics carefully negotiated the sitting little boy onto a stretcher while the doctor maneuvered with them, still holding the other end of the metal flag. They moved at a nauseatingly slow pace. Finally, the doors shut on the strange diorama of the three of them: barefoot Roman, Cycloptic child, and doctor in a sport coat. Everyone watched the ambulance leave.

There were mutterings. The bartenders were dismissed; the band disappeared. Questioning children were hushed. Fathers somberly finished their drinks. The crowd ebbed off into the parking lot. Engines turned over one by one, and soon only a few members remained. Lights began flicking off in the ballroom.

Yvette found her, unmoving, on the putting green where Sebastian had been.

—Oh, honey, she said. She picked flecks of grass out of Corinne's hair.

—What mess did you get yourself into?

She couldn't speak.

—It's just a silly pageant, Yvette said. It was a mistake. It's not like half of God's world doesn't have breasts on them. Corinne leaned on Yvette. It was her last summer on that putting green.

—They won't care in one week, Yvette continued. They're all too busy with their divorces and DUIs to pay attention.

—Why do terrible things happen? Corinne asked, and Yvette, who had already met many terrible things, who lived them in colossal family losses and daily discriminations, who was unaware of the misfortune in either of their futures, looked at Corinne and thought, Stupid Child. Stupid, lucky child that I love.

They didn't know then that in three years Corinne's family would lose the house, and her father would serve a two-year sentence for a white-collar crime that she still wouldn't understand the mechanics of, not a decade later. They didn't know that Yvette's sister had lupus, or that, six years out, Corinne's mother would check herself into rehab, then out, then in again, over and over, until she ran out of money but not out of gin. And it was impossible to know, twelve years out, Sebastian would be drinking on the top deck of the club, looking passable with his prosthetic eye, wondering if the little girl he'd chucked golf balls at, now a beautiful waifish thing in a black dress, would forgive him for his past indiscretions and follow him onto the dark of the fairway.

20

Occlusion

-DEIRDRE-

September 2009

I've been looking for her. Not that I believe in reincarnation, not logically. Not that I'm religious. But surely, out of six billion, her print may be identical in someone else's palm. It is also not completely impossible to discover her in another person, another object. Unlikely, but not impossible.

At first I thought I saw a refurbished version of her in a faceless mannequin displayed in the thrift shop off Delancey Street. She wore a miniskirt and knee socks, like a teenage porn star, but the hair was what got me: a long, black braid, drifting down the side, and also the narrow little breasts covered by a tank top, and the long, tapering fingers. The inside of the shop smelled like wet newspaper, the linoleum gouged and linty. I wove a disinterested route around the racks, eyes on the mannequin, trying to look like I had a purpose.

—Need help? asked the sour woman at the register.

I still looked young enough for every shop owner to think I was about to scoop a pair of jeans into my coat and run.

—How much is that? I asked. I pointed at the mannequin.

—The skirt or the socks?

—No, not that, I said, the whole thing.

Saying *mannequin* felt perverse.

The woman came out from behind the register. Her chin was unusually shiny, as if she'd had it polished. Her T-shirt advertised a surf club in Verona Beach and her bare thighs were dented with cellulite. A pink roll of fat poked over the lip of her jeans.

—What do you want to do with it? Did Ted send you? she said.

I had no clue who Ted was.

—You can tell that twisted bastard to get himself castrated, she said.

That sounded fair, so I left.

In the first year the mornings were the hardest, because I'd wake up and forget that she was dead. Then, simultaneously: guilt about forgetting, fury that I had to remember at all. There would always be a new clue designed to destroy me. Once it was her hairbrush, then her photograph in the composite, then her sociology textbook, unread. What if, when something reminds me of her, it isn't a reminder? What if it is Margot calling out to me?

—You know what would help? Marcia said. Visit Nathan and Kyra. Go see the baby. It'll distract you.

The equation was silly. Death could be solved by life. She must have come from a family that bought a replacement dog as soon as they buried the last one.

—Soon, I said. But I need to buy her a gift first. She must be broke.

—Oh, I think she's got plenty, Marcia said, suddenly sour, but I wasn't interested in asking what she meant by that.

One afternoon on the back patio a catbird approached me. She was a cocky little thing, with black eyes and a sleek gray body. Her head was small and smooth, without those funny Mohawk tufts that stick up on titmice.

—What does it feel like to be a bird in the rain? I asked her.

She blinked at me.

—What I mean is, does it bother you? Does it weigh you down?

She dipped her sharp little beak into her right wing and dug frenetically at an itch, which I took to say, no, not really, it's not such a bother at all.

—Are you scared? I asked her.

She puffed her chest.

—Are you missing something?

She departed.

She did not seem dead. She seemed taken. She seemed transfigured.

All of my memories took on a tawny glow. In one we were putting in our service hours for the sorority by raking leaves at an assisted living facility for the mildly deranged. Geese were migrating overhead in urgent V's. Dumber birds sat on telephone wire, spaced out like notes on sheet music. The trees here had been carefully planted in increments: an architect had planned ahead for roots, for shade, for unused benches. What a meticulous life.

None of the deranged came outside.

A round-faced man stood at his window and watched us the whole afternoon, his breath fogging the glass, then pressing his cheek against it and fogging it up again. We scooped leaves into enormous black contractor bags—body bags, Margot called them—and at one point she shoved a handful of debris down the back of my shirt, which I know, surely, I must have hated—the itch of it—but now I can't remember it that way even if I try. She was playful.

We found an empty purple lighter and an eggshell and bright

slivers of feathers hidden in the piles, and showed our discoveries to each other as if we were doing an anthropological examination on a planet unknown.

The man at the window waved at us, tentatively, and she waved back in enormous arcs. He beamed, pumping both arms at her, as if she was an old friend awaiting him at baggage claim.

—That's nice of you, I said, but I didn't wave with her.

The man was elated, savoring the feeling of being seen by her. Please, I thought, don't let him come outside.

—Sometimes, Deirdre, you have to be nicer than you want to be, she sermonized, and I must have thought she was being preachy but in the memory I can only see her as profound.

On harder days, I'd feel like she was just around the corner or in the next room. I walked faster, quieter, so as not to scare her. I called her name and no one answered.

Someone was driving her car, or her car's doppelgänger, down Craven Street. Her ancient purple Honda had an unmistakable eroding pattern of rust at the seam. The back windows were steaming. The headrest hid the driver. I followed it onto Route 10, where the road widened and I darted to the right lane and peered. The tint was so heavy it was probably illegal. All I could see was the spectral outline of a face. I waved frantically. The Honda sped up. I followed as far as Vernon and then it disappeared down a long, muddy driveway.

Amanda bookmarked passages from Job in her kooky Bible and left it at my door. Instead I flipped to John and read of Lazarus. Lazarus, who'd been so lucky. All Jesus had to say was *Lazarus, come out!* and he popped out of his cave in his shroud like it was Groundhog Day. I reread the passage over and over. Lazarus was dead in one verse, alive in another. I could kill him and bring him back with a flick of the iris.

Later, Jesus said: He who loves his life loses it. It sounded like a threat. I tried to picture a guy in sandals saying it, his hand resting on the head of a child, a sheep nibbling at the tasseled rope around his tunic. Putting children into the scene only made it seem more sinister. I wanted to ask her: How much did you love your life when you lost it?

I remember how, after I saw Tremaine Bechetti throw himself off an overpass, she googled him. Now, as her disciple, I googled, too. There were two Margot Grace Glenns. One had already died in 1947, at the age of sixty-six, down in Orlando. Wife of Thomas, mother of Marie and Edie. So that was impossible, of course, because if she had been uncreative enough to have a past life with the same name surely she wouldn't have chosen a life with a husband and two children in Florida, of all places.

The other Margot Grace Glen had dropped an *n* and lived as an orthodontist in Minnesota. I called the practice.

—Monarch Orthodontics, a woman lisped.

I clutched at the phone, stricken. What more was there to say?

—Monarch Orthodontics? the woman said again.

—Is this Dr. Glen? I whispered.

—She's with a patient, the voice said. May I ask who's calling?

—I'm sorry, I've made a mistake.

I hung up and walked down the hall to the bathroom. I ran a paper towel under the sink and pressed it hard against my face. When I pulled it away, two half-moons of mascara smiled at me. The shower radio bellowed about a dealership liquidation sale SALE SALE!!! My hands were bloodless. I ran them under water, too hot water, and studied the prints.

• • •

Maybe all of life is split in two.

There is the guileless side, where nothing is missing and it's a little boring in its ease, so we build problems for distraction.

The other side is about the losing of things, and we build problems because we think the answers will solve the ache.

The problems she'd constructed for herself were horrifically obvious in hindsight. Of course she was a druggie. Of course she used me as a distraction. Of course I was her enabler, I was her neglecter, and, on the worst days, her executioner.

If I hadn't gone to work that night— Some days I couldn't finish the sentence. If I hadn't gone to work that night, she would have shared her doses with me.

I thought of her parents. Her father was a contractor and not a great communicator unless it came to drywall or the Patriots, but her mother could wax so poetic that Margot used to refer to her as artistically depressed. She's probably bedridden now, curled into piles of blankets just as her daughter used to do. When Margot introduced me to her mother she called me her best friend. I don't know what I'd expected. Her mother blinked too much and spoke like she was recovering from laryngitis. It was like talking to a psychic.

Margot told me how no one else knew that she was adopted. She said she had no interest in her biological parents, and I believed her. Life for Margot began when her mother held her for the first time. She told me how her parents spent the first night with her in a dusty hotel near the airport, and whenever a plane took off the legend was that she wouldn't cry, but she would shut her eyes and frown deeply, like a nun interrupted from her prayers. She saved her tears for her father. She cried whenever he tried to come near her until she was nearly five months old.

I clutch at these tiny details and try to climb into the night: her parents look like pale, sore thumbs in Phoenix. Margot's mother is sweating and nervous, mixing formula over the bathroom sink, treating it as if it were alchemy. Her clumsy father is lying on one of the double beds, watching the little body wriggle in the detachable car seat, patiently waiting for a sense of kinship, like a bear ready to swipe at the first glimpse of trout.

Now the Delancey Street mannequin wore a sequined dress in magenta. It wasn't the same. The long braid had been coiled against the skull. I couldn't see the legs or breasts. The fingers, I noticed, were fused together, pointed like spades. I didn't go back inside. Over and over, I lost her.

But other days I couldn't walk a mile without seeing her new manifestation. A knock-kneed girl with an oversize backpack and hair skidding out of a ponytail waited for the bus. She rocked side to side and swung her lunch bag from one hand to the other while her mother read the paper, oblivious to her sway. The girl dropped into a hunch and stared under the bus-stop bench and studied until she reached under and came away with a piece of used gum, which she quickly popped into her mouth and chewed, her mother unaware. Impossible, I thought, and kept walking.

We stood on the back patio. In the memory it was nighttime, but somehow I could see the trees for yards, and the floodlights from the side of the house poured an amber light upon her face, and she passed to me and said, Do you think he knew he was going to die when he fell?

This was after I'd seen Tremaine Bechetti die on I-95. She was feeling more introspective than crass, my favorite version of her.

—I don't think so, I said. I think we all know we're going to die but we always think we have a shot at living when it's happening.

—Down to the last synapse, she said.

—Denial, I said.

—It's a shame.

—Let's talk about something else.

—Did I spook you?

I couldn't see beyond the floodlight after she said it. Trees rustled invisible.

—People are just unfinished ghosts, she said.

My sisters sat in the dining room and planned philanthropy events, mixer themes, and Bid Day shirts. One snuck a kitten into the house and hid it from Nicole. One slept with another's boyfriend. One yelled at her mom over the phone about her embarrassing Facebook posts. They were so wonderfully banal. They stood on the other side of the shroud and looked at me like, really? Why the drama?

I gave Amanda her Bible back at lunch.

—Did you find it to be helpful? she asked.

—I did, I said. Thank you very much.

She hugged it to her chest and nodded at her knees.

—I'm glad that it gave you peace, she said.

After she left, Twang said, Did she make you read Job?

—She did, I said.

—Jesus, that's the worst fucking one, she said.

—What's the best one, then?

—Ecclesiastes, she said.

—Really?

—No, she said. I've never read it. I just like the word, and I've heard Amanda talk about it before.

It wasn't just that I was missing her. I was missing a good death. She'd done such a bad job at dying. I thought of how, when I was little, I would watch Wile E. Coyote flatten himself over and over again under the weight of a botched scheme. He would stand in a puddle of deepening shadow and then look up at the last minute, eyes as big as sunflowers, but he never managed to move in time. Then he would appear in a new scene, completely resurrected, looking grumpy but intact all the same.

The Rosewood complex had sagging rooftops and ballsy raccoons. I parked in a spot that threatened to tow me. Kyra answered the door looking raw.

—She just went down, she said.

But then the baby wailed in protest from the other room.

—Short nap, I said.

I followed Kyra into the bedroom. The baby was quavering a vacillating little cry. I could see it stirring through the bars.

—Shh, Kyra said. It's time to meet your auntie Deirdre.

—Deedee, I said. Kids can't say my name.

—It's not like she's going to say it today anyway, Kyra snapped.

She lifted the baby from its crib.

—Meet Mona, she said, and there she was, peering at me, imperious and sullen. Her eyes were heavy lidded and her face was stretched, but there was no mistaking her.

—Oh, God, I said.

—I know, Kyra said. She takes your breath away.

The problem with grief is that it works inside of me like twine: sometimes it holds, and I can go about my day without its intrusion. But often, it takes nothing to make it unravel, and I am too distracted by the fray of it to do anything but chase her down before I mythologize her into what she wasn't.

• • •

—Monarch Orthodontics, a woman lisped.

—I'm looking for Dr. Glen, I said.

—May I ask who's calling?

—Her sister, I said.

—Hold on.

There was no hold music. The receptionist clunked the phone and I heard muttering in the background. It was almost closing time there. Dr. Glen was done with patients for the day. The line clicked.

—Candace? said Dr. Glen.

—No, I said.

I could visualize this woman so clearly. It was six thirty. She had taken out her contacts and put on frumpy reading glasses once her patients were gone. She was scribbling notes in a patient's file—little Kevin Wahler was lying about how frequently he slept with his retainer. The bite didn't lie. She sighed.

—I'm sorry, she said. My receptionist said you were my sister. I must have picked up the wrong line.

—It's fine, I said.

—Bear with me and I'll transfer you back.

—No! I said. Not yet.

Surely, I thought, if a shred of her was there now, she would hear me, she would know my desperation and listen.

—What can I help you with? Dr. Glen said.

—Why did you decide to be a dentist? I asked.

—Pardon me?

—What made you choose to be a dentist?

—Orthodontist, she said. Is this for a school thing?

—No, I said.

There was a pause. Dr. Glen was assessing. She was leaning back in her desk chair, chewing on a pen cap, thinking fast about how to get me off the phone. But she was a nice lady. She wasn't going to hang up on me, not right away.

—I became an orthodontist because I wanted to help people, she said, blithely, gently, as if she were talking to a classroom of third graders.

—That can't be why.

—Why can't it?

—It's too prosaic.

—How old are you? she asked me.

—Twenty-one.

—You are too young to think that helping people isn't a good reason to do something. Are you in college? Isn't college all about idealism?

—I'm a little depressed, I said.

—At least you know you are, she said. Lots of people are and don't know.

We were quiet again. I shivered.

—Is this one of those things where I need to call a suicide hotline? she said.

—No, I said.

—That's good. I used to be depressed, she said.

—Over what?

—The mechanism doesn't matter. The diagnosis does, she said.

—I'm sorry. That was rude of me to ask.

—When people have a bite that doesn't work it's called a malocclusion. Do you know what *occlusion* usually means?

—Yes.

—Define it.

—All right, I don't, I said.

—Isn't it funny how our egos are so precious that we can't even tell the truth to strangers? she said.

I broke the spell. She was going to impart some sort of grand lesson about malocclusion but I'd ruined it. It was late, she was tired, and she was talking to a liar.

—I'm going to let you go, she said. I'm sorry you're depressed. It gets better.

—Wait—

—I can't help you, dear, she said.

I couldn't picture her face on my own anymore. I'd recognize her if I saw a photo, but if I was drifting off to sleep I could only remember the details. The ugly Picasso tattoo. The little spot by her ankles that she'd always miss shaving. The bend in her right ring finger.

I found one of her old T-shirts pushed to the back of my closet. I picked it up and inhaled greedily but couldn't find her smell. She was gone.

I wrote it down, all of it, how she looked before: the black hair, the brown eyes, how she wore too many green shirts and not enough yellow, which was her color, how she was mean and spiteful and funny and tender. How she looked when I found her. I wrote it down and made it mine and then turned the page backward. It was a flipbook story. Over and over I brought her back and killed her, trying to find an answer in the syntax, trying to find a way to give her a better ending.

But not every memory could be transcribed. The sneaky ones were insidious, especially if I was unfocused or drowsy, and soon they were misshapen so that in one we were smoking on the patio in winter and in another we were standing in the stairwell in red initiation robes and in others I couldn't see her hands anymore, or her eyes, and in this one she was raking with me, the air suspended in orange, the geese lazy and roosting, and the trees floated overhead, trunkless, like clouds. We stuffed piles into bags like thieves in a heist, stealing our own landscape, and she stared at me in the strange orange of my memory, telling me to wave at the man in the window, a fully realized person, an unfinished ghost.

21

Margot at Coda

-MARGOT-

April 2008

Got antsy. Took some Molly but it was slow to roll in. Pissy in the meantime. Then D got called into work when Jade called out. Who the fuck is Jade. Told D to stop, admit she loves the attention there. Don't say it's for the money anymore. Called her a masochistic antifeminist. Told her not to go but she went all the same. Told her to go fuck off and she said right back at you. She couldn't slam the door; the others would know. But if she could, if she could've she would've.

D gone for the night, now, at a party as a literal slab, tits out and men and women eating off of her. Hot plate.

Packed the bubbler and felt, not less angry, but better. Not so furious, just pissed. Still antsy/zooming. Foot jiggling against other foot on the bed, watching it do its own thing, no brainwaves to help it go. In the mirror, across the room, reverse me peered. Small and bewitchy if I tilted the chin and widened the eyes. The bedroom has low light: pupils are huge and eyes are shining. Wished Kyra wasn't gone; had moved her out the month before when she'd gotten herself knocked up. Kyra would have been good for a night like this, would roll with me and then disappear with a guy and I could walk home blitzed enough to not be pissed at D. Ruby too lazy to go anywhere. Twyla too edgy, staring at corners earlier in the day, told her to cut back on the coke, but she lied and said she hadn't done any.

Called J.R. instead. An easy pickup. Met him down at Coda, in the black light basement, the bass so loud it sucks the air out of the room, no cover charge for me, fifteen dollars for him. Satisfying. Shot of coffee-flavored rum sinking in the root of my tongue. From then on, swallow first, taste later.

J.R.: Handsome, only sort of white. Makes me nostalgic for places I've never been. Tahiti. Senegal. Has slim ankles and skinny, weirdly long feet, as if everything's been stretched at the joint.

Then it hits, and I am reacquainted with the pulsating thunk of the bass that somehow manages to make me feel more important than I am, I love to put my hand on my collarbone and feel the vibrato, I am just a conductor for sound, I love the way the DJ leans into his board. Skirt on my legs feels like tiny hands petting my thighs. All of us on the dance floor are wearing Glow Sticks with connectors that transform into neon pink halos over our skulls, the air is warm and sticky with the breath of my people, some of the halos cracked and exploded in our fingers, wiped on shirts, all of us neon-gorgeous. J.R. is more beautiful than ever now, his teeth are brilliant under the black light, his mouth funnels into my ear and he offers to take me to the balcony so we can see this mass of humanity from above and I don't want to go, I don't want to leave my brethren but I also can't wait to see the other corners of this world awash with so much light. Edge of distress: to know that it is physically impossible for me to be every place at once: every bathroom stall; every street called Martin Luther King Boulevard; every gyno, palm reader, financial planner; every segment of space, though parts of me are knit through there, the gorgeous unravel of thread.

Above, looking down: the DJ demands that we throw our hands up in the air and so we do and I wave alone from the balcony, and they aren't looking at me but I know they're waving at me, for me, too. J.R. says, What did you take, and I say Molly and he says all right. He owl-eyes me. Who is your mother? I ask. He doesn't understand. She's Filipina, he says, but he doesn't get it, I want to know her, cosmically. I tell him she must be so proud. He is amazing, little Filipino boy, now a professor at a big university in America. I can't believe I'm with a foreigner, and he says, but I'm not foreign, I'm a citizen, a real citizen. It's important for me to merge with him here, I know, and we are all citizens, which I say. And he calls me ignorant, and I agree. We're all ignorant! Then he is gone but he is always with me and I am always with him, with all of us.

In the bathroom, peeing is a relief unlike anything I've ever known and it lasts forever, and the seat is cool on the backs of my legs, my face feels perfect in my palms, elbows on knees, all of my skeleton is relaxed on the toilet and God did I say peeing is a relief unlike anything I've ever known and it lasts forever? I meet a beautiful girl by the sinks. She has a piercing floating above her lip and her eyeliner is so exact and perfect and I ask her to do mine and she does, her hands on my face like my mom's, so warm, so gentle. My reflection in the tampon dispenser is full Cleopatra eye of Horus face of knowledge and I don't know how I pulled it off but I did and I know it and so does God. Beautiful Girl says Are you rolling Hun and I say yes and she says Are you thirsty Hun and I say no and she says Take this and gives me a tablet from her bag and I am amazed by her bag, Mary Poppins with eyeliner and medicine and I tell her that and she laughs and tells me to swallow water from the tap. Phrases in church that never made sense now have new meaning, and all are in the bathroom: The ceiling is our firmament of heaven. My face is light from light. Beautiful Poppins Girl is inestimable love.

Then my legs are moving like I'm crushing grapes on the dance floor. How many hours have I been there I want to ask but there is no time for question marks. Guy on the floor comes up behind me and grinds so I turn around, cannot be angry, he feels right, I am a fishing rod, unspooling, lure sunk, he is caught, it isn't his fault.

There is always a thing you want that will ruin you. But is *ruin* so bad, because Mrs. Latham said in eleventh grade A.P. Latin it just means to fall and people jump from planes all of the time, they have to jump, to reconnect with their land, to see it for what it is.

There is always a thing you want that will ruin you, I say to the guy on the floor and he says What and I repeat it: there is always a thing you want that will ruin you. Okay, he says, and there is no need to say more.

He brings me drinks that I don't count because counting feels obscene and man-made and it eats at the majesty of his human goodness.

I wake up in a cab in the center of town, guy is next to me, hand on my leg, feels fantastic but it is enough, I have to go, I say, and he says Where, and driver says C'mon already, and the window is down, outside it is gorgeous, cooing cold night, I open the door and reconnect with my earth, not far from the house now.

Pressing hands into the back of my eyes is in itself a tremendous experience, tiny fireworks made for me by my own brain, the geometry of them reminds me of the real thing, real fireworks. Bona fide. Fourth of July with my parents, grass ticking through the sheet one blade at a time, toenails speckled with old polish, Mom and Dad illuminated by the explosions, so loud the pows roll to the back of my skull and out again through my eyes. Other kids cry at the noise but I lean into it and Dad calls me the pyro princess, tells Mom to keep me away from the matches.

Thought of all the times long ago when I had been aimless and had nowhere to walk, where I had turned on the TV to drown out my own thoughts, where I had been afraid if a car radio did not work because I would have to think by myself if there had not been some sort of entertainment and distraction and that is a human thing, isn't it, a real thing, it is not original to feel that way and that is a relief. My heart is fast, then slow, then fast, working for me, a good heart. Good heart. Palm on chest. At the house, all quiet, my sisters—my sisters!—either out or sleeping. My room, astounding space, where love is made. Not ready to sleep yet. Take another Molly to stay awake. D still out. Will wait for her to come home. So much to share with her, so much to tell. Take Xanax to slow the good heart. Perfect alchemy, a balance to keep me awake and calm and wise like a priestess, and I will hold her cat-shaped face in mine, lie beside her tall, long body, touch her pale hair and tell her she is part of me, I am part of her, jealousy is a construct and none of this is real. Lie on the floor

Will wait for

Ruin, to fall

Dawn will come, flare of orange on the line, stars blotted out by the rising sun but they are still there, they are mine and ours,

Can see the stars through the ceiling,

vault, fingertip touching God,

neon halos

D will come

tiny choke, tugging for breath

forgetting the breath

grass ticking through one blade at a—

pulling for air now, none found

inestimable love

struggle and can't, struggle and can't. a portion of me knows what is happening, is frantic, one hand grabbing at the carpet on the floor, if I could just clutch one thing I could stay—

light from light

other portion says, This Is So Fucking Stupid! starts to laugh without air

so stupid! on this floor! in this shirt?

there is always a thing you want that will ruin you

D will come

how absurd it is to

eat ashes

pay dues

kiss men

take oaths

starve

pluck

sweep

hide love under covers, what for?

firmament of heaven

grass tickling my feet,

not afraid to—

grab at the closest neon halo

before it cracks and leaves a stain

22

Group

-EVA, BROWNIE-

July 2012

Ricki called me out of Room One and told me someone was there in the lobby for me, and I went hot, convinced that I was getting served with papers over the car I'd hit last week and driven away from. Maybe there'd been a camera in the lot, I don't know. And instead there was Brownie. Down the hall, I knew, the exam I'd left was turning into a euth. I could feel it through the building, heard the wife's voice when Dr. Blasser went to get the Telazol and Euthasol from the safe in the back.

Three years later and I couldn't remember Brownie's real name, hadn't followed any of my pledges online, hadn't gone to their graduations, and still here she was, Brownie, who somehow had known I was working at the vet in Hadley, who wasn't calling me Pledge Mistress anymore, but called me by my name, without asking my permission.

We talked. She still had the stammer. I don't know if it was always there or if I was the one who nicked her speech. It was possible I still had that impact on her. Even in scrubs, even out of the house.

When did I get off, Brownie wanted to know, and I told her late, so she insisted on taking me to lunch. I made her wait. The couple, crying, left exam Room One and were shepherded through the lobby by Dr. Blasser. Their cocker spaniel lay on a stained towel on the table. I got the blue bag and cut the vet wrap off its leg, pulled the cath, slid it into the bag, knotted it, and attached the red tag, big letters, GROUP. I took my time carrying it to the freezer out back. I took my time washing my hands. Back in the lobby, I found Brownie and Ricki, chatting about the Kardashians, no stammer.

—You ready? I said, and Brownie followed behind. I didn't hold the door.

—Thank you for this, she said in the parking lot.

—For what?

—For meeting with me.

—I want a burger, I said, and she followed me in her ugly little Mazda to a restaurant with french fries sole-crushed into the linoleum under the tables and sun that cut her hard in the eyes through the storefront. She had to know that seeking me out was wrong, but if I went any longer without being classy I'd come off mannish, and who knew who she would report this to. So I asked her how the girls were doing.

—Charlotte's getting a degree in social work in Texas, she said around a chocolate shake, and Missie's engaged to Mike.

—Who?

—Charlotte. Missie.

I pictured her pledge class, all too pale and almost fat, each one of them, and no blondes, not one, though one of them had a boyfriend that sold so he was good for parties.

—What were their pledge names?

Her face crumpled. It was dissatisfying to hurt her when I hadn't even been trying.

—You really don't remember them?

—I'm teasing, I said.

I think we'd called Charlotte Pancake because of her flat face. Missie could have been Twinkle or Chubba, if I was picturing them right. Pancake had been the best at her tasks. No hesitation when we'd put her in the trunk of Twy's car and driven her with a blindfold. No pause during the puzzle test. Could drink better than the other girls, never cried. Didn't talk back. Hardly talked at all. Margot was dead by then, but Ruby took her on as a second little to keep the line going. They were a good line, a no-bullshit line. I couldn't remember what line Brownie had been in.

—Did you graduate? I asked.

—Yes, Brownie said, and she unslouched herself out of the seat, pushing her chin up so the sun couldn't blind her anymore.

—Cum laude. I did okay.

—You did okay, I agreed. You were a solid sister.

She didn't smile.

—What makes for a good sister, to you? she asked.

Over at the registers, two girls in yellow uniforms were talking shit about their boss, I could tell by their peaky little faces and chips of words like *asshole* and *sycophant* or *psycho*, I couldn't tell for sure. Brownie repeated herself.

—How do you define a good sister?

—Is this for an article or something?

—For me, Brownie said.

—A good sister is decent and honor-bound, vibrant and composed, I began.

—I know the poem, she said. You taught me the poem. In your own words.

—I haven't got a fancy answer, I told her.

The girls at the register were dealing with a woman in a walker now, a woman who was squinting hard at the enormous menu hung above them, asking about the cost of extra fried pickles.

—You should know what a good sister is, I said. If I taught you right, you should know.

—If you taught me right, she repeated.

—Yes.

There were roadblocks, spring-loaded nets, pits covered with leaves all around me. I knew it.

—So the blow job game was supposed to make me more sisterly?

This was what she needed.

—It was a game, I said.

—A game.

—A bonding experience, yeah.

—A bonding experience.

—Don't repeat what I say. You're not a dipshit.

—Where'd you get the idea?

It wasn't that creative. She wanted me to be a mastermind, but the truth is I'd been smoking with Spide and Dubbs from Zeta Sigma and then we'd taken a bus to Northampton, and it was cold and most of the shops were for retired hens except for the sex shop, which had this awesome display of a Christmas tree made out of bras, all the cups stacking each other, and some pasties to make the ornaments. And inside we'd found a discount bin full of dildos, which was hilarious, all these stupid packages of dongs rubbing up against each other like lobsters in a tank, so I'd bought a pile and brought them back to the house for the pledges to practice on. It was Elina who brought the camera. And I didn't plan on having the brothers there, they just stuck around after dinner. The rules popped up as we went. If you gagged on your dildo you took a shot. If you used your hands weird then Spide or Dubbs would joke around and correct you. The more we drank the funnier it got, and eventually

Pancake got fed up when we told her she couldn't deep throat right so she yanked the dildo off its little suction cup on the table and flung it at the wall, where it cracked the glass of the composite from 1989.

And in that story was another story, I remembered, a story from Spide about their pledge class.

—You girls have it easy, he'd said. He was wedged deep into the couch, knees wide, a sea of suction-cup dildos on the table before him. He looked like he cut his own hair.

—Everyone says they get it worst, I said.

—I'd suck a fake dick instead of going through our rites again, he said.

—Fag, said Dubbs, bored.

—What are they?

Spide had a thin smile, a top lip more defined than most, cut sharp, lines already at the corners, a face I could have hated or kissed, depending on the lighting.

—A real brother wouldn't say his rites, he said.

Twinkle wiped saliva off her chin and yawned. Her dildo wasn't funny to her anymore, so she'd started flicking at the head, watching it sway back and forth.

—You, he told her, lips on. Go on now.

She made eye contact with him while she took the whole thing in her mouth.

—Atta girl, he said.

There was a suckling silence.

—Fine, he said. I can show you what we do.

—Why don't you just tell me? I said, but he was already standing, taking off his sweater, his shirt, turning around. On his back, a spatter of dime-size scars.

None of the girls were sucking anymore.

—The problem with burns, he said, is that when you know they're coming you can't help flinching. And if you flinch you get an extra, each time, until you stop.

—But what's the point? asked Brownie.

—Shut up, Brownie. Maybe I had said it, maybe Spide did, or a pledge. I don't remember.

He was looking at her now, bare-chested. His stomach was soft, and his chest hair was sparse and straight.

—Duty comes with sacrifice, he said quietly.

It sounded noble and trite and fake even then, but some of the pledges looked impressed.

—Now, he said. Who's ready to practice on me?

—Fuck off, Spide, I said.

He was grinning. He made a slow show of unzipping his fly.

—I said fuck off.

—I'm trying, he said.

He was looking at Brownie again. She had virgin's eyes, wide and unblinking. Her arms were crossed and she sat back, far. She looked at him, at me, at him.

—He's just joking, I told the girls. It's just a game. You all can go.

—Thank you, Pledge Mistress, they said.

And they were gone. I saw Dubbs slouch out through the back patio. I did not look behind me to see if Spide followed him.

One time, at work, on the end of a long, floundering night, I'd pricked my ring finger on the Euthasol meant for the tabby in Room Two and my hand went numb. The fingers were still pink. I could move my wrist. And about four minutes after we'd dosed the tabby and Dr. Blasser had pronounced her dead, my hand resurrected itself, warm and tingling. It had been, to me, an event. And it reminded me of how few events I had in new adulthood, how, in college, everything had been important. So many days since I'd graduated, and now if someone had asked me what I'd done with my day, I wouldn't have a new answer. Often I'd be on the phone, and I'd have this feeling like I had news, but I never did. The mailman put the wrong bill in my box. My health insurance plan was changing. A cat had chewed off its own leg in a trap and we'd amputated the necrotic bone. That was what I had now. Cat legs and deductibles.

And now in the restaurant Brownie was crying, God, the ugliness of her crying.

—Get it together, I hissed. The girls at the register were staring.

—I thought you were so relevant! she wailed.

—Who says that? I said. I mean, really, who says that sort of thing out loud? Christ, Brownie.

I'd never noticed before, but her neck, her neck was horrifically long. Wide eyes, large teeth. Three years later, and my duty had returned. I wanted to leave her and couldn't. Her humiliation was my job.

—I'll go if you don't pull yourself together, I said.

She wiped her nose with a rough paper napkin.

—The problem is, I can't tell if you're dense or evil, she said.

—Does it help if I can't either? I said, smiling.

But she wouldn't let go.

—I don't know if you let him on purpose or not, she said.

—Who are we talking about?

—Spide, she said.

—What about Spide? I said.

And now we sat in a dare, because we both knew. We both knew that after the game, after I'd shooed the girls, after I'd gone to my room, I'd gone back to get my cigarettes from the den.

He had his hands around the back of Brownie's neck, fingers laced, and he was pulling her into him. His face, that top lip snatched between his own teeth, eyes half-open even when I opened the door. He saw me and didn't care.

—Brownie, I said, and when she stopped bobbing and turned I could see snot, tears, saliva, her entire countenance in an ooze.

—Brownie, I said again.

Spide was flagging and aggravated.

—Get out, he said.

That lip. That lip.

—I didn't authorize this, I said. My voice was higher than I wanted.

Brownie was weeping now, full sobs that stuttered her whole body. She pulled her knees into her chest. Lawsuits, I thought. Fucking litigation and suspensions and depositions. Jesus Christ, Brownie.

—Come on now, Spide coaxed her. Come back, we're almost done, you're doing good.

—She's not into it.

—She's still here, isn't she?

We both stared at her. She was pitiful.

—Goddamn it, Spide said. God fucking damnit. I knew you bitches were pussies.

—Get out, I said.

He was still half-flaccid. Incredible. I couldn't stop staring.

—I'm not done here, he said. And he reached to the floor and grabbed Brownie by the ponytail, pulling her up.

—Are you a quitter? he asked.

I couldn't look at her face anymore.

—I said, are you a quitter?

She didn't answer.

—The brothers won't like this, he said.

At the time my reasons felt valid. Zeta Sigma was the brotherhood we'd always wanted to match with. Spide smoked me up when I needed him. But mostly it was damage control, my job was damage control. It was stupid and dramatic and pointless, but it was my pointless code, my code, and no one could take it from me.

—Go, Brownie, I said, and I knelt.

It was fast and easy. Toward the end, he grabbed my head and pushed so I didn't have a choice but to swallow. But maybe that was for the best, because I didn't want to wash my face or get caught in the hall with a stain.

We didn't talk when he was done. Instead, I took my cigarettes and stepped onto the patio. He followed.

—What's the deal with her? he asked.

—With Brownie?

—Yeah.

—I don't know, I said. She's a pussy, I guess.

Spide pulled a jay out of his pack of cigarettes and lit it. He passed it to me. I pulled.

I could still taste him. I ran my tongue over my teeth and gums, trying to swallow him away.

—Your pledges need work, he said.

I knew before I even lit my next cigarette what I would do.

—Come here, I whispered, rolling my eyes up, my lips parted, the fuck-me face, I knew. Let's go again.

And when he leaned in to kiss me I pressed the butt of the cigarette, hard, deep, in between his eyebrows. He didn't see it coming. No flinch.

I don't even remember how the punch felt, just that he landed it square, and I ran into the house laughing.

Spide's blister would heal and look like the scar left by a bad zit. Later that year, I'd get hammered and screw him twice. The last time, I waited for him to come and then I bit his shoulder until he bled. But that night I was done with him.

I found Brownie in her room. She had showered. I brought her lousy bourbon.

—Drink, it'll warm you up, I told her.

—What do we do? she asked.

—Drink, I said.

She obeyed. Three swallows.

—Who do we call?

—Who do we call? I said. You shitting me?

—I mean, the police, or the dean?

—There's no one to call, I said.

—But I was—

—You were what? I asked.

—I was—

—You can't even say it, I said. You can't even say it because honestly, can you tell me it was a crime? You put your lips where you didn't want. Is that a crime?

—But he—

—I don't give a shit what he did, I said. He's a dumbass. You're not a dumbass. You picked that situation. I told you all to leave. What did you want from him, a rose? Stop crying.

She obeyed, again. She was good. Not as good as Pancake, but she was good.

Her feet were white. I went to her dresser and dug out some socks.

—Put these on.

—What did he do to you? she asked.

—He didn't do anything to me.

She was so pathetic I could have vomited. I hated this job, this stupid mothering job. I was never going to have children. Gobs of sympathy that I couldn't fake. And snot. And rehashing. All of it a colossal waste.

—You get to pick how you want to see this, I said.

She didn't look at me, her head bent over her feet, rolling the socks on one at a time.

—This can be one stupid shitty night, or it can be a pussy crime, I said. Your pick. If you think you're totally blameless, if you're some sort of Snow White character, if you think you didn't want this, then go ahead and call the cops. See what happens.

—Has this happened to a sister before? she asked.

—You mean, has a sister called the cops?

She nodded.

—Brownie, if they called the cops they're not our sisters anymore.

And now in this shitty fast-food place, on a lunch break from the dead, I was talking to the same bleary face.

—I should have filed a report, she said.

—Forget that. His word against yours. A mess.

—Not against him, against you, she said.

—To who? Nationals? The Panhellenic Council?

—You were my leader, she said. It was your duty to guide me. To keep me safe.

—Can I make a suggestion, Brownie? Don't make yourself a victim just because you're bored.

She opened her mouth.

—Don't, I said. Don't carry on like you've got some great psychic angst that you lug around at all hours. Your trauma is just something you use to fill your time. And you have a lot of time, don't you? You're in some wasteland of a job and you need something to tell the guy you met on Tinder on your fourth date and you pick the horror of sorority life. But that house gave us purpose. And when you're alone on a Friday night, crying about something that happened for five minutes three years ago, I want you to remember that. I want you to find something else to do with your useless hours, instead of scheming to harass your pledge mistress on her lunch break.

She was stunned. The bitches at the register were staring. This was a great opportunity. She could lash back at me now, she could call me a hypocrite and a cunt and a wild failure. If she'd done that then I could have had a new best friend, a nihilistic pal. But only stories work that way.

On the drive back to work I called Lisa, no answer, and didn't leave a voice mail. I wanted her to verify that none of these younger bitches mattered, none of it mattered. I'd done my job. I'd herded them into initiation, listened to their forgettable complaints, made them stronger, taught them respect. Of course they'd resent me. No one gives the drill sergeant credit.

At reception, a customer asked the date and I couldn't remember.

And Ricki asked, for the third time that day, who was my favorite Kardashian?

23

Say Yes

-RUBY-

June 2014

The dress was satin, knee length, with the color listed as "biscotti." Lisa sent me a link to pretend to get my approval before she told me I had to buy it. Subject line: *Say Yes?*

I replied,

ur the only person id wear this shit for.

Yayyyyy, she replied, sans exclamation points.

I checked the sizing. (It went up to twenty-two.)

That Saturday we met in her hometown at a dress shop with posters all over the walls of brides walking through meadows. Many of them smiled down at their feet, like there was a secret hiding for them in the grass. One lone black bride was pictured in the corner, petting a horse while her black husband smiled down at her from his saddle.

Lisa's little sister Anna sat on a pleather sofa and mashed at colorful little circles on her phone screen.

—Hey, Anna, I said. The little cretin wiped her nose with the back of her hand and went back to tapping.

—Anna, say hi to Ruby, Lisa demanded.

Anna let her hair fall over her face. She bent her knees and scooted her butt to the end of the couch. The salesgirls, all wearing pencil skirts and blazers, looked pointedly at her sneakers on the pleather but didn't say anything.

—Wanna see my dress? Lisa asked.

—You already bought it?

—Last week, she said. I couldn't wait. Don't be mad.

—I'm not mad, I said.

I wondered who came with her to pick it out but didn't ask, afraid that she'd say she brought Eva and her mom. If they had been with her then there was no way it could have been a spur-of-the-moment thing. It would have been a purposeful exclusion.

—What's your size? the salesgirl asked me.

—Eighteen, I said.

I checked her face. (I was always on the lookout for shame.) But she was good. She came back with my dress and didn't say a word.

When you get to be my size, they start pinning pants differently on hangers. They tuck some of the fabric in so it won't look as wide as it really is from the side profile in a store. They hide my bra sizes, too, usually at the back of the rack or, in fancy stores, in drawers underneath the displays. This dress was no different. They had folded the sides of it inward, like an accordion, and I thought of how nice it would be if I could do that to myself, if I could fold sections of my skin as needed and then fully expand when it was safe.

Lisa rustled in the dressing room beside me. A team of saleswomen stood outside the door, listening for rips.

—My feet are a disaster, Lisa said over the partition.

She was right. Years of dancing had warped them.

—You'll wear nice heels, I said. None of that rhinestone strappy sandal stuff.

—I'll have to, she said. If I don't people will scream.

—The bunion bride, I said.

—Fuck you, she said, and then came out of the dressing room and drummed her fingernails on my door until I opened up, half-zipped.

She looked like the posters, smiling at her feet and all. She'd chosen a sleek satin thing that pulled in tight around her body and then shot out at the thighs in an explosion of tulle.

—You look great! I said, which sounded inauthentic but I meant it, she really did.

—They're calling it a mermaid cut, she said. It might look idiotic in thirty years. My daughter will look at our photos and ask me what the hell I was thinking.

—Good thing you're not wearing it in thirty years, then.

—You're supposed to cry, she said, and I could tell that she was teasing, but she probably wished I didn't sound so serene, as if I were supporting her choice for dinner rather than her wedding gown.

—Zip me? I said.

The zipper didn't close. The salesgirl brought a twenty and a twenty-two, and when I zipped into the twenty-two I found myself feeling relieved and disgusted at the same time.

—It works.

—It looks good, she said.

—I plan on losing more before the wedding.

—You don't have to do that, she said. Then she added, Do you want to order a smaller size?

—No. If I lose the weight I'm sure I can get it altered.

—Say *when* you lose weight. Not *if.*

—*When* I lose weight, I agreed.

We went to the mirror at the center of the store like they do on TV and the salesgirls fanned around us. Lisa stood on a little platform while I stood behind her. It felt like one of our old sorority ceremonies. The salesgirls probably did this fifty times a day. I wondered if they had scripts. They said all the right things. Angelic, and stunning, and lucky husband, and princess.

Anna, disinterested, mashed at the buttons on her phone until Lisa forced her into the fitting room and she came out with her hands over her chest.

—Everyone will see my boobs, Anna said.

—I gotta tell you, kid, you don't have any yet, Lisa said. Anna slammed the door to her dressing room hard enough that she knocked a screw loose out of the top hinge.

My sorority sisters never treated me differently because of my size, and they never spoke to me about it directly. My pledge name had been Baby Ruth, but they'd said it with affection. They made me eat clay off of a tennis court during hazing, but contextually it was funny. I could have said no if I'd really wanted to. And sure, they may have hidden me in the Chapter Room during recruitment presumably so I could track Potential New Member reports, but that was because I was good at organization, and who wanted to be talking to a bunch of dumbass potential new members on the first floor anyway? And when we took pictures, they would shift me to the back, but I was tall and that made sense and honestly I liked being in the back row, protected by a squad of lean bodies in front of me, bodies that I could be like if I chose to, bodies that could even be similar to myself one day (if the doctor ever found the thyroid problem I suspected or if they invented a good pill or I had a procedure). From Bid Day to graduation, my sisters had accepted me for who I was, within reason. No one said a word about my weight, except for Lisa, who didn't see the point in ignoring its reality.

—Why are you sort of fat? she asked me when we were still pledging.

We were crashing in the study after our first mixer. My mouth was dry but I wasn't as plowed as she was. I never was as plowed as the rest of them. It was my superpower. She was on the floor, shoving marshmallows into her mouth and chugging water.

—Why are you skinny? I asked.

—It's not the same thing.

—I dunno how to answer your question, I said.

—Was it trauma or something? Are your parents fat? What'd you eat?

—They're not fat, I said. And it's not like one meal made me fat. It's habits, I guess.

—Does it bother you? she asked.

—Sometimes, I said.

(All of the time.)

—Why don't you do something about it?

—Genius, I said. You're a fucking mastermind. Why hadn't I thought of that before?

—What have you tried?

—Everything, I said. Intermittent fasting, points systems, the diets where they mail you your food, that diet where you don't eat flour, those pills that make you shit out grease, and cleanses. All of it. Multiple times.

—I guess you didn't try it long enough, she said. Have you tried the grapefruit diet?

—If you ever suggest another diet I'll sit on you, I said.

She laughed and then started gagging when she swallowed a marshmallow wrong. She rolled onto her hands and knees and I smacked her knobby little back until she hacked a white blob onto the carpet.

• • •

The bridal shower was held at a golf club near Josh's family's house. A pair of lesbians had thrown a brunch on the patio just hours before and when we arrived they were taking down a banner that read TWO CHICKS GETTING HITCHED!

—That reminds me, I said, did Deirdre ever RSVP?

—No, Lisa said. I didn't expect her to, anyway.

Eva was clopping beside us in a noisy pair of sandals. Her pinched little face was completely twisted against the sun.

—You think Deirdre will stay queer? she asked Lisa.

—I think so, Lisa said. But I don't think she'll ever stop looking for Margot.

That was the closest we came after graduation to mentioning what happened. And really, what more was there to say about it? They hadn't dealt with the body like I had. They knew I'd done CPR. They knew I'd gone to a counselor for a while. Before Margot I'd wanted to be a nurse. Now I worked as a sales rep, distributing sample packs of allergy medication at doctors' offices. The medical assistants would stop me in the waiting room, take the samples, and usher me away before I could meet the doctors.

During the shower Eva sat beside Lisa and carefully recorded every goddamn present that was opened. Lisa's mom sat on her right side. Anna sat Indian style on the floor and didn't even open her eyes when her mom chucked balled-up wrapping paper at her head to get her attention. I didn't want to intrude so I sat slightly out of the circle and wove the ribbons into a crown.

Lisa had an aunt with a rosy face with full cheeks that made her look like an old-timey barmaid. She saw me sitting outside of the circle and waddled in my direction. No, I thought. Please don't. But it was too late; she recognized me as one of her tribe. She noisily dragged a chair through the group and settled beside me, breathing heavily.

—It's too hot for girls like us, she said.

—I don't think so, I said.

She wiped at her chest with a napkin. Her hair was plastered to the sides of her face. She was like a caricature of a fat person. I threaded ribbons together and pretended that it was the most engrossing thing I'd ever been asked to do. Lisa unwrapped a box of wineglasses and Eva nodded like it was a very significant gift and began jotting the information down.

—How many wineglasses was that? Eva asked.

Lisa's aunt opened her purse, pulled out a Baggie of grapes, and began peeling the skin off with her teeth before popping them into her mouth.

Someone tried to toss a ribbon on my lap but it slipped onto the floor and I had to do an awkward reach to snag it. The aunt happily snatched it up and handed it to me.

—Thank you, I said.

I did not turn to her or make eye contact.

—Girls like us gotta stick together, she said.

—I don't know what you mean.

—Yes you do, honey, she said.

She offered me a grape. I declined.

I ate nothing at the bridal shower but when I got home I locked the door to the apartment and grazed directly out of the fridge. I stared at the cold leftover burrito in my hands and watched it disappear, one bite at a time. A part of me was yelling that I needed to cut this shit out. I could be Audrey Hepburn. I could have cat eyes and arms so small that they could barely hold up dinner gloves. But before I finished the burrito I was planning my next entrée, trying to remember exactly which boxes of cereal were open in the pantry.

During college I'd go to support Lisa in her recitals. The dancers before and after her would do some stomping and then pitch themselves up and down stage until their time ended and they collapsed onto the floor as if someone had punched the energy out of them. Lisa was different. Her movements were smoother than the other dancers but they also weren't as risky. She would wear pastels and dance to pop songs about heartbreak and she'd usually end in a position with her hands over her heart, looking mawkish and begging.

After her recitals, Lisa would smoke me and Eva up in her car. She got high, she said, so she could feel more connected to her body, just like she felt when she was dancing.

—What does that mean? I asked her once. Are you usually disconnected if you're not dancing?

—No, but now I'm more connected, she said.

She grabbed at her own elbows to emphasize her point.

—You sound insane, Eva said.

—Nah, she said. Imagine how you feel when you suck some idiot's dick and that's how I feel when I dance or when I'm high.

Eva grinned at her and pulled the recline lever on her seat, hitting me in the knees. Even though the three of us would smoke together Eva never really addressed me directly. I was invisible to her, but I didn't want to be seen by her anyway.

—So you're saying you feel peaceful in your body, I said.

—Yeah, she said.

(And the truth is I didn't know what that could feel like.)

The only notable thing about Lisa's bachelorette party was how the bartender looked at us, Lisa wearing her white sash and stupid tiara, me wearing a T-shirt that read TEAM BRIDE. He had spiky hair like it was still 2005 and he kept sliding free drinks our way. He asked us how long we'd known each other.

—Seven years, Lisa said. This girl is my best friend.

She wrapped an arm around me and held me tight. She smelled like pineapple juice. I clutched at her, my best friend.

—You're sort of an unexpected pair, he said.

He was looking at me.

—Fuck you, Lisa said, and we got our girls and hopped to another bar.

The next morning the group ate cold pizza out of the hotel fridge. Our room overlooked the parking lot, where the sun was ricocheting off the roofs of cars. We kept the curtains closed. The room was dark and stale and frigid.

—I feel like someone took out my brain and replaced it with flannel, Lisa said.

I sat on her bed and bounced slightly.

—Asshole, she said.

—Bitch, I said.

She rolled over and rested a hand on her belly.

—I can literally hear my stomach slosh when I move, she said.

—You keep talking like I'm going to feel sorry for you, I said.

I pulled marshmallows out of my bag and handed them to her.

—This is why we're best friends, she told me.

Eva was lying on the floor with her hands flung over her face. In the adjoining room, Elina and two of Lisa's coworkers were yelling something about the water pressure in the shower.

—I think I ate six thousand calories last night, she said. She paused. How's your diet going?

—Subtle, I said.

—I'm just asking.

—I don't know why you ask me about my diet but you didn't go whining to any of our sisters when they'd purge in the laundry room bathroom.

Lisa put a pillow over her eyes.

—I probably should have said something, she said. I guess the problem with fat is that you wear your vulnerability on the outside. Nobody cared if Shannon's throat was eroded as long as she didn't open her mouth and say Ah.

—It's some shallow bullshit, I said.

—It is, she agreed. But if you want to be fat and adored you'll have to go to one of those African countries where they worship that shit.

—I hope you throw up this morning, I said. I hope you barf and it gets in your hair.

—Back at you, she said.

She crammed a marshmallow in her mouth. I was waiting for the year when her metabolism would slow down and we could be the same size. We would share clothes. She wouldn't ask cagey diet questions. (I was starting to suspect this wouldn't happen until Josh got her pregnant. But I was patient.)

One night in college, shortly after I'd taken Margot on as my little, I took her to a bar downtown. It was early, and there were no drunk freshmen yet, but she was already trashed. She kept trying to take a drink out of her straw and missing, so the thing poked her in the cheek. I took the straw out and bent it into a star.

—Let me ask you, she began. But she didn't finish. She was staring into the mirror behind the bar. She lost herself.

—Come back, I said.

—Let me ask you, she began again. Do you want a normal life? Like house, husband, kids and stuff.

—Yeah, I said.

—You do? You really do?

—I really do, I said.

—Why?

—Because I don't know if anyone will want me to build a normal life with them, I said.

—Oh, she said, and she put a hand on my knee like she'd just heard terrible news.

Margot in the bar mirror was small and mousy. We looked like we came from different species.

—You could have a normal life, she offered. There are plenty of guys out there who—

—Do you want a normal life? I asked.

—Oh God no, she said. But that's probably because I'm always assuming I'll be stuck with one.

(When I think of this moment I wonder if she could see what was coming. I wonder if she wanted it like this. And, if I think of her in the bar for too long, I'll start remembering what she looked like, how her ribs popped under my hands when I tried to help her the morning she was found. I have to leave it here.)

We spent the morning of the wedding getting our nails done at a salon downtown. Lisa picked out the color of the polish. Her sister Anna refused to have anyone touch her hands. She sat on top of them the whole time, perched in a chair by the door like a little gargoyle. At one point, Eva smiled at me and told me that I had pretty hands.

We all left the salon in disposable flip-flops and sang sad country songs on the drive over to the chapel. I felt like I had in my sisterhood, like I was a part of something, connected to a tribe, and, by extension, safer than I'd felt in a long time.

A hairstylist and makeup artist were waiting for us at the chapel. Our dresses were lined up next to one another on their hangers. There was a lot of sweet chatter about Josh, and his kindness, and how happy Lisa was going to be. There was a lot of talk about Lisa's prettiness, and whether or not the makeup artist should lighten up the eye shadow, and how each of us should have our hair curled.

We were running behind.

The first guests were arriving when we went for our dresses.

Our matching robes dropped to the floor.

I took my dress into the bathroom, not willing to be seen by the others. I wrangled legs and belly into my Spanx. I pulled the plastic sheath off of my dress. I peeled it apart and stepped in. I held my breath and tugged the zipper, at first gently, then harder. I stumbled into the suite. My tribe could fix this.

—It doesn't fit, I said.

—The zipper's probably stuck, Eva said. Hold your breath.

I sucked in all of the air I had and willed my lungs upward. I thought of feathers. I imagined little pockets of air separating my spine. But soon I ran out of air and had to exhale.

—Damn it, I almost had it, Eva said. Hold on.

I inhaled a second time and this time I thought of being connected to the body. I willed it to obey. I pictured each organ and imagined layers of fat folding themselves together, like pants on a hanger, compressed for appeal. Eva yanked and then unzipped the dress to the bottom.

—I'm going to do a fast pull, she said.

This time I leaned against the wall and pressed my palms against it, breath held, the tension so strong that I felt that if I squashed myself any farther I'd collapse into a diamond, and Eva yanked and the zipper sliced up my back and settled.

—Thank fucking God, Eva said, and I exhaled a sigh of relief that was so momentous that the force of it immediately ripped the zipper away from the seam. I felt my back pour out of the new gap, like water bursting through a broken dam.

—We can fix it, Lisa's mother said quickly. We can fix it. All we need are some safety pins and—

—A new dress, Eva said.

Lisa came out of the back room. She was in her slip, holding her gown in her arms like it was a fainting lady.

—Everything okay?

(I tried to say no, I really did.)

—Ruby's dress isn't cooperating, Lisa's mother said.

(This would have been the moment to extricate myself. But I was being selfish. I didn't want to go.) I pictured the dress crumpling into a giant hand, the middle finger extended at all of us.

We dug through the drawers and searched for safety pins. They began weaving them into my back. Someone looked for a scarf to drape me with. The chapel manager knocked at the door.

—Ten minutes, she said.

—I can't do this, Lisa said. I'm not ready! I can't do this.

—You're going to be fine, I said. Josh is the love of your life.

—It's not about Josh. It's you!

—Lisa, I begged.

The others were staring at me. I kept my back to them.

—Lisa. Get a grip. It's not that bad. I can wear a shawl or something.

—You had six months! she cried. You had six months to not treat yourself like human garbage and fit into one fucking outfit.

—Maybe the dress is the wrong size, Lisa's mother said.

—It's not, Eva said.

—I can fix it, I said desperately. I can wear something else. I have the outfit I wore to the rehearsal dinner—

The makeup artist rested a hand on my shoulder. I knew it was over.

—Everything will be easier to talk about after the ceremony, Lisa's mother said gently.

I didn't wait. I blundered into the parking lot. Guests were hurrying to the chapel now. I recognized Lisa's grandmother, and her fat aunt, and in the distance I saw Janelle and Corinne walking together in tiny little sundresses, envelopes and directions and clutch purses in hand.

Corinne began to wave at me and then dropped her arm. I ran to my car, my back exposed, sweating, and sat with my head on the steering wheel.

Anna had followed me. She slapped at the driver's-side window with a flat palm. I rolled it down.

—Can I come with you? she asked.

—No, I said. Fuck off.

—I hate them, too, she said.

—You don't, I said. And I don't either.

Anna waited for me to have an epiphany. She waited for me to unlock the car. Music was playing inside of the chapel.

—Go, I told her. You have to. And when you're an adult you can decide if you really want to hate them.

—I thought you'd get it, she said.

She walked back to the chapel.

During the ceremony, Josh did that sweet thing that men do when they're really moved where he stopped blinking in case a tear would slip out of his control. Lisa vowed that she would never make Josh put up Christmas lights by himself, and Josh vowed to move the clothes to the dryer instead of letting them get moldy in the wash. Josh's grandmother took a hanky out of her old-lady purse and dabbed at the crepey skin around her eyes. The groomsmen smiled warmly at the bridesmaids, admiring their tanned legs, their tiny little waists. Not a zipper, not a hair, not a button was out of place. When Josh and Lisa kissed, as if on cue, the sun burst out from behind a cloud and the chapel was illuminated in a gorgeous warm light.

At the reception, the sisters gathered together and lit some tapers and sang our sorority's marriage song to Lisa, a song that included the horrendously cheesy lyrics *even though you've gone and married / your sisters' love you'll always carry.* Later, the photos were posted on Facebook: Lisa, Eva, Corinne, and Janelle, a perfect quartet.

It was, Eva told me, the perfect wedding.

24

Ouija

-CHORUS-

They say when she died the glass in her class composite shattered.

They say when she died the flower arrangements on the dining room table burst apart, the petals popping off of their stems like corks out of bottles.

They say when she died the Chapter Room doors locked and didn't open until her body was taken from the house.

We put out a scrapbook of her. It was supposed to be comprised of pictures that represented her different attributes but none of them were appropriate for visitors to see. Here she was sticking her tongue out at the camera, here she was out of focus, here she was, beatific and twisted with half-closed eyelids, hovering over a series of fat white rails cut and ready on the Pledge Room table. Her composite photo was sufficient, but she looked, as Eva put it, like she was trying to remember her own name. So all the scrapbook held was her obituary, and some articles on her death, and one article about a donation her parents had made in her name to a rehab center in Boston. That accounted for six pages. The rest of the book was blank.

Ruby said she could hear Twang talking to herself in her room after she died. They shared a wall, and Ruby, who was fat and never had a reason to go out, sat at home and snooped and stewed.

—Talking how? we asked. About what?

—About her, she said. To her. She's talking to her like she's still alive in the room.

—She's probably on the phone, we said.

Ruby stared at each of us with withering skepticism.

—Who would she talk to on the phone? We're all *here.*

—What does she say to her? we asked.

—Most of it's just current events, she said. But sometimes Twang starts telling her to ignore the man.

—What man?

—That's the thing. There is no man.

—That's some spooky shit, we said, and Ruby melted into the couch and hugged a throw pillow to her chest, pleased that she had finally gotten a desired reaction out of her reporting.

They say, on the one-year anniversary of her death, that the heat shut off in the house and the sisters almost froze to death in their beds while they slept, unaware of hypothermia creeping through the sills.

They say, on the second anniversary, that a sister recognized one of her shoes, a size seven UGG boot with her initials on the sole. It was found standing upright near the end of the upstairs hallway, as if it had been on a journey for its mate. And Jennifer, who had never said a word about what happened, who hadn't even been that close with her, took the boot into her room and refused to let anyone else see it. We don't know what she did with it.

On the day that she was supposed to graduate, the sisters of her pledge class took their photos on the front lawn with white stoles denoting our house. Kyra stood off to the side with her baby sleeping in its stroller, its little head tilted to the side in an eerily sharp angle as it slept. Kyra didn't notice the baby's lolling head. Instead she directed Marcia and Janie and Shannon and Lucy and Deirdre and Alissa into place, but a gap kept forming between Lucy and Shannon, as if an invisible influence were forcing them apart. There was a lot of scrutiny over the photos later, looking for hints of orbs, or a face in a window, but nothing was found.

And then, one year later, they said that something was found in the photos, but by then the pictures had been lost, or deleted, or burned, depending on who was asked.

One night we yanked the mattresses off of our beds and threw a sleepover in the hallway, trading nips of rum until we all passed out and Pancake and Twinkle woke up at the devil's hour and said they saw her hovering over them.

—What did she look like? we asked.

—Pretty, Pancake said. She wore a white dress and had her hair up.

—It wasn't a dress. It was more like a toga, Twinkle said.

She looked happy, Pancake said. As happy as a ghost could be, anyway.

—She was sort of overdressed, really, Twinkle said. It was like a fancy toga. Lots of braided gold sashes.

—Why wouldn't a ghost wear loungewear? Pancake asked.

• • •

Finally, the last girls who would have known her graduated.

Her class composite went missing.

When our favorite shirts or dresses disappeared from the basement dryers we blamed her. She was cold, or she wanted to stay in style, or maybe she just wanted to punish a sister who spoke badly of her.

We lost the scrapbook. We blamed the new pledges, who probably threw it out when they were doing spring cleaning.

They said she had black hair.

They said she had red hair.

They said she was gay.

They said the statue of Hestia looked just like her, that it had transformed and adopted her face after she died.

One sister said she was drugged at a party, and a girl with a long black braid and full red lips grabbed her by the hand and took her out of some creepy guy's room before he came back from the bathroom. The girl led her outside and called her a cab, and when our sister got into the car the girl disappeared.

They said she was having an affair with a married professor, a guy in the anthro department, who looked a little bit like Indiana Jones but had soft, flabby man arms that hinted at middle age.

They said she killed herself.

They said it was just weed, or oxy, or she'd bought a little blow from a guy selling at Zeta Sigma, or she had a heart defect and had died stone sober.

• • •

They said she died with a dick in her mouth.

They said the professor killed her, in the dining room, with a candlestick, blunt force trauma to the back of her skull, after she begged him to leave his wife. Better than in the bathroom, by a lezzie sister who'd been stalking her, who burned out her eyes in a jealous rage with a curling iron. Or in the Chapter Room, by the ghosts of our founders, somewhat homely women in inexplicably dirty chemises, who wrapped their hands around her neck and squeezed. And someone said no, she died in Room Epsilon, or maybe it was Kappa.

They said that she was in the room during initiation. That, when all of the pledges were blindfolded and led down the hallway in their red robes, she was the cold hand leading them into the firelight. If an acolyte looked to her right during the ceremony, they'd glimpse the side profile of her pale face, luminous in the dark.

They said we could find her in the back stairwell if we went in there with the lights off and called her name, three times, sotto voce. Her body was half-human, half-snake, and if you were quiet after you called her name, you would hear her slithering over the stairs, seeking you out with her forked tongue.

Then they said we could find her in the back stairwell if we went there with the lights off and called her name, six times, sotto voce, and she would come out from the corner and claw at the caller's eyes with her long, moldy fingernails, her face once lovely, now putrid, trying to make the sister look just as mutilated as she did in her rot.

Fifteen years after her death a sister brought a Ouija board out of the pledge study closet and gathered a group of us together in the living room. We stacked the logs and lit the fire. Some of us, halfheartedly, rolled a finger in the ash bucket and slipped it in our mouths. We lit candles. Each of us touched a finger to the planchette.

—Are you here?

—*Y—E—S.*

The log popped and spit an ember onto the hearth.

—Who's moving it? we asked.

—I'm not! we insisted.

—Are you happy? we asked her.

—*N—O.*

We were more saddened than afraid.

Some of the fingers on the planchette were cold, some were hot and sweaty, some were delicate, some were forceful.

—How did you die? one girl asked.

—*G—O—O—G—L—E—I—T—B—I—T—C—H—E—S*, the board said.

One sister admitted that she was pushing the planchette and we banished her laughing into the shadows. But we didn't google, not then. We pulled closer to the fire.

—Are you happy? we asked.

—*D—D—D—D—D—D—D*, the board said, and someone knocked the boxed wine off of the table and we were done for the night.

In our respective bedrooms, the rooms of sisters we no longer knew, we typed her name into the search bar and read. We knew the girl, but not as well as the ghost. In each room, we reached the same conclusion: we would not share her earthly story. We would not say her name. We would not alter, perverse or protective, the legend that she had become. She belonged to us now, our dear sister, and we were the keepers of her story.

25

The Chapter Room

-CHORUS-

May 2009

In 1864, founders Virginia Wheeler, Lucinda May, and Joanna Howard . . .

The room was candlelit and overheated.

bonded together to form a private society of womanly compassion and support . . .

Necklace clasps dug into the backs of necks, legs were crossed at ankles, toes crammed into pumps.

These women, in their youthful wisdom . . .

The girls sat in order of seniority. In the front row, Elina sucked a peppermint down into a wafer, then crunched it on *wisdom.*

Sought love and support in a time of hatred . . .

Janelle stared at Stella's side profile and wished she'd suffer a brain aneurism. Nothing deadly, just something that would leave one side of her face all droopy.

While their homeland was torn apart by war . . .

Upstairs, Deirdre imagined, Margot's ghost drifted aimlessly down the hall. Ghost Margot was wearing her favorite black clubbing dress with her hair pinned sweetly at the nape. Ghost Margot was not covered in piss or vomit. Ghost Margot had flawless skin and immaculately drawn eyeliner, the battle regalia of the dead. Ghost Margot still knew how to have a good laugh, though, and likely was the reason why Amanda inexplicably had a panty liner stuck to the back of her cardigan.

These remarkable young women built a sacred sisterhood upon the bedrock of peace.

The newest sisters sat in the back, still in awe of the pomp of candles and chanting in unison. Bedrock of peace. That's nice, thought Twinkle. She pictured a mermaid napping on a boulder in the Bahamas. What was the word for a mermaid from the Bahamas? Bahamian? Bahaman? Bahamener? Bahamamaid?

As president, it was Corinne's job to intone the final line:

Let there never be strife among us, she said.

From this day until our last, they replied, bored.

Candles were blown out. Fluorescents flipped on. Out of the cover of candlelight, the older girls straightened in their chairs and recrossed their ankles.

It was happening now, Deirdre knew. Upstairs, Margot's ghost drifted from Room Alpha, to Beta, to Gamma.

—Madame Secretary, please review the minutes from last week, Corinne said.

Minutes were accounted for. Old business was reviewed. New business was offered to the table. It was time.

—I have new business, Deirdre said.

Corinne, who had clearly been expecting a seamless, business-free meeting that ended promptly at nine fifteen so she could review tapes of her most recent failure in the Miss Northeast pageant before bed, paused before responding. Ignoring would be impossible. If only she hadn't sounded so assertive!

—Yes, sister?

Twyla, who had been half-asleep throughout the meeting, now sat upright in her chair, stricken. Something was wrong. Something was wrong upstairs.

—I move that we initiate Margot Glenn into her rightful place within the Omega Chapter this evening.

—Deirdre, Corinne said, I told you before—

—I know she's not eligible. I know. But she deserves it all the same.

—Madame Secretary, please read the Omega Chapter Enrollment portion of the guide to our sisterhood, Corinne said.

THE OMEGA CHAPTER

A sister, after a lifetime of honorable repute and service to her house, is to be enrolled into the Omega Chapter upon her departure from this earth. A sister may be active or alumna upon the time of her transition. A sister's enrollment into the Omega Chapter must be performed by her home house at a time deemed appropriate by the executive board. Noninitiates and disaffiliated sisters are (regretfully) not eligible for the passage into the Omega Chapter.

—Read the last line again, Corinne said.

Tracy complied.

All were silent.

—Margot was an active sister, Deirdre said.

—She was, Corinne agreed. And she was a damn good sister. For God's sake, Tracy, stop taking notes on this. Go off book.

Tracy, who had been frantically recording the minutes of the exchange, closed her notebook and gaped. Hands around the room began to rise, but Corinne ignored them. If one spoke, they all would want to talk and then this would spiral into another night on the repercussions of Margot's fuckup.

—None of us will ever forget Margot. Her loss was a devastation to our house. I'll always remember her sweet smile, her kind words in the hall—(Deirdre remembered, acutely, the time Margot had gotten high with Corinne and proclaimed to her face that she was more boring than a cooked ham). Yet, and I hate the crassness of this statement, if she had survived her suicide—

—Overdose, Deirdre said.

—If she had survived her overdose, then she would have suffered consequences at the hands of the executive board for engaging in drug use as an active sister in the sanctity of our home.

—Bullshit! shouted Eva. Corinne, you were high as shit on the back patio like five hours ago and now you're talking about drug use like it doesn't happen. Such bullshit!

—You're right, Corinne said. I was high, Twyla was high, and Ruby was high. But the difference here is that none of us almost cost the chapter. None of us made a reason for an army of cops and reporters and those finicky bitches from Nationals to show up. We didn't risk the value of the house over a stupid—

—Oh, I'm sorry your sister's death was an inconvenience to you, Deirdre said. I'm so sorry that you had to fill out some paperwork and fake cry at her memorial service, you fucking—

—Shut up, Elina said.

The room fell completely silent.

Footsteps plodded upstairs.

—It's him, Twyla whispered, and the whole room turned to stare at her, this strange sister, covered to the wrist in a gray cardigan.

—Are you all right? Amanda asked. She touched Twyla's shoulder, but the girl didn't move.

—My father's here, Twyla whispered.

Corinne had hit her threshold. —That's great. I'm sure he's a swell guy. Now, if you could all kindly pull your shit together so we can get to—

And then the unearthly keen of the fire alarm sounded and the entire Chapter Room was doused in the rusty water of the sprinklers overhead.

Candles extinguished, girls shrieked, Tracy threw herself over the meeting notes as if they were a newborn, and in the commotion of flood and fury, no one noticed that Twyla stayed in her chair, chattering, staring at a spot in the corner of the room. And no one saw Deirdre in the back stairwell, bent double, laughing. And no one saw Eva step outside and take a drag, no one saw Tracy frantically shielding her fake eyelashes from the downpour, no one saw Lucy and Shannon shove past each other, hard, and no one saw the newly initiated pledges ever, so in that regard, at least, things went on as normal, even in the exodus to the dry first floor. It was the last time no one was seen.

Upstairs, the girls found a manifesto taped to each bedroom door. It read:

> *A sleeting night in the heart of February, two weeks before the fall pledge class is initiated, and our housemother, Nicole, is burning white sage in her apartment. We can smell it on the first floor. Ice pings against windows . . .*

But this is not a ghost story.

Acknowledgments

I am forever grateful to my agent, Robert Guinsler, who left me a voice mail that changed my life. I owe many thanks to kindred spirit and editor Alison Callahan, and her ever-patient assistant, Brita Lundberg, along with a team of heroes at Scout Press, especially: Jennifer Bergstrom, Jennifer Long, Jennifer Robinson, Meagan Harris, Wendy Sheanin, Abby Zidle, Diana Velasquez, Lisa Litwack, Jaime Putorti, Monica Oluwek, Caroline Pallotta, Alicia Brancato, and Chelsea Cohen.

I'd like to thank my colleagues at Monroe College, especially Carol Genese, for giving me the luxury of time to write.

I would not have written a scrap of this without the guidance or encouragement of Lou Ann Walker, Susan Scarf-Merrill, Ursula Hegi, Andrew Botsford, Terrence Lane, Chris Cascio, Jessica Johnson, or my literary dad, Roger Rosenblatt.

To my family: I love you and hope none of you ever read a word of this book.

Ten years ago, on another continent, I met someone who believed me when I said I was going to be a writer. It was the luckiest day of my life. Max, you are my best friend and biggest supporter.

Finally, to my real-life sisters, Greek and otherwise: Many people have asked me if I've modeled the women in this book off you. I always tell them no, my real sisters are much kinder, funnier, and smarter, and therefore far too wonderful to put in a piece of fiction. How did I get so lucky?